CORAL MOON

Brandilyn Collins
Seatbelt Suspense™

Other Books by Brandilyn Collins

Kanner Lake Series

1 | Violet Dawn

Hidden Faces Series

1 | Brink of Death

2 | Stain of Guilt

3 | Dead of Night

4 | Web of Lies

Bradleyville Series

1 | Cast a Road Before Me

2 | Color the Sidewalk for Me

3 | Capture the Wind for Me

Chelsea Adams Series

1 | Eyes of Elisha

2 | Dread Champion

BRANDILYN COLLINS

KANNER LAKE SERIES

CORAL MOON

BOOK 2

ZONDERVAN®

ZONDERVAN.com/
AUTHORTRACKER
follow your favorite authors

ZONDERVAN®

Coral Moon
Copyright © 2007 by Brandilyn Collins

Requests for information should be addressed to:
Zondervan, *Grand Rapids, Michigan* 49530

Library of Congress Cataloging-in-Publication Data

Collins, Brandilyn.
    Coral Moon / Brandilyn Collins.
        p. cm. — (Kanner Lake series ; bk. 2)
    ISBN-10: 0-310-25224-5
    ISBN-13: 978-0-310-25224-5
    1. Murder — Fiction. 2. Resorts — Fiction. 3. Supernatural — Fiction
  4. Idaho — Fiction. I. Title.
  PS3553.O4747815C67 2006
  813'.6 — dc22   2006037474

Interior design by Beth Shagene

Printed in the United States of America

---

07 08 09 10 11 12 • 10 9 8 7 6 5 4 3 2 1

SCENES AND BEANS™
The Kanner Lake Blog

Life in Kanner Lake, Idaho—brought to you by Java Joint coffee shop on Main

HELP CREATE THE KANNER LAKE WORLD

Write a post for Scenes and Beans—
and win a signed copy of Violet Dawn!

Scenes and Beans, the Kanner Lake character blog, features many of the Java Joint folks you'll meet in *Violet Dawn*. Their entertaining posts are written in real time, according to events in this story. And they're created by you—the readers of the series!

Visit Scenes and Beans at *www.kannerlake.blogspot.com*.

For details on auditioning a post, go to *www.kannerlake.com/scenesandbeans.html*.

Want to discuss *Violet Dawn* with your book club?
Insightful questions about the story and how
it applies to your life can be found at
www.kannerlake.com/discussions.

For Sister #2,
Sheila Lovell.
A quiet strength
and a brilliant, witty mind.
When you left home,
I mourned for days.

I do not know how the suns and worlds are turned.
I only see how men will plague themselves.

— Mephistopheles, Faust

INTRODUCTION

Dear Reader,

In this second book of my Kanner Lake series, I offer you a story that's a bit ... different. My task in life, after all, is to keep you off balance, not quite sure of what new trials you must endure at my hands. Certainly *Coral Moon* offers you the same cast of colorful characters you came to know in *Violet Dawn*. You will also meet some new folks. The town has settled into relative quiet after its *Violet Dawn* traumas. Java Joint is enjoying a higher rate of business. The Kanner Lake blog is up and running, with thousands of loyal readers across the country. Chief Edwards keeps law and order; S-Man types away on his science fiction manuscript. Winter has nearly passed and spring is around the corner. Ah, yes, beautiful, pristine Kanner Lake has much to look forward to. Except—

What is that feeling in the air? Something strange and dark. Something unsettling.

As a reader of my books, you know the drill before turning the page: Strap your seatbelt on tight, keep your hands inside the car, and don't forget to *b r e a t h e ...*

But if this particular roller coaster becomes airborne, if plunging ride gives way to startling flight ...

Well, at least I gave you fair warning.

Brandilyn Collins
Seatbelt Suspense™

CORAL MOON

PART ONE

Messages

ONE

Kill tonight — or die.

The words burned, hot acid eating through his eyes, his brain. Right down to his soul.

Only a crazy person would obey.

He slapped both hands to his ears, squeezed hard against his head. Screwed his eyes shut. He hung there, cut off from the world, snagged on the life sounds of his body. The *whoosh* of breath, the beat of his heart.

The words boiled.

His skull hurt. He pulled his hands away, let them fall. The kitchen spun. He dropped into a chair, bent forward, and breathed deeply until the dizziness passed.

He sat up, looked again to the table.

The note lay upon the unfolded *Kanner Lake Times* newspaper, each word horrific against the backdrop of a coral crescent moon.

How did they get in here?

What a stupid question. As if they lacked stealth, as if mere walls and locked entrances could keep them out. He'd been down the hall in the bedroom watching TV, door wide open, yet had heard nothing. Hadn't even sensed their presence as he pushed off the bed and walked to the kitchen for some water.

A chill blew over his feet.

His eyes bugged, then scanned the room. Over white refrigerator and oak cabinets, wiped-down counters and empty sink. To the threshold of the kitchen and into the hallway. There his gaze lingered as the chill worked up to his ankles.

It had to be coming from the front of the house.

His skin oozed sweat, a web of sticky fear spinning down over him. Trembling, he pulled himself out of the chair. He clung to the smooth table edge, ensuring his balance. Then, heart beating in his throat, he forced himself across the floor, around the corner, and toward the front door.

It hung open a few inches.

They were taunting him.

He approached, hands up and fingers spread, as if pushing through phantoms. Sounds of the night wafted on the frigid air—the rustle of breeze through tree limbs, distant car tires singing against pavement. He reached the door, peered around it, knowing he was a fool to seek a sign of them. The air smelled crisp, tanged with the purity of pine trees. The last vestiges of snow dusted his porch, bearing the tracks of his footprints alone.

He closed the door and locked it. As if that would do any good. He sagged against the wall, defeated and sick. How stupid to think they would leave him in peace. Hadn't he seen this coming? All the events of the last few months ...

Shoulders drawn, he made his way back to the kitchen and his inevitable fate. Each footstep drew him away from the life he'd built, reasoning and confidence seeping from him like blood from a fatal wound. His conscience pulsed at what he had to do.

The message sat on his table, an executioner beckoning victim to the noose. He fell into the chair, wiped his forehead with the back of his hand. He read the words, fresh nausea rising in his stomach. No misunderstanding their commands. They had a chess score to settle. He was their pawn.

He pushed back against the chair, arms crossed and hugging himself, the way he used to do as a boy. Dully, he stared at the window, seeing only his own pitiable reflection. For a long time he watched himself, first transfixed in fright, then with the evolving expression of self-preservation.

If he just did this one thing, his debt would be paid. They'd leave him alone.

For another hour … two … he sat, forcing down the queasiness as he thought through dozens of details. How he should do it. What could go wrong.

By the time he rose near midnight, he'd laid his plans.

Gathering the necessary items, shrugging on a coat, he slipped out into the cold and soulless night.

TWO

Leslie Brymes awoke to a promising day of argument and scorn.

She stretched, groggy eyes roving the master bedroom suite of her newly rented house. Sunlight seeped through her pink curtains, casting the walls and carpet a hazy mauve. Her flannel sheets were soft and warm, coaxing her back toward slumber ...

She resisted.

As sleep morphed into awareness, her mind began to pop with names and workday duties. Eleven a.m. — interview Bud Grayson by phone. Two p.m. — Myra Hodgkid at her house. Leslie smiled, imagining the arguments of these opponents and the article she would write. Nothing like a little controversy to sell newspapers.

She slid out of bed and made her way to the bathroom, interview questions trooping through her head. *Mr. Grayson, how much did publicity from the country's fascination with the Edna San murder have to do with your decision to build a hotel in Kanner Lake? Ms. Hodgkid, why do you oppose the hotel when it promises new tax revenue for the town?* As hot water in the shower hissed and pounded, Leslie considered others she might talk to, the word count she would need. Above all, how to push her story from the *Kanner Lake Times* pages into bigger newspapers and onto TV. The national-interest hook might still have some life in it, especially with the recent airing of her interview about the Edna San case on *Crime America*.

For that, she had to give her roommate a lot of credit. Paige hadn't wanted a thing to do with any public appearances, yet didn't try to stop Leslie from being on the show. Paige knew how much Leslie wanted it to boost her career.

The twenty-five thousand dollars hadn't been bad either.

Leslie stepped out of the shower, anticipation zinging through her veins. She donned a bathrobe and towel-turbaned her wet hair, then parked herself in front of the closet, considering what to wear. She pulled out jeans with sequins and little pearls on the thighs, laid them on the bed, then eyed them critically.

Perfect for the sweater.

Leslie headed down the hallway toward her roommate's door. She knocked hard. "Hey, Paige. You gonna let me borrow that sweater today?" Her movement sent the towel turban into a slide until it covered one eye. She pushed it back in place. "Paige!"

The door swung open. Paige stood before her, clad in black jeans—and the teal sweater Leslie wanted to wear. Set off by the top, Paige's vivid blue-green eyes were stunning. Even with no makeup and her brown hair uncombed, the girl looked gorgeous.

Leslie thrust a hand on her hip. "You rat. How did you know I'd want to wear that today?"

Paige shrugged. "I didn't. But you can have it. I'll wear something else."

Leslie's turban slipped again. She gave up and pulled it off. Wet hair slapped against the back of her neck. The cold sensation shot a frisson between her shoulder blades. *Ooh.* Sudden willies rattled her body, and the hair on her arms raked up.

She shivered harder.

Something touched the back of her neck.

Leslie gasped and whipped around, eyes stabbing the hallway.

"What's wrong? Leslie?"

She barely heard Paige's voice. Felt only the prickle of her nerves, the lingering sensation of icy fingers on her skin. A strange, indefinable heaviness descended, thick and dark. Leslie trembled, wanting to run, unable to move. Waiting for ...

What?

The feeling sucked away, a shadow on a fast-ebbing tide.

She blinked, senses assimilating. Double-checking.

It was gone.

Her fingers cramped. Leslie realized how hard she was clutching the wet towel. She eased her grip, turned around to face her roommate. Paige stared at her.

"Are you okay?"

Leslie drew a breath. "Did you feel that?"

"Feel what?"

"You telling me you didn't feel *anything*?"

Paige looked right and left. "What are you talking about?"

Leslie's shoulders relaxed a little. *Okay. Fine.* She was just a little spooked this morning, that's all.

But she could have sworn ...

"Never mind." She slipped the towel around her like a shawl, pulled her wet hair on top of it. "I just ... went off for a minute." She forced a smile, knew it came out crooked. What had they been talking about? "Oh, the sweater. Don't worry about it. I'll wear it another day."

Paige's eyes rounded. "I swear your face went white. You sure you're not sick?"

Leslie managed a laugh. "Sick in the head, maybe." With a flutter of her hand, she headed back down the hall. She could not tell her friend what had just happened—whatever *it* was. Paige had been through enough, and the last thing she needed was any more weirdness in her life. In the past month she'd begun to blossom, her shy smile quicker, her confidence on the rise.

Leslie wasn't about to put even the smallest speed bump in her roomie's road to recovery.

In her own bedroom, Leslie chose a blue sweater and slid into her jeans. She pushed the strange occurrence from her mind.

Twenty minutes later in the kitchen, Leslie dropped a bagel in the toaster. While it toasted she slipped outside to fetch the *Spokane Review* off their front sidewalk. She snatched it up, the cold March air already seeping through her sweater, and hurried back into the house. *Blessed spring, come soon.*

Her bagel spread with cream cheese, Leslie settled at the table to peruse her competition. Dratted big city daily. Hitting the streets once a week on Wednesdays, the *Kanner Lake Times* couldn't cover news anywhere near as fast as the *Review* did. What's more, the *KLT* was only six pages long. Leslie took a large bite of bagel. Well, so what? Neither could the *Review* cover Kanner Lake news as thoroughly as her paper. Fortunately, most of the townsfolk subscribed to both. Besides, how many of those reporters had been on national television? All she had to do was keep her nose to the grindstone, and she'd skip over bigger city newspapers altogether, go straight to TV.

Yeah, girl, keep believing it.

She checked the cat-shaped clock on the kitchen wall, its black tail ticking away the minutes. Just before nine. Time to head to the office.

Leslie shoved the last bit of bagel in her mouth, chewing as she rinsed her plate and knife and stuck them in the dishwasher. Within minutes, teeth brushed and lipstick applied, she was headed out of her bedroom, bearing her small briefcase and a camera slung over her shoulder. The day beckoned, and Leslie Brymes would take it by storm.

"Bye, Paige!" She drummed pink fingernails across her roommate's door as she walked by. Leslie knew Paige would be reading the Bible—a habit she'd picked up lately. Paige didn't have to be at work at Simple Pleasures until ten.

"See ya!" Paige's voice muffled through the wall.

At the front closet Leslie stopped to slip into a puffy jacket, pushing the camera back on her shoulder. She walked out to the porch, ensuring that the door locked behind her, and tilted her face toward a hazy blue sky. Kanner Lake had half a chance of seeing some sun today. Thank goodness the temperature had climbed into the midthirties, just warm enough to have melted recalcitrant patches of snow. It had covered the ground since the beginning of December.

Leslie stepped off the porch and veered right, following the branch of sidewalk that led to the driveway, which curved up to the double-car garage on the far end of the house. Thanks to full boxes in the garage, she and Paige were parking outside until they unpacked everything. As Leslie approached the driveway, the rear right bumper of her bright yellow VW edged into view, followed by the pink daisy petals on the passenger door.

Someone sat in the car.

Leslie pulled up short. She leaned forward, frowning. The frame between the passenger door and windshield blocked the person's face. Who was that?

She ventured three steps, watching the form materialize into full view. The person didn't move.

Over his head—hers?—draped a green towel.

Fear spritzed Leslie's nerves, followed by quick denial. It was just Paige playing a joke. Somehow she'd proved Wonder Woman enough to beat it out the back and slide into the car before Leslie stepped through the front door ...

Three thoughts hit Leslie in rapid succession. Paige didn't play jokes. Her towels were blue. And she never could have made it out here in time.

What was going *on* today? First that feeling in the hallway, now this.

Leslie moved two more steps. Was this a new neighbor, looking for a few laughs? Some kid, who should be in school?

The figure remained still as stone. Leslie couldn't even detect a breath.

Spider-fingers teased the back of her neck.

A year ago Leslie could have convinced herself this was a practical joke. Lots of people knew she and Paige had just moved here. Any number of her friends could have staged this prank. After all, she hadn't locked her car. But after the events of last summer, Leslie Brymes was no longer the naïve twenty-year-old she had been. Life—even in quiet Kanner Lake—had proved it could explode with the vengeance of a volcano.

Leslie eyed the cataleptic figure and felt the tumble of rocks in her chest.

Slowly, she set down her briefcase. Slipped the camera down her arm and laid it on the cement. Hands free, she forced herself to the end of the sidewalk.

Where the driveway began, she stood within six feet of her VW. Close enough to make out the narrow-shouldered torso, wearing a white blouse, emerging beneath the towel. The covered head was quite a few inches away from the ceiling. A woman? Short, diminutive.

Still.

Leslie refused to dwell on the possible reasons for that.

Maybe this *was* a trick. Maybe it was a life-sized doll. If someone was looking to spoof Paige's terrifying find of last summer, they'd done a good job. Leslie glanced over her shoulder, seeking a snickering culprit, but saw only empty street.

She turned back toward the car, eyes catching a streak on the passenger door. Dark red, about three inches long, over the edge of a pink daisy petal.

Leslie's feet rooted to the pavement. She dropped her gaze to the concrete, seeking … Spatters of blood? Footprints? She saw nothing. Honed through her recent coverage of crime-scene evidence and the testimony at last month's trial, the reporter in Leslie spewed warnings. *Notice everything, touch nothing. Grab the notebook and pen from your briefcase, take notes—*

"No."

This *wasn't* real. Couldn't be. It was a sick prank, nothing more, and when she got her hands on the person who'd set her up, she'd *strangle* him. Or her.

Propelled by her indignation, Leslie strode forward, grabbed the door handle, and jerked it open. "Listen, whoever you—"

The figure didn't flinch.

All sound died in Leslie's throat. Her stunned gaze fell on thin legs in blue polyester pants. Gnarled and bloodied hands curled in the lap. Pinned to the person's chest, a piece of plain white paper, with the number one on it, circled in black felt-tip pen.

Leslie froze, screaming at herself to back away. Her legs wouldn't move.

She knew then. Even so, she sought hope. Swallowing hard, she reached out a finger, poked the woman's arm.

Stiff.

Experience and terror cried for her to stop. This was a crime scene, and nothing should be touched. But fear of the unknown overcame her resistance. Leslie lifted her hand—and jerked away the towel.

Blood crusted a battered head and cheeks. Open, glazed eyes. The face—Leslie knew it.

Her feet back-stepped, hand flying to her mouth. Leslie stumbled, sought the breath to scream and found none. Strangled into silence, her lungs swelling shut, she fled to the porch and pounded on the locked front door.

THREE

The piece of paper—folded twice and smudgy with footprints—lay on the floor by her locker. Pulling sixteen-year-old Ali Frederick's attention like a magnet.

Clutching her geometry textbook, Ali stared at it. Had to be a personal note. Students didn't fold up their homework like that. It was regular paper, with faint blue lines and a ripped punch hole. Could have come from anybody's notebook. Someone must have dropped it. Maybe didn't even know it was missing yet.

Had Sarah lost it? The girl whose locker was next to hers had just left, yakking a mile a minute with her best friend, Kara, about some TV show.

Ali glanced down the hall. Sarah would be easy to find, with her reddish hair and long legs. There she was—three classrooms away. Too far. Ali looked around for someone else who could have dropped the paper. Had anybody noticed she'd seen it? Her classmates made lots of noise, all laughing and talking. They changed books at their lockers, slamming metal doors. Their footsteps kicked up a stale smell of dust and sweat. Too many bodies in one place.

No one was paying her any attention.

Her eyes returned to the paper.

Kinda weird, the way it pulled at her. And it was so close. Almost like somebody'd left it there for her to find.

Before she knew it, she'd bent over and picked it up.

Ali opened her locker door, holding the paper close to her waist. She pulled out her history textbook, stuck the paper underneath its cover, then slid her geometry book onto a shelf and closed the door. Suddenly she was afraid to turn around. What if the owner of the note had seen her? Someone like Marla or Tracy or Kristal, who had it all, and wouldn't mind telling her what they thought of her snooping.

If she'd been attending this school longer, it wouldn't matter. If she had friends here, well, so what if she read somebody's note? But she'd lived in Kanner Lake less than a month and had started attending the high school this week. When you're brand-new and trying to fit in, you don't want to go looking for trouble.

Someone bumped Ali's shoulder. She jerked around, heart skipping.

"Sorry." Some heavy-set guy raised his double chin and lumbered by. No smile.

Ali exhaled. "It's okay."

She *felt* the note in her textbook—like it called to her. She wanted to read it, but there were too many people around. She hurried down the hall and upstairs to her second-period class, and slid into the back-row seat closest to the door. Up front, Mr. Harkins leaned against his desk, joking with Terrence, the short, skinny class clown. Ali slapped her binder and textbook down on the desk. Her homework, a two-page essay on the role of women in the workforce during World War II, lay in the front pocket of the binder. They'd had three days to do the assignment, but it had taken her less than two hours, even with the research. So far, all the homework at Kanner Lake High had been like that. Not that the teachers were bad or anything. But after being homeschooled since kindergarten, Ali was way ahead of everyone else.

Now if she could only make some friends.

She pulled out the essay and laid it on top of her binder.

A male voice sounded behind her — the voice that had made her tingle the first day she'd heard it.

"... in Spokane on Sunday. Daryl's driving. Can you go?"

Ali bent over her desk, pretending to look at her essay. Her gaze cut left to see Chet and Eddie — she didn't know any last names yet — walk up the aisle and choose seats across from each other. Chet was wearing a blue sweatshirt that made his eyes look extra good. His light brown hair was gelled just right, and he moved with this ... ease. Ali watched his hand — it waved so casually as he talked. And the way his tall body folded into the chair. In front of Chet, some blonde chick named Kim turned around and flashed him a smile of perfect teeth. She said something, and Chet gave her head a little push.

Jealousy shot through Ali. She lowered her eyes.

I will never look as good as her.

Well, so? Ali didn't consider herself exactly ugly, either. She had big brown eyes that her dad always said were "gorgeous." And her body was okay. She just needed to learn more about makeup, plus do something with her hair. The reddish brown color was pretty good, but it was all one long length, except for the bangs. She looked like one of those hippies from the sixties.

The bell rang.

"Okay, people, let's have it quiet!" Mr. Harkins pushed off the desk. "Time to hand in those essays."

Students groaned and binders clicked open. Ali passed her assignment to the guy in front of her. The papers rustled their way up to the front.

She looked down at the history textbook. Time to read the note.

Ali opened the book.

She held the cover up so nobody on her left could see. The note felt gritty as she unfolded it with one hand. Pressed it flat.

Just a few scrawly lines in the center of the page. Ali bent over to read.

The first sentence made her eyes go wide.

The second sent pinpricks down her arms.

After the last line, Ali felt shaky. Refolding the note, she crammed it in the back of her book. Then sat staring at her desk, heart pounding.

It's not real. Just some stupid game.

But she couldn't believe that. Something told her it was real, all right. That note had some kind of power. It had called to her, and she'd picked it up like some dumb sheep. And now, somehow, she was going to pay.

FOUR

Kanner Lake Police Chief Vince Edwards studied the file on his desk, drinking a Java Joint "biggie" coffee. His office door stood open, the small station quiet. Young Frank West, the other officer of their five-man force on duty today, was out aiming radar on Lakeshore.

Lining the top of Vince's desk were photographs of his wife, Nancy, and their son, Tim, whose twenty-second birthday would have been two weeks ago, and of their daughter, Heather, who lived in Spokane with her husband and little girl. Vince picked up the photo of Nancy and Tim, taken just before Tim shipped out to Iraq. Vince said a quick prayer for his and Nancy's marriage, which had almost unraveled after Tim's death, and for help with their grief. Then he prayed for Heather and her family.

Vince had never been much of a praying man, but the curveballs life had thrown him in the past year and a half had made him think twice about the Creator.

He took another drink of hot coffee, glad for the sleeve around the cup to protect his fingers. Gladder still that the case file before him could now be closed, however sick its solving had made the parents of Billy Yates and Carl Stedener. Vince shook his head as he closed the folder. *Dumb kids*. Windows in four buildings broken by vandals over a period of three days — and what was the common factor? Double sets of boy-size footprints in the snow. And the tracks of a three-legged dog.

Only one such beast existed in Kanner Lake: twelve-year-old Billy Yates's brown mutt. A cross between some kind of spaniel and a chocolate lab, "Spud" had lost a limb when he got hit by a car the previous year. Half the townsfolk, animal lovers that they were, sent gifts to Spud. The mutt was up and adapting to his new hopping gait long before the squeaky mice and bacon-flavored bones stopped coming.

Note to Billy—when you own a dog with one set of tracks in a million, best leave him home during a crime spree.

Brimming with denials at first, Billy caved when presented with the irrefutable evidence. He copped on his best friend, Carl, and, of course, poor Spud. All three of them—busted. The criminal canine got off easy (after all, he'd already lost a leg), but the boys would be putting in a lot of weekend cleanup hours at the businesses they'd hit. Some of the more crusty codgers in town, like Wilbur Hucks, had declared Spud should be taken away from Billy. No criminal deserved so brave a canine. But they'd been outvoiced by others who insisted that Spud, a one-kid dog, would also bear the punishment.

Vince agreed—for Billy's sake as well as Spud's. You just don't separate a boy and his dog.

He gazed through the open blinds of his window, out toward Main. The day was overcast and chilly, but the snow was gone. Across the street, Missy Stafford, mother of four, stepped out of the post office and drew her coat tighter around her big body. Sixty-year-old Ralph Bednershack, owner of the IGA grocery store, rushed by her on the sidewalk and waved. Ralph's face was turned away from Vince, but there was no mistaking his distinctive never-on-time trot. Missy waved back.

Thank heaven Kanner Lake had drifted back into normalcy, Vince thought. Well, except for the controversy over the hotel that Californian wanted to build. Hard to believe a month ago dozens of journalists had swarmed the town, feeding the country's fascination with the "Edna San Burial" case.

Vince's personal phone line rang. He put down his coffee and reached for the receiver. "Chief Edwards."

"Ch-chief?" The female voice sounded hitched, tight.

Vince sat up straight, instantly alert. "Yes, who is this?"

"Paige."

Paige. A chill shot through Vince, followed by a dozen imagined scenarios, none of them good. With everything this gal had gone through, he'd never once known her to cry. Now she sounded close to it. "What's happened?"

"Vesta Johnson's been murdered."

"What?"

"Somebody put her in Leslie's car, in our driveway. Sometime last night. Leslie just found her."

Vince blinked at the paperwork on his desk, all peaceful thoughts vanished. Vesta Johnson — in her seventies. Sweet lady with no enemies, a hostess at every New Community Church potluck.

A dozen questions pelted him. Where to begin? "You say she's in Leslie's car?"

"Yes."

"You said 'our driveway.' You two rooming together now?"

"We just moved into a house at the end of Madding Court. Number 235."

Vince grabbed a pen and jotted down the address. "Are you sure Vesta is dead?"

"Yes. I ... I saw her. Her head's all beaten and bloody. And she's stiff."

Vince closed his eyes, thoughts roiling. Then his policeman's mind took over. *The body's been touched.*

"Paige, are you both all right? Where's Leslie?"

"We're ... okay. She's here. But she was too upset to call."

Vince pushed back his chair. "Okay, I'm on my way. Listen. Just stay in the house with your doors locked until we get there. Don't touch *anything*. Not the car, not Vesta, or anything around it. Hear me?"

"Yeah, okay. Just ... hurry." The last word cracked.

"I will. Hang on."

Vince smacked off the line, begged the dawdling dial tone, then punched in Frank West's cell phone number. It was an automatic response to keep the call off the radio, where Jared Moore, owner of the *Kanner Lake Times*, could pick it up via scanner.

As Frank answered, the irony hit Vince. What good was keeping the information off a scanner when the *Kanner Lake Times* reporter *found* the body?

FIVE

As Paige hung up the phone, Leslie tried to pull herself together. Her brain felt as withered as a desert flower. Paige didn't seem much better off. She hovered at the kitchen counter, eyes blank.

Leslie couldn't push the picture of Vesta's bloody face from her mind. "Thanks for calling." Her voice sounded thick, even to herself. "You held it together way better than me."

Paige nodded.

They looked at each other. The police should arrive within five minutes, but that seemed like forever. What were they supposed to do in the meantime? What *could* they do? Leslie could hardly think. She knew she was in shock. Which was a good thing. Shock clamped down emotions, and she sure didn't want to feel what boiled inside her right now.

Paige's gaze drifted out the back window. "Chief said we're supposed to wait here. Not go outside." She crossed to the kitchen table and sank into a chair.

Like we'd want to go back out there. Leslie slumped into the seat beside Paige. Hard to imagine she'd been headed out the door ten minutes ago, laser-focused on interviews. Somewhere deep inside, her reporter's brain screamed for details and answers to this new story, but she couldn't begin to listen. This was too raw, too real. She *knew* Vesta Johnson. Respected and loved her.

How could this have happened?

Leslie drew her arms around her chest and stared across the room, seeing Vesta's battered face. "Why?" she whispered. "Why would anyone do this?"

At New Community Church, Vesta had greeted Leslie every Sunday. *Leslie, what a good job you did on the paper this week. ... How beautiful you look. ...* Vesta stood about five feet four, but the sparkle in her eyes and her energy gave her a presence far greater than size. She hadn't been a pretty woman, but beauty flowed from her spirit. Her eyes were gray, her nose large. Her wide mouth was always smiling, always saying kind words. Forceful words, too, when needed. She didn't hesitate to speak out against behavior that "flew in the face of God's will." But even then, Vesta exuded love for the person, as if cut to the core that one of God's creatures would insist on self-destructive behavior.

Vesta was the first to take food to someone who was sick, or to mourners after a funeral. Sometimes people who called themselves Christians didn't act much like it, but Vesta *lived* her faith. She'd lost her husband of fifty-one years just fourteen months ago. Many said she was better off without him. He'd been selfish, demanding, and bad-tempered. Apparently, Henry mocked Vesta's faith all his life. Still, Leslie had never heard her speak a word against him.

Leslie looked at Paige. She was staring at her tightly clasped hands, her face like carved wood. "Paige?" Leslie leaned toward her. "You okay?"

Paige raised an empty gaze. "Yeah."

Guilt welled in Leslie. What had she been thinking, pounding on their front door when she had her own key? She should have calmed down before telling Paige what had happened. Instead her own terror had knifed into her friend, and Paige had run out to the car to see for herself. Then stumbled back to the porch, white-faced.

"Hey." Leslie touched Paige's arm. "You can't blame yourself for this. It was my car, not yours. Whoever did this—it has nothing to do with you."

Paige watched one of her thumbs rub over the other.

"You hear me?"

Paige shook her head. "Death follows me, Leslie." The words fell hard and flat, like sheeted steel. "Now Vesta has paid for it."

"No. Not this time. She's in *my* car. *Everybody* in this town knows that car. No way a yellow bug with pink daisies is going to be confused with a dark blue Explorer. Whatever sick mind did this, he—or she or *it*—aimed it at me." Leslie's voice cracked. "Vesta lives on the other side of town. Someone killed her, most likely in her own home, and took the time to bring her all the way over here. *Why*?" She pressed back in her chair, shaking inside.

No, no, please, shock—don't leave me yet.

But she couldn't stop the thoughts. When Paige had found Edna San's body on her property last year, there was a reason it had been placed there. Had to be a reason this time too.

Is it because I'm a reporter?

Then why not choose Jared Moore's car? He *owned* the *Kanner Lake Times*, plus he lived just three blocks from Vesta.

There must be another explanation.

An idea rose in Leslie's mind, so dark, so horrible, that she couldn't speak it. Paige wasn't the one who should feel guilty here. Maybe she—Leslie Brymes, Vesta's friend—should. Maybe she had done something to *cause* this murder.

Could that possibly be true?

Leslie lowered her head into her hands. No way. Please, God, it couldn't be. Because if it was, she would never, ever be able to forgive herself.

SIX

Minutes after hanging up the phone, Vince pulled his vehicle to a stop at 235 Madding.

He hadn't run code to the house—no flashing lights, no sirens. And he'd informed no one but Frank, although phone calls would soon be flying if Paige's information proved correct. His first order of business was to assess the scene for himself.

Through the car window, he focused on Leslie's bright yellow VW in the driveway. He could see a body inside. Unmoving.

From a kit on his passenger seat, Vince extracted a pair of white latex gloves. He got out of his car and pulled the gloves on.

He scanned the house and yard, surveyed the homes across the street. He saw no one. Kids would be in school, parents at work. Stay-at-home moms with little ones would be inside on this chilly morning. The quiet was typical for a dead-end street. The road ended at a fence, an open field beyond. Five years ago, before this little subdivision was built, this ground had been farmland.

A black-and-white gunned up the street. Frank West slid out of the car almost before the engine cut and strode over to Vince with grave anticipation. At twenty-five, Frank was a good-looking kid, his chiseled face and brown eyes enough to put females in a flutter. He'd only been on the force a little over a year. The investigation of the Edna San murder had given him just enough experience to consider himself well seasoned.

Kid would learn soon enough.

"Got here as quick as I could." Frank's gaze slid past Vince toward Leslie's VW and hung there. Anxiety twinged his features, then was gone. Vince understood. Being called to a potential homicide was one thing, coming face-to-face with the evidence was something else.

"Thanks." Vince started up the driveway, eyes roving the pavement for possible evidence—a tire track, something left behind. Frank fell in step. They followed the driveway as it right-curved at the top toward the garage. Approached the car from the rear.

Leslie's VW sat about six feet from the front lawn's edge. Paige's Explorer was parked on the other side of Leslie's car. The passenger door to the VW was closed, but not fully latched. Below the handle ran a three-inch smudge of dark red, almost surely blood. The victim's, or the perpetrator's? Vince drew even with the window, edging over to make room for Frank. They peered inside.

Vince's heart went cold.

It was Vesta Johnson all right, but not like he'd ever seen her. Mouth hanging slack, head battered, rivulets of dried blood on her face. It must have been a violent, gruesome death.

Oh, Lord, why?

The last time Vince had heard this woman's voice, she was greeting him at the IGA, asking how Nancy was, saying she still prayed for him and his wife. Vince couldn't imagine who would do this to her.

"God have mercy." Frank straightened and crossed himself.

Vince's gaze traveled down to Vesta's chest—and stopped. If his blood had chilled a minute before, it now turned to ice.

A pinned piece of paper, with a circled number one.

For a long minute he could only stare, disgust and dread whirling in his head.

"That number …" Frank pointed without touching the glass.

"Yeah." Vince's voice hoarsened. He stepped back and motioned Frank aside. With one gloved hand he opened the VW's door, leaned in, and placed the backs of his fingers against Vesta Johnson's carotid artery. Even through the latex, her skin felt like cold stone. "She's been here a while."

A towel lay in her lap.

Towel. Vince stared at it, making an immediate connection. His brain sifted through facts he thought had been laid to rest …

Maybe not. Maybe it just covered something.

He pinched a corner of the towel and lifted it up.

Underneath lay Vesta's hands, bloodied, folded in her lap. Almost as if they'd been posed.

Vince let out a long breath, dropped the towel back in place, and drew away from the car. Two possible scenarios ran through his brain. One: Leslie's investigative reporting was getting too close to someone's secrets. Or two: this murder was unfinished business from Paige's discovery of Edna San.

He turned to Frank—and spotted Paige and Leslie huddled some distance away on the branch of sidewalk curving up to the driveway. Shivering. They wore no coats, but Vince knew their trembling was from more than the cold.

Following his gaze, Frank turned. "Oh. Hi." He strode toward them, hands up, palms out, as though warding the girls from evil. Vince had noticed the kid's soft spot for Paige ever since Frank met her under dire circumstances last July. Subsequent events in her life—and the dignity with which she'd faced them—seemed to reinforce Frank's attraction. Not that he would admit it. Didn't have to. It was in the way he spoke her name, the straying of his eyes toward Simple Pleasures, where Paige worked. Now, seeing the way Frank shielded the girls from the body, Vince knew his response was as much personal as professional.

Frank drew to a halt in front of the girls, in quarter profile to Vince. Paige hung back, but Leslie reached for his arm and clung to it. Frank patted her on the head, then eased toward Paige. "Sorry you had to see this." He looked to Leslie, almost too late, to include her in the statement.

Paige nodded, arms drawn across her chest.

Leslie threw a glance toward her VW. "I found her."

"I know." Frank took a step back from Paige. "Chief Edwards and I will be here for a while. But we're going to be real busy."

Leslie and Paige murmured vague responses.

Vince turned away, pulled by all the things he must do. He needed to get on the phone to the Idaho State Police. This thing was way beyond Kanner Lake's resources—the pinned number on Vesta Johnson's chest screamed that fact. But first, immediate questions had to be answered.

He shut the car door as he'd found it and walked down the sidewalk to Frank and the girls. Dozens of details spun through his brain. After calling the ISP, he needed to secure this crime scene. Had to send someone over to Vesta Johnson's house ASAP, look for signs that the murder had taken place there, and if so, secure that site as well. He'd call in his other three officers, but even with their help, he wished for more manpower.

Vince neared the trio and stopped. Frank edged away from the girls, transitioning from the personal to the professional mode. He stood by Vince, legs apart, arms crossed.

"Leslie, Paige." Vince's tone mixed concern and confidence. He made eye contact with each of them. Paige's electrifying blue-green gaze was clouded with pain and ... something else. Defeat? He tucked the observation in his mental file. Leslie drew herself up straighter, fear and resolve flicking over her face in quick succession. "You two doing all right?" Vince asked.

Paige nodded. Leslie bit her lip and looked to Frank. "Hey, no problem. I'm a reporter, remember?"

Vince had to admire her pluck.

He put a hand on his hip. "I'll have some help out here as fast as I can. But I've got to get a few things straight. Leslie, you say you saw the victim first?"

She nodded.

"Did you open the car door?"

"Yes."

"Was it closed all the way before you opened it?"

Her gaze dropped to the sidewalk, and she frowned. Her chin came back up. "Yes."

"Sure about that?"

"Yeah, I'm sure."

"Okay. There's a towel on the victim's lap. Is that where you found it?"

Leslie pulled in a long breath. "No. It was on her head, covering her face."

Oh, man. Covering the victim's head reeked of shock value. The perpetrator would know whoever found the body would be compelled to pull it off. And the possible symbolism of the towel still shrieked in Vince's mind.

"So you took it off and dropped it in her lap?"

A shudder seized Leslie. She folded her arms and emitted a weak "Uh-huh."

"Did you move anything else?"

"No. I did just ... touch her arm with one finger. That's all."

Vince could imagine it. Anyone would have done what Leslie did. "Okay." He looked to Paige. "On the phone, you said the body felt stiff. Did you touch her too?"

The question had to dredge up a swamp of memories for Paige. The last body she'd found, she'd done substantially more than touch it.

"No, that's what Leslie told me. I didn't even open the car door, just looked through the window." Paige looked Vince in the eye, as if daring him to disbelieve.

"All right." He offered her a brief smile. "Thanks." He glanced over his shoulder at Vesta Johnson in the VW. The body screamed for him to fast-turn the wheels of justice. "You two should get back in the house where it's warm. I'm going to make some calls, and we'll have a lot of people out here before long. While I'm waiting for them to arrive, I'll need to secure this scene. Leslie, you understand your car will have to be impounded?"

She sighed. "How long?"

Vince shook his head. "Maybe sixty days. That's standard. But it's not up to me. When we find who did this—and we *will*—it's possible the prosecutor will insist on keeping your vehicle until the trial is complete."

"Oh." Her shoulders sagged. She looked past Vince toward the VW and its horrifying cargo, a sick expression on her face. "But you know," her voice fell to a whisper, "I'm not sure I can ever drive it again."

Time was ticking. Vince urged the girls back into the house, telling them to gather some things. They'd need to stay somewhere safe for a few nights—preferably at Leslie's parents' house. The murder scene, including their rental house, would be sealed off for at least today. Paige would also have to find other means of transportation for the day, since they'd need to check out her car as well.

Vince began spouting orders to Frank. The kid would call in officers Al Newman, Roger Waitman, and Jim Tentley immediately. Al, known as C. B.—short for Charlie Brown due to his round, bald head—and Roger would report to Vesta Johnson's house. Jim was to come here.

"Frank, get the tape out of your car. Let's seal off the area."

As Frank hurried toward his vehicle, Vince pulled out his phone to dial the ISP. If only it were Monday morning between eight and nine, when the Idaho State Police had their staff meetings in Coeur d'Alene. Perfect time to catch everybody together. Punching in the number, Vince calculated it would take forty minutes to an hour for a couple of homicide detectives to show. Maybe another two hours for a team of crime techs.

In the meantime, he had more than enough to keep him busy.

He hit the last digit, his gaze pulling to Vesta Johnson's still form—and the piece of paper pinned to her chest. *A circled number one.* He closed his eyes. As far as he was concerned, that message could mean one thing.

He had the beginning of a serial killing on his hands.

As the phone rang in his ear, Vince's mind flitted over faces and names of people in Kanner Lake. People he'd known all his life. He was their friend, family member, neighbor. Their protector. At the mere thought of all the folks he held so dear, a terrible question smoldered in his chest.

Who could become a circled number two?

SEVEN

He hadn't slept all night.

Hard to do with blood on your hands. Blood on your clothes. But they could be washed. What about the blood on his soul?

As if he had one left.

He pushed himself out of bed, stumbled to the bathroom for a long shower. As Lady Macbeth had washed her hands, he washed his entire body. Scrubbed and scrubbed until his skin glowed red.

They'd watched him kill last night, smirking with vindictiveness. He hadn't seen them, but he felt their presence.

He stilled, towel in hand. What if they'd stayed after he was gone? Left something to implicate him? What final vengeance — make him do their dirty work, then see that he was caught.

Trembling, he slipped into clothes, aware of his locked bedroom door. What if they were out in the hallway right now, waiting for him? With him dead, who would ever know . . .

He crept near the door, leaned his ear against it, listening. He heard only his drumming heartbeat.

His fingers found the cool knob and quietly rotated its lock. He hesitated, muscles tense. Then gathered his nerve — and jerked open the door.

Empty hallway.

He let out a breath. Then a low, derisive chuckle.

Get hold of yourself, man.

He walked down the hallway, into the kitchen. His eyes snapped to the table.

Funny. From here, he couldn't see their death message. And he hadn't touched it.

He approached the table, his sock feet silent on the beige linoleum.

The note was gone.

He stared at the table, seeing only a newspaper. Had they crept in during the night, snatched away the evidence?

Mind reeling, he turned away. They were supposed to leave him *alone* now. Hadn't he done what they'd demanded?

His hands fisted against his chest. Okay. So they'd been here again. But only to take away their message. He could live with that, couldn't he? And now it was done, all of it. He could get back to normal.

So do it.

With a deep breath, he crossed the kitchen to the refrigerator. Pulled out food. Bacon. Eggs. Bread for toast. Mind on hold, he broke the eggs into a hot pan, laid the meat beside them.

By the time the cooked food sat on his plate, steaming and salty smelling, the burn in his belly had dwindled to a tiny ash heap.

He sat down to his breakfast and pulled the newspaper toward him. He'd read it yesterday, but—anything to keep his mind busy. He skimmed the cover, turned the page—

And jerked back.

A new message lay inside.

Before he could tear his eyes away, his mind had registered the terrifying words. The demand shot like venom from a spitting cobra, streaming poison through his veins.

Another victim's name. Another killing.

It wasn't over.

Not at all.

48

EIGHT

As soon as she and Paige stepped back into their house, Leslie's shock wore off. *Poof*—just like that.

She sagged against the entryway wall, feeling her face drain of color. Paige grasped her arm. "Are you okay?"

Leslie shook her head hard. An uncapped well of emotion bubbled up her throat. "I'm sorry." She pushed around Paige. "I just can't ..."

She stumbled to her room and slammed the door.

Sobs broke from her as she collapsed on the bed. Leslie buried her face in the covers, fingers clawing the fabric—and cried. She didn't even try to muffle the sounds. Paige would understand and would know to leave her alone.

Grief poured out. For the loss of Vesta, the sweet woman who would never hurt a soul. For the injustice of her death, the senselessness of it. For the sorrow of everyone at church, in town.

"God, *why* did You let this happen? *Why*?"

Fear and guilt swirled with the sadness, making Leslie cry all the harder. Why *her* car? What had she done to cause Vesta's death? To deserve this?

Leslie hacked and choked until her throat closed, her nose clogged, and her head pounded. Still she couldn't stop. So many if onlys. If only she'd had a chance to tell Vesta how much she loved her. If only this had happened to somebody else, in some other town. Selfish, she knew, but still … If only God had stopped it. If only she understood.

If only she could find out who did this.

I swear I'd kill him with my own hands.

As her energy drained away the tears began to subside. Finally, exhausted, Leslie could cry no more. Did she even have an ounce of water left in her body? Her mouth had gone dry and her eyes scratched.

With a ragged breath she rolled over on her back and stared at the ceiling.

For some minutes her mind coasted, unable to hold a thought. She wiped her face, pushed hair out of her eyes. Pulled in deep breaths. Then tried to pray.

Logical thinking returned in spurts. And with it, pulses of her fighting spirit.

She had to pull herself together. This was too big for her, too terrifying. Either she'd be strong and overcome it, or she'd be trampled. She wasn't about to let the latter happen. Look what she'd done last summer. Fought in the face of death—and won. She could do the same again. True, she couldn't bring Vesta back. But she sure could help find out who did this.

She *was* a reporter, after all.

Leslie sat up, shoulders slumped. Gathering her strength, she pushed off the bed and headed to the bathroom for a much-needed drink.

Her emotions threatened to rise again. She beat them back.

She needed to keep her mind busy, that was the key. And the best way to do that? Simple. Shove her reporter hat down so hard on her head it wouldn't blow off in the gale.

With growing resolve, Leslie guzzled a glass of water, then planted herself in front of the bathroom mirror to fix her makeup. To play the part, she'd better look the part. Okay, her eyes were red and her nose all swollen, but from here on out—whoever did this was in for one major battle.

She reached for a washcloth.

Ten minutes later, she looked fairly presentable. Leslie turned away from the mirror, jaw set. First on her agenda: see what Chief Edwards was doing out front. If he'd discovered any evidence, she wanted to know about it.

Just watch me, whoever you are. See what I do to find you.

With a deep breath, she left her bedroom and headed to her briefcase for her notebook and pen.

NINE

Ali was standing at her locker before third-period class when Kristal passed by, talking to Kim. Ali heard the words "... found the note." *Oh no.* Kristal was petite, with a doll-like face and shiny black hair. But her personality was strong. Ali could feel the heat coming off her.

She busied herself shoving things around in her locker.

Chet and Eddie passed, books at their sides, Eddie waving a hand in the air as he talked. He was a lot shorter than Chet, and muscular, dark hair down to his shoulders. Chet walked in that graceful way of his, like he had nothing to fear from anybody. Ali watched him move down the hall.

Kristal and Kim stopped at the door to Room 14. Kristal turned toward Ali—and their eyes met.

Ali blinked away. But not before she saw that guy who'd bumped into her go up to Kristal and say something.

They were talking about her.

Ali slid her history book onto her locker shelf, took out the science text. She glanced back at the little group. They all had their heads close together. Kim looked at Ali.

Ali's heart beat hard. She felt like she had when she was six years old and her mother caught her taking a quarter off her dad's dresser. That sick, you're-in-real-trouble-now feeling.

Kristal called Chet, and he and Eddie turned around. She motioned a frantic *come here.* Chet and Eddie walked back toward the trio. Now there were five of them talking.

Ali moved things around on her locker shelf, like she was all innocence. *Why* had she picked up that dumb note? But how did they know she had it?

Maybe that guy who'd hit her shoulder saw her pick it up.

She glanced at them again — and saw Chet looking at her. Ali jerked her head away, a little shiver running through her. She banged the locker door shut and clutched her books to her chest. The bell would ring soon. She'd have to pass them all to get to class, but she couldn't bring herself to do it.

Fine, then. She'd walk the other way, go up to the second floor and come back down the other side.

Ali hurried off, feeling stares at her back. Some girl called her name. *Go, Ali, just go.* She walked faster, head down.

A hand grabbed her shoulder. "Hey, wait up."

Chet's voice.

She pulled to a halt, swallowed hard, and faced him.

He looked down at her with a brief smile. "Hi."

He smelled so good. Kind of spicy and sweet at the same time. Was that cologne or just *him*? Ali could lose herself in that smell, and in his blue eyes. This close, she could see they were different shades, lighter in the middle, darker on the outer rings. "Hi." Her voice sounded tinny.

He gave a little shrug. "We haven't talked yet. I'm Chet."

"Oh." She nodded. "I'm Ali."

He looked so tall next to her, probably over six feet. She was only five-five. He had a faint scar underneath his chin.

Ali felt her cheeks go hot. She glanced down the hall. Kristal, that guy who'd bumped her, Eddie, and Kim — they all watched like hawks.

"Um." Chet scratched his jaw. "There seems to be a little problem, and I wondered if I could talk to you about it."

Ali gripped her books tighter, afraid he'd see her heart smacking against her chest. "Okay."

Kristal strode toward them. She pulled up beside Chet and pinned Ali with a stare. "You picked up something that belongs to me, didn't you?" Her dark eyes flashed.

Chet glared at her. "Kristal, I told you I'd handle this."

"Why should *you* handle it? That note's mine."

The rest of the group began to drift toward them, leaning forward to catch every word.

Kristal planted a hand on her hip and faced Ali. "Nate said he saw you pick a folded piece of paper off the floor last hour. Funny, I just happened to lose a piece of paper about that time. Think there could be a connection?"

"Kristal, you don't have to be so—"

"Shut up, Chet."

He looked up at the ceiling and sighed. Eddie, Kim, and Nate came up beside him.

"Well?" Kristal wagged her head at Ali. "I'm waiting."

Something shifted in Ali. It was hard enough being new to the town and school—new to *any* school. She'd had to leave all her friends in Montana when her dad was transferred to work in Spokane. Plus, her mother, who used to be so energetic and fun, was now real sick from cancer and all the chemotherapy, and couldn't homeschool Ali anymore. Ali didn't want to be here. Didn't want to be living this suddenly complicated life. And she sure as all get out didn't want to face this nasty girl right now.

"I did find a note." Her voice sounded small. "But there was no name on it ... "

Kristal tilted her head. "Did it have a little drawing of a coral moon at the bottom?"

Coral moon. Ali had barely noticed it. "I think so."

"Okay, then it's mine. And if you saw the drawing, that means you read it. You had no business doing that."

"You're cursed." Nate's eyes bugged. "That's what the note said—any outsider reading it is cursed." He elbowed Eddie. "Wonder what's gonna happen to her?"

"Will you lay off?" Chet sounded disgusted. "Nothing's going to happen to her."

"How do you know?" Kim shot back.

Kristal's eyes bored into Ali. "I don't like people snooping around in my things."

"I won't tell anybody." Ali tried not to show how scared she was. She *was* cursed, she could *feel* it. No wonder her parents had told her to stay away from supernatural stuff. They said it led to trouble—now look at her.

Eddie blinked. "Hey, maybe she was *meant* to read it."

"Yeah, right, Eddie." Kristal tossed her head.

"No, I mean it. Maybe the Powers wanted to bring her in."

A chill shot through Ali. She bit her lip.

"You're scared, aren't ya?" Nate rounded his mouth and nodded like some old professor. "Scared of the curse."

Ali couldn't speak. Why were they so mean? The memory of dressing for her first day of school four days ago flashed through her head. She'd tried on five different outfits, worrying in the mirror. Like it had done any good. One more minute of this and she'd break down in front of everybody. "I have to get to class." She moved to go around them.

Kristal caught her arm. "I want my note back."

Ali pulled away. "I don't have it. I tore it up and threw it away in the bathroom."

"Oh, yeah, *sure* you did."

"No, really—"

The bell rang. Ali jumped, then took a deep breath. "Look. I'm sorry for reading your note. I won't tell anyone. Okay?"

Kristal's eyes hardened. "Nate's right. You'll pay for it."

The thought terrified Ali. It was true, wasn't it? She'd felt it as soon as she read those words. Almost as if an invisible evil pressed against her. Besides, she was already paying. Now she'd *never* make friends at this stupid school.

Tears sprang into her eyes. Ali felt her face crumple. "I said I'm sorry, what more do you want? Just leave me *alone*!"

Head down, books gripped to her chest, Ali ran to class on trembling legs.

TEN

Helen Communs dragged her finger through the bowl of dough and stuck a glob in her mouth. *Mmm.* She closed her eyes. *Heavenly.* Nobody made chocolate chip cookies like she could, even if she did say so herself. Besides, the whole town agreed.

She pulled out a baking sheet and placed it on the counter, glancing at the clock. She wanted to give the cookies plenty of time to cool before packing them up for the Quilting Ladies luncheon. At seventy and with arthritic hands, she couldn't ball the dough as fast as she used to.

Better get crackin', ol' girl.

Humming an old hymn, Helen dug out a tablespoon of dough and started rolling it in her palms. She placed it on the sheet and repeated the process. Couldn't help but take another taste or two while she worked. The dough was every bit as good as the baked cookie, but she wouldn't tell Lyda Hill that, because the old worrywart would start on her spiel about eating uncooked eggs—

Leslie Brymes.

The name shouted straight into her head. Helen stilled, a spoon of dough hanging in the air. Goodness, why had she thought that? Strange, the way it—

Leslie Brymes!

Helen dropped the spoon into the bowl. Okay, now that—

Pray. Pray.

The voice inside her resonated. So strong, so compelling, Helen couldn't help but obey. She knew the voice. Well, not that she'd ever heard it before like this, but she *knew*.

She grabbed a paper towel, ignoring the pain in her fingers, and swiped her hands. Hurried to the living room and her favorite chair. As she reached it, sweat broke out on her face. Raw terror rose within her, and both knees turned watery. She fell into the chair, heart thumping, casting wild glances around the room. What *was* it? Was she having a heart attack? Was she going to die?

Something was coming. Something...

Pray.

Helen's mouth opened and prayers spilled out. Loud. Desperate. She hardly knew where they came from. Her voice stuttered, and tears flooded her eyes, but she kept at it, praying for Leslie Brymes. That God would protect the girl. Give her strength. Guidance. Keep her alive.

Alive?

The words continued to flow. Helen leaned over, eyes squeezed shut, panic knocking around her ribs until she thought they'd break. As strong as her horror grew, the prayers felt even stronger. She rocked back and forth, begging God for Leslie's life, for protection over Kanner Lake. What had happened, she didn't know. Only that it was bad. And that what was coming would be worse.

And it would be here soon.

Oh, God, help us all.

Helen crossed her arms over her chest and prayed on.

ELEVEN

Behind the Java Joint counter, Bailey Truitt watched as Carla Radling's fingers lifted from the computer keys. *Uh-oh,* Bailey thought. *Here it comes.*

"For heaven's sake, Wilbur, you can't say that!" Carla sleeked a lock of black hair behind her ear and glared at the seventy-seven-year-old.

Wilbur pressed back in his chair at the corner computer table, indignation on his wizened face. "I can so, it's *my* post. Bailey said I could say anything I want."

Bailey kept quiet, one hand resting on a damp rag. Of all people to help Wilbur Hucks write his post for the "Scenes and Beans" blog, it was Carla. Those two couldn't be together one minute without arguing. The saving grace was they secretly enjoyed it.

"Tell her, Bailey!" Wilbur bobbed his white head. "You said when you started the thing last year as long as we don't talk about Edna San's murder—"

"Fine, Wilbur, but that doesn't mean you can say whatever you want about other people in the town." Carla put a hand on her well-dressed hip, aiming an exasperated look at Bailey. Clad in gray wool slacks and a maroon cashmere sweater, Carla was ready for a day in her real estate office. "You know what he wants to say? That Fr—"

"Would you *hush*!" Wilbur smacked the table. "You don't have to tell the whole world!"

Carla stared at him in utter wonderment. "You're fixing to put it on a public *blog*, and you don't want me to tell the few people in this café?"

Bailey wiped the cleaning rag across the Formica, watching as Wilbur cast a purposeful look around the room. She aimed to stay out of this one as long as possible. Wilbur's gaze traveled toward the corner table by the door, filled with usual occupants Bev Trexel and Angie Brendt, both retired schoolteachers. Bev stared back at Wilbur, a hand stuck in her blue-white hair, her powdered and wrinkled face full of stern disapproval. Prim and proper Beverly never would give Wilbur, with all his rough edges, the benefit of the doubt. Angie, wearing a bright pink sweat suit, listed her stout body toward the dueling duo, all ears for Carla's revelation. Her round cheeks were spotted red, one veined hand wrapped around her middler-sized mocha. Three tables over from Wilbur and Carla, Ted Dawson bent over his laptop computer, typing away on *Starfire*, his science fiction manuscript. Oblivious to all around him.

Wilbur made a face at Bev. She shook her coiffed head and turned back to Angie, dismissing him with all the dignity she could muster.

He folded his arms and faced Carla. "There are *ears* in this shop. You tell what I'm gonna say in my post, the whole town'll know it before tomorrow. Then who'll read the thing?"

Bev flicked a beleaguered look at the ceiling.

Carla pushed back her chair. "Okay then, Mr. Know-It-All. Get somebody else to type your post. I've got to get to work anyway."

"Well, that's a fine how-do-you-do. This how you treat people who want to buy a house? Tell 'em to get somebody else to help?"

Carla raised both hands in a wide shrug. "Yes, Wilbur, that's what I do. Just tell them to go somewhere else. Which is why I'm so successful at my job." She shoved in her chair, oozing irritation. "And now if you don't mind, I'm needed in my office. I'll be sure to tell anyone who calls to come here and let *you* find them a house." Picking up her nonfat biggie latte, she snatched up her red leather purse and flung it over her shoulder. "He's all yours, Bailey." She stalked toward the door.

Oh, boy. "Have a good day, Carla."

Chilly air filtered into the shop as Carla made her exit. Bailey turned to wipe down her espresso machine.

Wilbur uttered something Bailey couldn't hear, which was probably just as well. "Bailey?" He let out a long-suffering sigh. "You gonna help me with this thing or not?"

Bailey glanced through the windows toward the street. Nobody making their way toward the café at the moment. "Yes, Wilbur, I'll help you." She stepped around the counter and crossed toward him. "But if someone comes in, I'll have to stop. And you know I'm not going to let you say anything gossipy."

The old man grunted. "Fine, fine, be the boss. Just 'cause you started the thing." He heaved a sigh and frowned at the computer, as if it were all the machine's fault. "Women."

"Okay." Bailey slid into the chair in front of her computer. "Let me just read what you have so far." She leaned toward the monitor, squinting a little. At fifty-five, she didn't have the keen eyesight of Carla, who was barely past thirty.

It's me, Wilbur Hucks, coming to you once again through this here cy-whatza from Kanner Lake. (My know-it-all friend, Carla, just informed me it's called cyberspace. Well, how's a man to know? I've heard the word space, but I've never met a cyber in my life.)

Yesterday I went to the doc for a checkup on my heart. Remember I told you I had a triple bypass last summer? Anyway, doc says I now got one of the strongest tickers he's ever seen on a man my age. I'll probably live to 120. Hah. That's long enough to rile Carla. She says if I live that long, will I at least quit showing everybody my scar? Little pip-squeak. I came by my scar honestly and with more than a little pain, so I figure I got a right to show it to whoever I please. Last week I showed it to our new neighbor, that cute little Fredericka. (My wife was there, and so was Fredericka's husband, so don't go gettin' any ideas.) You shoulda seen the gal swoon! I thought it was the scar, but now I'm thinking it was my sexy chest. After all, Fredericka used to . . .

Bailey leaned back and turned a penetrating gaze on Wilbur. His eyebrows raised in all innocence. "What?"

She shook her head. "Wilbur, I know what you were going to say, and Carla's right—you can't do it."

He folded his arms, puffing his cheeks with air. Irritation shone in his watery blue eyes. "Drat it all, Bailey, you're young enough to be my daughter; you got no right tellin' me what to do—"

Bailey heard the café door open. She turned around.

"Howdy, Belle Bailey!" Pastor Hank Detcher flashed his smile from the threshold, then pointed both fingers like a double-barreled gun at Bev and Angie. "Mornin', girls."

They called their greetings as Bailey patted Wilbur on the arm. "We'll talk about this later, okay?" She rose to cross the café. "Morning. You're late today."

Hank shrugged off his coat, hung it on the back of a chair. "Yeah. Had an in-home visitation." Like many men in Kanner

Lake, Hank wore blue jeans and worn leather boots. A thick red sweater cast a ruddy hue to his cheeks. He was in his midfifties, his brown hair thinning and crows-feet etched into the corners of his warm brown eyes. He looked over at Wilbur. "Mornin', old man. You blogging?"

Wilbur snorted. "Tryin' to, if these women would stop bossin' me around."

"Wilbur"—Hank threw the words over his shoulder as he headed for the counter—"they'll never stop, and you know it. That's part of their charm."

Sighing, Wilbur pushed from his chair and made for his regular stool at the counter. Hank slipped onto the next one, withdrew four dollars from his wallet, and laid them down—three dollars for the drink, plus his usual tip. Bailey was already making his biggie latte.

"So what's going on this morning, other than you being henpecked?" Pastor Hank drummed his palms on the Formica in front of Wilbur and tossed Bailey a wink.

Wilbur opened his mouth to answer—and the Java Joint phone rang. Bailey set down the foaming latte and turned toward the rear portion of the L-shaped counter to pick up the receiver. Behind her, the men's voices faded into the background. "Good morning, Java Joint."

"Bailey?" The voice sounded as thin and fragile as an ice sliver. "It's Wilma Redlin. I'm . . . I was told Pastor Hank Detcher might be there?"

Bailey stilled. "He sure is here." Wilma was a resourceful and independent woman in her late sixties. Her tone was usually strong, and she'd never set foot in Hank's New Community Church, as far as Bailey knew. The woman held fast to her belief in spirits, crystals, and pyramids. "Is everything all right?"

"Something awful's happened." Wilma's words choked.

A slow trickle chilled Bailey's veins, and she *knew*. Not what or who, but … something. Twice in the past she'd been gripped in the same hard fist of precognition. The first—ten years back, the day her mother died at sixty-eight from a sudden heart attack. The second, almost five years ago when her husband, John, had the car accident that damaged his brain and left him an epileptic.

Dear God, who is it now?

"It's Vesta Johnson," Wilma said, as if she'd heard the prayer. "She wasn't feeling well yesterday, so this morning I've been calling over there, but got no answer. I finally decided to go across the street and ring her doorbell. Just when I reached her porch, a policeman pulled up, and then another one came. They told me they'd been called out to check the house, and I wasn't to touch anything." Wilma pulled in a shaky breath. "They went around to the back, and I followed at a distance. They told me to stay outside, but they were in the house for so long I couldn't stand it anymore. Vesta's been my friend for *years*, you know." The words pinched off.

"Yes, Wilma." Bailey clutched the phone, her eyes closed. A part of her wanted to flee the shop, anything to avoid hearing more. "I know."

Wilma was crying now. "Vesta's gone, Bailey. I peeked into her kitchen and saw blood on the floor. Then I screamed at the police until they told me what happened. They said she was murdered and found in somebody's car."

No. Not Vesta. Energy faded from Bailey's limbs. She reached out, laid a palm against the wall. Leaned her head against the back of her hand. Vaguely, she registered Pastor Hank's voice asking what was wrong.

"I need to talk to her preacher because …" Wilma's uneven breathing pulsed over the line. "Bailey, you there?"

"Yes. I'm here." Bailey could hardly speak. "I'll get him for you."

"Henry's come back!"

Bailey's mind couldn't process Wilma's blurted words. "Henry?"

"Johnson. Vesta's husband."

Bailey pulled her head up, focused bleary eyes on the wall. Henry Johnson had died over a year ago. "I don't—"

"That man was mean as a snake, and now he's proved it. I heard him tell Vesta once he could just strangle her 'cause of her 'stupid religion.'" Wilma's voice rose. "Bailey, his shoes were on Vesta's back patio. That crazy pair of red sneakers he always used to wear. I hadn't seen those shoes since Vesta and I cleaned out his closet a *year* ago. We threw them away 'cause Vesta said Goodwill wouldn't want 'em. Now there they are out of nowhere. And they have *blood* on them." Wilma's tone wavered. "I have to tell Vesta's pastor what's happened. I've never been one for prayer, but now ..." She drew a breath. "We need all the help we can get, Bailey. Henry Johnson's done returned from the dead, and we got to get him back on the right side of the grave."

TWELVE

Clutching notepad and pen, Leslie peered at an angle out her front garage window. Chief Edwards had slipped from view. She shuddered to think what he was doing—probably examining Vesta's body. Frank had already disappeared down the road. Leslie knew he'd seal off the street. No one would enter without his permission, and all names and times of coming and going would be recorded. No fun for area residents.

The image of Vesta's bloody head seared her mind. For the hundredth time Leslie shook it away.

Yellow crime-scene tape stretched in front of the house, wound around a neighbor's tree on one side, and the pasture fence on the other. *POLICE LINE, DO NOT CROSS*. Leslie couldn't read the words from where she stood, but she knew them all too well. As much as she'd seen the tape last year, on her own property it screamed all the more of violation, its color uglier, its flutter in the breeze more gut-wrenching.

Leslie had already made some necessary phone calls. First to her boss, Jared Moore. Die-hard, nose-for-news Jared was shaken at her story. Vesta had lived in his neighborhood and often passed the Moores' place on her walks. "Would you please call Bud Grayson and Myra Hodgkid?" Leslie asked him. "I had Bud at eleven and Myra at two. Tell them I'll reschedule their interviews when I can."

Jared promised to take care of it.

Next, her parents. Leslie's mom taught third grade and couldn't be reached, but she caught her father at his insurance office. He was horrified to hear a killer had been so close to his daughter.

"You're coming home today, you and Paige. And you're staying here until this guy is caught."

No kidding. No way did Leslie want to sleep in this house tonight.

Third call: Enterprise Rent-a-Car in Coeur d'Alene. They promised to deliver a four-door midsize right away. Leslie hadn't bothered telling the guy he'd be stopped at the end of her street by a policeman. He'd find that out soon enough.

After that she'd thrown some things into a suitcase—enough to last for a few days.

Now Leslie watched out her garage window, trying to see what Chief Edwards was doing. She was feeling stronger by the minute—or so she told herself. It helped to imagine a wall inside her chest, building brick by brick, holding back the emotions. She knew policemen had their own walls. Had to, with all the trauma they saw. Chief Edwards no doubt was working very hard right now to keep his in place, out there next to Vesta's battered body ...

Leslie forced her mind to the to-do list on her notepad.

One—take Paige to Simple Pleasures. Paige had no wheels either, although she'd probably get her car back by tomorrow.

Two—head over to Hayley Street where Vesta lived, talk to her neighbors. Had they seen or heard anything last night? Could they imagine anyone who'd want to kill Vesta?

Three—Frank. She would question him as she and Paige drove off the street, using all the charm she could muster. Which wouldn't be hard in hunky Frank's presence—

Chief Edwards stepped into sight.

Leslie craned her neck. He was examining something in the grass next to the driveway, camera in hand. He stooped down, peering closer. Then disappeared.

What was he doing?

Leslie hurried into the kitchen and toward the front door. As she passed by the hall she could hear Paige in her bedroom, closing a suitcase zipper. Leslie eased outside on the porch, watched Chief Edwards walk toward the street. From his car he pulled out four wooden stakes and carried them back up her driveway. Intent on his work, he didn't notice her. On the grass, he pushed the stakes into the soft ground, creating a rectangle. Started winding yellow tape around them.

Pulled by her need to know, Leslie walked halfway down the sidewalk. "Chief. What did you find?"

He turned around. "Leslie, you shouldn't be out here."

"I know, but what did you *find*?"

He gazed from her to the ground and back. Hesitated, as if weighing whether he should answer. "A shoeprint. Now get back in the house."

"Oh." More questions surfaced, but Leslie resisted. She knew better than to push him any further right now. Even so, hope surged as she returned inside and shut the door.

A shoeprint. How fortunate, considering the killer could have stayed on the concrete.

A piece of evidence like this could lead them right to the murderer.

THIRTEEN

When he was six, he saw his sister's ghost.

His parents were summoning her spirit in the living room. They lived in Southern California at the time, his father an architect and his mother answering phones at a car dealership. Tamara had been dead three months, succumbed at age nine to leukemia.

His parents went crazy with grief. Their salvation – or damnation, depending on how you looked at it – was their entry into the world of séance.

At the funeral home, Tamara lay in a white casket. Now years later, he could still picture the room – beige walls, blue and brown carpet. Rows of folding chairs with padded gray seats. His parents led him by the hand into the room, asking the big man with the serious face for some time alone before friends arrived.

He cried and begged to stay outside.

The strong smell of flowers sickened him. Tamara's casket sat half open on a long pedestal, revealing his dead sister from the waist up.

Was the rest of her still there?

His parents yanked him closer. He cried louder, dragging his heels.

Tamara's face looked white and waxy. Like the grub worm he'd dug up in the backyard a few days ago – just about the time he heard his mother's wail from the window of Tamara's room. The sound terrified him. He watched the worm thrash in his palm in rhythm with his mother's cries, thinking that was the cause. He shook the worm onto the ground, praying for it to stop twisting. After that his mom would be all right ...

But it squirmed even more. His mother's crying grew louder. And his father joined in.

The worm convulsed and lay still.

He'd killed it.

Then he learned his sister had died.

At the casket, his mother lifted him up and over Tamara's body. He flailed both arms, screaming for her to stop. "Hush up and kiss your sister," Mom spat. He could smell the tobacco on her breath. She lowered him head first, down toward the grub worm cheeks and lips. The horrible sight came closer, closer. If he touched it, he would turn to stone.

"No!" He writhed and kicked, bracing his arms against the raised lid. His mother yanked them back and pinned them against his chest. Pushed him down. His screams rose, then muffled as his mouth mushed against rock-hard lips.

His mother held him there.

Greedy Tamara sucked the breath out of him.

When he came to, he was lying on his back in the corner of the room, his dark-faced father towering over him. "How *dare* you treat your sister like that?" The words lashed. "After she loved you so much."

Two weeks later they held their first séance.

They made him leave the room, saying his sister wouldn't come with him around. He was glad to hide in his bedroom. Still, they were calling the ghost to *his* house, and Tamara might show up anywhere. What if she knew he'd killed her along with the grub worm? She would haunt him forever. And if she'd looked so horrible in her casket—imagine how she'd be *now*.

His parents had never taken him to church, but he knew they'd believed in God. Until Tamara died. Then they wanted nothing to do with Him. They wouldn't even speak His name except in a curse. Instead they turned to the "Black Powers," hoping to see Tamara again.

He didn't know where they learned their spells. From some book? Each time it was the same. His mom and dad would plead with the Powers, their voices low and intense, then louder and louder. The sound chilled him to the bone. The air in the house would turn heavy and cold, and goose bumps would pop down his arms.

He started hiding under his bed.

Door locked, he would slide into his place, resting a cheek on folded arms. When his neck got sore, he'd face the other way. He learned to press his feet against the wall. Something told him as long as he did, his sister couldn't sneak up behind him. Deep down, he knew that was stupid. Ghosts could go anywhere, right? It's not like she needed *room.* In fact, what was to keep her from coming right through the wall? Still he clung to the belief, telling himself even ghosts had to follow the rules. And this was one of them—no sneaking up on a boy under the bed when his feet touched the wall.

The chanting wasn't as scary in the daytime, but after dark it terrified him. He turned on every light in his room. And he prayed. Hard. He wasn't sure to What. He just knew he couldn't face this alone. He needed ... Something. Someone big and strong, who knew all the ghost rules.

Maybe that Somebody even *made* the rules.

One summer night his parents' chants droned on and on. The sun was still up when he slipped under his bed, but now, peeking through the two-inch space between the covers and carpet, he could see the light fading. Fear bit at him. He pressed the balls of his bare feet hard against the wall. He didn't dare slide out to turn the light on. The minute he did, his sister would jump him.

The edge of light on his carpet pulled away ... away. Then disappeared.

He breathed harder, air sucking in and out of his mouth. His sister would hear it. If she hadn't guessed his hiding place, she'd find it now. The quieter he tried to be, the more oxygen he needed. And it was so hot! His skin grew slick with sweat.

His hiding place darkened.

A sudden wailing chant from his parents filtered through his door. His muscles locked tight. His breath sputtered, and the sweat turned cold. He started to shiver.

This was it — the night Tamara had been waiting for. Now she'd catch him in the dark as his parents called for her. He stared at his blue bedspread, watching it fade to black. He couldn't see the carpet beyond it anymore.

The rules change after dark.

The horrifying thought shot through his heart. He wiggled backward until every part of his feet pressed against the wall, from toe to heel. The position raised his lower legs off the floor, straining the muscles behind his knees. How long could he stay like that?

What if it didn't do any good?

Maybe he should slip out — real quick — and run for the light switch.

He'd never make it. Tamara would be there.

His leg muscles tingled ... burned ... shook. The bedspread disintegrated into blackness.

Blood pounded in his ears. From the living room the chants rose and fell, scraping his nerves. His legs started to shake, then his whole body.

He was going to die. He'd join his sister in the World of the Grave, and then she would eat him whole.

His leg muscles jerked so badly he couldn't keep his heels against the wall. Only the balls of his feet and his toes. After a while, just his toes. Endless minutes passed. All energy ran out of him until he thought his tired heart would quit. Even his muscles couldn't shake as much. Then they stopped completely. His breathing slowed.

Sleep tugged at him — which was worse than shivering. It stretched his thoughts long and colorless, like pulled taffy. He couldn't give in. Could *not*. The minute he fell asleep, his sister would come ...

Footsteps.

The chanting had quieted.

There, again! Someone walking on the carpet.

He lifted his head enough to bring his ear up off his arms. Listening.

Another step.

His heart thrashed with the ferocity of a scared bird's wings.

His eyes had adjusted to the darkness just enough to see the edge of the bedspread —

And the vague shape reaching underneath the fabric. Lifting it up.

Glassy eyes stared at him.

All breath sucked from his throat.

Tamara's mouth stretched into a slow, hideous smile. "I found you." Her voice ground gravel.

He screamed. Jerked up his head and banged it against the bed. Slid out from under and pushed to his feet. He stumbled through the dark toward his door, flung it wide, and pounded down the hallway. Burst into the living room, startling his parents, their faces flickering in the light of a dozen candles. Howling, he jumped on his father's chest and pounded with both fists.

"Stop it, stop it, *stop it*!" He hit and kicked and shrieked until his father shook him off like some savage locust. He hit the floor, his mother pouncing on top of him, yelling that he'd ruined it all just as they'd almost broken through, and now she would hate him forever. He wanted to say they *had* broken through, that his sister was in his bedroom, ready to eat him, and did they want to lose him too? But his mother slapped and punched, driving his head once, twice, three times to the hardwood floor. The pain, her screams, the smell of candles blended into toxic smoke, circling above his head, vacuuming the air from his lungs —

The world careened to black.

He awoke the next morning in bed, still in his clothes, face bruised and the back of his head tender enough to make him cry.

His parents never spoke of the incident.

In time his bruises healed — those on his skin, anyway. Whenever his parents chanted — two, maybe three times a week — he slipped into the garage, turned on the lights, and locked himself in his father's car. New ghost rule: no coming after him as long as his back pressed against the seat and his feet were flat on the floor. That meant no lying down, sometimes hour after hour, and he'd feel so tired.

But it kept his sister away.

FOURTEEN

As Leslie finished jotting a note about the footprint in her notebook, her cell rang. She placed the pad on the kitchen counter and pulled the phone from her jeans pocket. Checked the incoming number. Not one she recognized. "Leslie Brymes."

"Hello, Leslie." An older woman's voice. Soft, but tinged with anxiety. "This is Helen Communs from church."

A pang shot through Leslie. One of Vesta's many friends. Another widow. "Hi."

"I hope you don't mind me calling. I got this number from Jared."

Sounds of cardboard shoving across a floor filtered through the kitchen door. Paige was keeping herself occupied, sorting through boxes in the garage. "That's okay. How are you?"

"Oh, well, I . . . I heard the news. About Vesta."

Of course she had. "Yes. I'm sorry. I know she was your friend. Mine too."

"Everybody loved Vesta."

Leslie closed her eyes. "I know."

Helen Communs cleared her throat. "Look, I wanted to tell you something. This morning—before I'd heard anything—I had an experience. I heard God speak to me. Not in an audible voice, but in my head. Never happened to me before. But when it happens, boy, do you know it. He told me to pray for you."

"Me?"

"Very strongly. Tell you the truth, I was petrified. I knew something terrible was coming. I prayed until the feeling passed. Not long after that, I heard the news. But I also want to tell you ..."

Leslie looked out the window to her backyard, waiting. She could feel the woman's reticence, and it scared her. The way Mrs. Communs spoke—as if she knew something and didn't know how to say it.

"I hope I'm doing the right thing in telling you, Leslie. It's just that the feeling was so strong. You need to be careful. This thing's ... not done yet. I don't know what that means, I just know it's true. Watch who you trust. Most of all, keep praying. I promise you, I'll keep at it too."

Leslie tingled all over. She licked her lips, searching for a response. She should feel safer, knowing God had called someone to pray for her in such a way. Right? But the thought that she needed special prayer ...

"Thank you, Mrs. Communs. For praying. And for telling me."

"Oh, well, of course. I'm so sorry this has happened to you. And Vesta—it's still hard to believe."

"Yeah," Leslie whispered. "It is."

They said good-bye, and Leslie folded her phone closed, pressing it between her palms. *This thing's not done yet ...*

A shiver knocked between her shoulder blades.

She shook it off, slid the phone back into her pocket. Pushing her notebook and pen out of the way, Leslie leaned over the counter, closed her tearing eyes, and began to pray.

FIFTEEN

Vince finished taping off the print and checked his watch. Ten-fifteen. Idaho State Police ought to be showing up any minute. His own officer Jim Tentley, who was supposed to report here, hadn't been located yet. He wasn't at home and hadn't answered his cell phone. Vince couldn't blame the guy for leaving it behind on his day off.

Rocking back on his haunches, Vince gazed at the print, surprised he'd missed it before. It was a good, clear one on a bald spot in the water-ravaged grass. On the other hand, he'd first walked up Leslie's driveway watching the pavement, then had been occupied with the contents of her car.

The footprint looked like it came from a sneaker. Right foot, man-sized. Pointing straight toward the VW, as if the guy stepped back, found himself on ground, and stepped forward again. The tread pattern dissolved a little toward the inside heel, indicating heavier wear on that part of the shoe. The guy could have a tendency to roll his foot inward when he walked.

Vince pushed to his feet, gaze traveling from the print to the car. Why would the perpetrator have stepped backward some six feet from the VW? The footprint would make more sense if the car sat closer to the edge of the driveway—

His cell rang. Vince pulled it from the clip on his belt, checked the ID. Roger Waitman's number. He flipped open the phone.

"Roger. What'd you find at Vesta's house?"

77

In his midforties, Roger had been with the Kanner Lake police almost fifteen years. The man was a bit on the crusty side, plenty opinionated. Slim as a reed, but wiry strong. A no-nonsense cop.

"No sign of forced entry, but the back door was unlocked." Roger's voice had the hoarseness of a years-long smoker. "Blood in the living room—substantial on an armchair facing the television, with splatter on the wall and ceiling. My initial guess is, she was watching TV when someone approached from behind and hit her on the head."

Vince grunted. Was Vesta hard of hearing? He didn't think so. An intruder would have to be mighty quiet to walk right up behind someone without being heard. "Anything in the rest of the house?"

"Nothing in the bedrooms or bathrooms that we could see. There are drops on the kitchen floor, close to that back door, that look like blood. Like maybe she was picked up and carried out that way."

Why?

The answer to that question would lead Vince to the perpetrator. Why take the chance of moving the body all the way across town, being seen by someone? The act was so in-your-face, so purposeful.

And so targeted at Leslie.

The sound of an engine filtered from the street. Vince turned, spotted an ISP vehicle pulling up to the curb.

"One more thing, Chief."

That slight dip in Roger's tone. Vince knew he was about to be told something he wouldn't want to hear.

"Yeah?"

Two officers got out of the Idaho State Police car. Grant Dyland, a six-foot-four lumbering guy in his early fifties. Had a reputation for knowing his stuff. And Steve Harrough, about ten years younger and a good six inches shorter.

Vince raised his hand in a distracted wave.

"Vesta's neighbor, Wilma Redlin, was here," Roger said. "We could barely keep her out of the place. On the back patio is a pair of men's red tennis shoes. Woman freaked, Chief. She insisted they belonged to Henry, Vesta's dead husband. Said he's come back from the grave, because she threw those shoes away herself when she and Vesta cleaned out his clothes a year ago."

Dyland and Harrough started up the driveway, carrying their tools. A camera, notebook, some evidence bags.

Tennis shoes. Vince's eyes cut to the footprint he'd marked off. "Does the right shoe have mud on the bottom?"

"Yeah, matter of fact. Other one looks clean."

The state troopers hit the curve in the driveway, focused on the VW. Vince backed up a few steps to give them more space as they approached the car, then focused on Roger again. "Did you notice the shoe's tread by any chance? Does it look worn toward the inside heel?"

"No, I didn't. Want me to check?"

Vince didn't really need this information now. The lab would make the ultimate call whether the print matched the shoes at Vesta's house. When the techs arrived, they'd make a mold of the evidence. Their kit would contain the two necessary powders to be mixed with water, then poured over the print. The mixture would dry almost immediately, then be lifted off, yielding a thin, hard, strong piece of plastic. The mold of the tread would be compared to the shoe and its unique wear pattern.

Still, ultimate call aside, Vince wanted a sense now of what he was dealing with. A dead man back from the grave? Henry Johnson hadn't been Kanner Lake's favorite citizen, but Vince wasn't going to accept that explanation.

All the same, a dark feeling sidled through his gut.

"Sure. Take another look at it."

Dyland and Harrough were peering inside the VW, exchanging observations. They would wait for a briefing from him before they started their work. Vince felt a twinge of envy at their easy objectivity. What a different story it was when you knew the victim. He lowered the phone. "Thanks for coming. Be with you in a minute."

They nodded.

"Okay, Chief?"

Roger's distant voice sounded from the phone. Vince put the cell back up to his ear.

"I checked and yeah, I think the tread's a little worn."

Vince stared at the yellow tape wound around the stakes, assimilating the information. His mind flitted over the assertions—too soon yet to call them fact. A dead man's shoes used in the murder? The body brought here—then the shoes returned to Vesta's house? That would be crazy. Who would do that? Why?

Maybe more than one person was involved . . .

But where could the shoes have come from?

Vince shook his head. So many questions, and—for now—no satisfying answers. Bottom line, Wilma Redlin had to be wrong. Either she and Vesta hadn't thrown the shoes away, or this was a different pair.

"Why do you want to know all this?" Roger asked.

Vince laid a hand on the back of his neck. "I found a print. Can't know for sure, but it sounds like it might be a match."

"Terrific. Maybe the dead husband *did* do it."

"Roger, don't even kid about that. The wrong person overhears and guess what. You want it to end up in the papers?"

"Hey, it won't come from me. But this Wilma Redlin is another story."

The dread in Vince's gut grew stronger, which annoyed him. He turned away from the ISP officers, focused on the modest white house across the street. Of *course* they were dealing with a sick case of flesh and bone, not some ghost. The very thought was ridiculous. Still, nothing about this crime made sense. Vince didn't want illogical bits of a puzzle. He wanted cut and dried. And a suspect arrested—today.

Before he had a second victim on his hands.

"Okay, Roger, thanks." Vince's words clipped. "The ISP's here. I'll get them started, then come see what you've got over there. Although I need to get statements from the residents of this house first. Until I can get there, you and C. B. secure the scene."

He snapped the phone closed without waiting for Roger's reply.

Before turning back, he took a minute to breathe. Too many disparate thoughts in his head, too many colored threads in one tangled mess. He needed concentration enough to sort it all out. A possible match—so soon—to the footprint should be good news, but Vince couldn't shake his ambivalence. With all this weirdness attached, it may be just as well if they didn't match.

He slipped the cell phone into his pocket. *Lord, I need Your help with this one.*

As he briefed Dyland and Harrough, Vince's unease increased, and he couldn't pinpoint why. Dyland's eyes bugged at the story of the tennis shoes, and Harrough shook his head. "Man, Edwards, what is going *on* with Kanner Lake these days?"

Two cars showed up from Enterprise—one for Leslie and Paige, the second a return car to take the first driver back to Coeur d'Alene. The girls wanted to leave right away, and Vince had to say no. They'd need to be questioned before they went anywhere.

With the girls returning inside—none too happily—the ISP officers pulled on gloves and opened the VW door.

Dyland squatted down by the seat. Vince stood to his right on the other side of the open door, Harrough leaning in to see from his left. Dyland pointed at the note on Vesta's chest and let out a low whistle. "Not too subtle, is he."

Harrough glanced at Vince. "You know her?"

Vince inclined his head. "Small town. Not many I don't know." His throat tightened. "She was a wonderful lady."

Dyland looked up at him, a solemn veil drawing over his face. His deep-set eyes met Vince's in unspoken empathy. Vince nodded, grateful for the expression. These homicide detectives saw a lot of death, and like others in their field, had learned, for the sake of self-preservation, to harden themselves to it. For Dyland to let his guard down, even momentarily, meant much to Vince.

Harrough cleared his throat. He gestured toward Vesta's bloodied hands. "She must have fought."

Vince thought about it. "That, or the first blow didn't kill her, and her hands went to the wound."

The scene played through his head in vivid Technicolor. Vesta, sitting in her chair. The *crack* of the first blow. Her strangled cry, fingers flying to the pain. A second blow. The thump of her body hitting the floor.

He drew a deep breath and turned toward the street, hand on his hip.

"Look here." Dyland pointed to Vesta's right leg, close to her hands. "A hair."

Vince leaned over the car door, squinting. "The victim's?"

"Don't think so. Let's take a closer look."

Harrough stepped away to retrieve a pair of tweezers from their kit. He handed them to Dyland, who lifted the hair and held it up for Vince to see.

It was coarse and white, about three inches long. Vince looked at it and blinked. Twice. Two thoughts ran through his head.

No. Couldn't be his.

Why didn't I see that before?

But he hadn't spotted the footprint at first either. Missing one was strange enough. Missing them both ...

Vince stared at the piece of evidence, pinpricks dancing up his arms. No denying the coincidence. The hair looked like it could have come from Henry Johnson. The man had sported the thickest, coarsest white hair Vince had ever seen. About that length too.

Vince felt his mouth open. "Okay."

Dyland lowered the tweezers. "Got any ideas?"

He hesitated, then shook his head. "No."

The detective gave him a long look, then turned to Harrough. "Might as well take it for the techs."

Harrough produced a bag. Dyland dropped the hair inside, then labeled the evidence. Vince could not tear his eyes away. The prickling on his arms jumped like electricity to the back of his neck.

A minute later Dyland found a second hair on Vesta's knee.

What in the—?

Vince stepped back from the car, thoughts in a whirl. Planting both hands on his hips, he stared at the ground, seeing nothing, trying to wrap his mind around this craziness. A scene from the previous year ran through his mind—Henry Johnson, the last time he had seen the man alive.

Henry had hunched in front of an IGA checkout, gnarled knuckles jammed against the counter, face thrust toward Ralph Bednershack in contorted rage. A shock of his white hair stuck straight out, as if his indignation trembled his very scalp. "I told you I'm not payin' for that meat! It was spoiled, and we had to throw out every last piece of it!"

"Ralph, please, it's not his fault." Vesta shot a look of abject apology toward Ralph. "I left it sitting in the refrigerator too long, that's the—"

"Nobody asked you to open your yap, Vesta!" Henry had glared at her. "One of these days someone's gonna shut you up for good."

The words echoed in Vince's head.

He pulled in a long breath. He would find an explanation for all this, of course. Somewhere out there—in the land of the living—lurked his suspect. That person *would* be caught. These … coincidences would fall into place.

Even as he told himself this, Vince could not deny the sickening feeling that snaked through his gut—a profound and new sense of evil, one whose origin he couldn't define. As if he stared into a dark cave inhabited by monsters.

"Edwards?" Dyland's voice snapped his attention. Vince blinked, looked toward the detective. Dyland raised his bushy eyebrows. "Hey, man, what's up? You look like you just saw a ghost."

PART TWO

Pursuit

SIXTEEN

When the doorbell rang, Leslie was on the phone, trying to convince her frightened mother—who'd just heard the news—that she was okay. Which was true—sort of. In the background, thumps and bumps filtered from Paige's room. She'd carried three boxes in there and now channeled her energies into unpacking.

Leslie breathed a sigh of relief at the doorbell. *Finally.* "Mom, I gotta go. That's probably Chief Edwards at the door. He needs to talk to me and Paige."

Within minutes the three of them were seated in the living room, Paige and Leslie on the couch, and Chief Edwards in an armchair, pad of paper and pen in hand. His worried features betrayed his emotion, as much as he tried to hide it. Leslie felt sorry for him. She would do her best not to make his job any harder.

The chief began by asking about last night. What time had they last seen their cars? What time had they gone to bed? Did they hear any noises outside?

They'd heard nothing. She and Paige had already discussed that. Not even a vague memory, some noise perhaps thought a dream. They'd both slept like rocks.

"You did hear something this morning though, Leslie," Paige said. "When you were in the hallway."

Thanks for bringing that up. Leslie shrugged. "I didn't really hear a noise. I just ... sensed something." The chief waited for her to continue, but she said no more.

"What do you mean, sensed something?"

Oh, great. "I felt weird, like something was at my back. A kind of presence. It touched my neck. I know it sounds silly, but ..."

Surprise flicked across his face, as if her words triggered something in his own consciousness, then it was gone.

Had she imagined that?

"I did go out to my car last night, though," Leslie added. "Around maybe nine o'clock. I'd left my cell phone in it and didn't realize until I went to charge it."

Chief Edwards made a note. "Okay. I need to ask a few personal questions. Do you want to continue like this? I can interview you separately, if you'd like."

Paige shrugged at Leslie. "I'd rather stay together."

"Me too," Leslie said. "No secrets here."

"All right." The chief looked to Leslie. "Any new friends in your life that you might suspect? Any strange phone calls? Any men you happen to be dating?"

Dating? I wish. How about putting in a good word for me to Frank?

Leslie shook her head. "I'm not going out with anyone right now. Been too busy at work. And no new friends or strange phone calls either. I mean, life's been pretty normal since the trial last month."

"Well, I've been making lots of new friends." Paige lifted her shoulder. "Just people in town, you know? As far as hanging out, it's been with Leslie's group of friends that go back to high school. And I'm not dating anybody either."

It would be some time before Paige was ready for that, Leslie figured. Paige was just learning to stabilize her life. Dating brought far too many complications.

Chief Edwards wrote in his notebook. "Either of you turn down someone who asked you out?"

They shook their heads.

Like a flaming arrow from nowhere, a picture of the circled number one on Vesta's chest shot across Leslie's mind. The arrow pierced, its message branding into her brain. She stilled. *How* could she have not thought about that note until now?

Paige hadn't mentioned it either. But then, Paige hadn't opened the VW's door. Maybe she hadn't even noticed it.

"Chief," Leslie blurted, "why is that number on Vesta's chest?"

His eyes held hers. Leslie stared back, silently pleading she was wrong.

"What number?" Paige's voice sharpened.

Leslie kept her eyes on the chief's face. "A circled number one."

Chief Edwards cleared his throat. "Can't know for sure. But there are certain ... conjectures." He tapped his pen against the paper. "Let's just say I want to get this crime solved as soon as possible. And, Leslie?" He pointed at her. "That piece of information needs to stay out of the papers."

Leslie's mouth firmed. "For Vesta's sake and the town's—it won't come from me."

"Thanks." The chief's gaze moved from her to Paige and back. Paige was staring at her lap. "You both need to be aware of people around you. Anything unusual or suspicious, I want you to call me immediately." He pulled a piece of paper from his notebook. "Here's my cell phone number. And I want to make sure I have yours."

Leslie rattled off her number. Paige didn't carry a cell phone yet. Chief Edwards wrote his own down twice, tore the piece of paper in half, and leaned forward to hand them each a copy. Leslie's thoughts pulsed with a dozen scenarios of why either of them might need to make that call.

The chief looked to Leslie. "What stories are you working on right now? Any bit of investigative reporting that may have upset someone?"

Whoa.

The thought pierced right through her. She hadn't considered the possibility, not at all. Is this what she might have done to cause Vesta's death—ticked somebody off with a mere story? So a friend of hers is killed and stuffed in her car, just to get even? That would be *insane.*

Leslie leaned back against the couch, stomach churning. If Vesta died because of something she'd written, she could never write again.

She pulled in a deep breath. "I can't think of anything. I'm sorry. Just the idea …" She looked out the window, blinked a few times. "The big story now is the hotel controversy. I was supposed to interview Bud Grayson by phone this morning, and Myra Hodgkid at her house this afternoon. You know they're at each other's throats over this thing. Mr. Grayson had about won the city council over when Myra and her 'Give Kanner Lake a Break' cronies started all their petitioning against the hotel. You saw yesterday's edition?"

Chief Edwards nodded.

"Okay, then you read the cover story, 'Investment or Attack?' Today I was supposed to learn from Grayson his latest data for projected tax revenue from the hotel. Then I was going to quote that to Myra and see how she'd refute the positives for the town. Frankly, I don't think she cares about the extra money and jobs. She's just part of the old guard that wants to keep Kanner Lake like it's always been, and that's that."

The chief eyed her. "Sounds like you're on Grayson's side."

Leslie folded her arms. No way could she let herself believe anything she'd written had led to this awful crime. And besides, what did that story have to do with Vesta? "Privately, maybe, but I don't let it show in my reporting. I always quote both sides."

The chief scratched his cheek. "Leslie, if this murder does link to the hotel, who in your opinion would it benefit more?

Grayson and his investors, and all the business people who support them, because the crime might give Kanner Lake new publicity? Or those against him, who might think another traumatic
event would scare him off?"

Leslie stared at him. Now this was more like it. What a reliev-
ing question. Had some crazy person on one side or the other
turned to murder? If so, nothing she'd done or written had
caused Vesta's death ...

"I have no idea." Leslie's thoughts whipped in the sudden·
wind of possibility. The people she'd need to talk to, the rumors
she could follow. "But I'm going to find out."

"*No*, Leslie." Chief Edwards pointed at her. "*I'm* going to find
out. Got that?"

"Absolutely. I get it." Leslie held up a hand, nodding hard. Not
meaning a word of it.

As the chief turned to Paige with questions, Leslie made a
mental list of the first people she would call.

Watch who you trust. Mrs. Communs's warning.

Sure, she'd remember that. While she followed up on this
lead.

SEVENTEEN

By the time he finished breakfast, he'd resigned himself to their new demand. Already, he looked toward darkness.

Strange, how all dread had vanished—along with his conscience. If these feelings were still inside him, they lay deep, precious coins sunk to the bottom of a lake. He tried peering down into himself, searching for them, but saw only blackness.

The loss of humanity was a frightening thing.

Breakfast dishes in the sink, he spread a street map of Kanner Lake on the kitchen table. He knew all the roads in town, but he wanted to look at the layout of things. Beside the map sat a phone book and pencil.

Leslie Brymes would not stay in her own house tonight; he could bet on that. Probably run to her parents.

He pulled the phone book close, checked for *Brymes*. There— Matthew and Linda, 244 Sutter.

He circled the street on the map.

Eyes narrowing, he leaned back. Leslie Brymes. Blonde and pretty. Big brown eyes, nice lips. And ambitious. Had even gotten herself on TV. She was mighty young to wield so much power.

In his past life he might have dated her. If he'd wanted to, he'd have gotten her. Now the mere thought curled his lip.

His gaze drifted out the window. The trees stood resolute and green, winter over. A week ago snow had frosted their branches. Funny how the end of it had melted last night—the night of his first Kanner Lake killing. *This* should be the winter season, the time for cold, long nights. Yet nature mocked him with spring.

Back to the phone book. He flipped pages and ran his finger down the small print to another name. Wrote down the address and circled it on the map. *Hm.* Helpful location.

Leaning over the map, he studied how the two marked streets connected. The best path from one to another. The paths from each to his own house. Looked good. Very doable.

It was still morning. He had hours to figure all the details.

Meanwhile, he had other things to do.

He pushed back from the table and headed for the closet to fetch his coat. His "normal" life in Kanner Lake awaited.

EIGHTEEN

"You sure you're okay, Paige?"

Leslie pulled her rental car into a parking space near Java Joint and cut the engine. Since they'd ended their interview with Chief Edwards, her thoughts had raced like some NASCAR contender. So many people to talk to, so much to explore. The work built up her protective wall, kept her mind busy. Without it, she'd flash for the hundredth time on Vesta's face, all beaten and bloody...

"I'm fine." Paige managed a smile. "How are you?"

Leslie wagged her head. "Peachy keen."

Paige eyed her. "I know that look. Just promise me you'll be careful. The person who left that circled number one may be watching what you do. This isn't just a story to investigate, Leslie, it's people's *lives* on the line."

Leslie drew back. "As if I don't know that?"

"Of course you know it. But I know *you*. You'll throw yourself into your work as a shield, rationalizing that maybe you'll turn up some evidence. And maybe you will." Her voice tightened. "But so help me, Leslie, if you get yourself killed in the process, I will never forgive you. You're the friend I've always wanted, and if I lose you now, you're *toast*, hear me?

"Yeah. Burned toast, even."

At Leslie's feigned seriousness, Paige let out a huff. "You're a pain sometimes, know that?"

They slid from the car, Paige turning to cross the street toward the beautifully decorated front windows of the Simple Pleasures gift store. "Sure you don't want a coffee?" Leslie asked. "You can go decaf, you know."

Paige shook her head. "I'm late enough as it is. Tell them hi for me." She waved good-bye and jaywalked across Main.

When Leslie stepped through Java Joint's door, Wilbur, Jake, and Bailey greeted her as one. Hunched on his stool, Wilbur eyed her like a hawk. Beside him sat Jake, dingy red baseball cap shoved over his big ears. Jake was sixty-five, a skinny man with a scrawny neck and bug eyes who'd retired a year ago from his job at a lumber mill. Loved to gossip, and now had more time for it than ever.

At his usual table, S-Man perched in front of his laptop, dark brows almost touching as he focused on the screen. His collar-length brown hair looked half combed. Hearing Leslie's name, he glanced up, blinked a few times, and his expression cleared. "Hey, Les."

"Hi, Ted."

His recognition of her presence spoke louder than the concern of the other three put together. Ted was usually so wrapped up in writing, the world could fall down around him. He'd started his novel ten months ago when an accident at his logging job left him on disability with a broken right leg. Every day he'd claimed the same table at Java Joint, pecking at his keyboard. The cast finally came off, but the injury left him with a permanent limp. He'd not been able to return to his job. Now he wrote all the more furiously, driven by his mounting bills to launch a career as a novelist.

"Leslie, honey, how are you doing?" Bailey stood behind the counter, empathy brimming in her brown eyes. "Come on and have a seat; your drink's on the house today."

Gratitude washed through Leslie. Hospitality was Bailey's way of comforting. The woman wouldn't press for news and juicy details. She'd just serve, and wait until Leslie was ready to talk.

Wilbur *tsk*ed. "How come *my* drink wasn't on the house?"

"Wilbur, hush." Jake nudged him with an elbow.

The older man hitched his shoulders. "Just trying to add a little levity."

Leslie sank onto the stool beside Jake. No need to order; Bailey knew what she wanted. Ted limped over and took the last stool next to her.

Oh, no, here it came again. All their obvious worry made her throat tighten. She gave Ted a wan smile. "How's your book, S-Man?"

No fooling Ted. His dark chocolate eyes bored through her. At thirty-one, he looked like a young Stephen King, with the same intense expression. The man was laconic, unemotional, and distracted—and that was when you could pull him from Sauria. But Leslie saw the concern in his face.

"Going good. Be done in a few weeks, then it's off to the agent who asked to see it."

Leslie nodded. Her mouth kept moving, a disconnect from her brain. "That's terrific. You know we're all pulling for you. Ted Dawson's going to be famous someday."

"Can we chitchat later?" Wilbur's tone bulged with impatience. "I want to know what's goin' on. Where's Paige?"

"Now, Wilbur, she'll talk when she's ready." Bailey set the biggie latte before Leslie. "Here you go, hon."

A crack fissured up the brick wall inside Leslie. She took a deep breath, steadied herself. "Thanks, you all, for worrying about us. Paige had to hurry to work, but she wanted me to tell you she's fine."

Tersely, Leslie covered the basics—how she'd found Vesta in her car, her and Paige's interview with the chief. Much to Wilbur's and Jake's disappointment, she offered no inside details, such as the message the killer had left, or the footprint. No way could she trust those men to keep such things quiet.

"And now I have a lot of work to do." She slid off the stool. "If any of you hear something important, I want you to call my cell phone right away, okay? Bailey's got the number." She picked up her coffee drink. "And look, all of you, *please* be careful. Whoever did this is still out there. And who knows if he'll do it again."

As she turned to go, she caught Bailey's eye, and instant communication flowed. Bailey had something to tell her. Leslie blinked away before either of the two old geezers caught the look. S-Man was already beating a path back to his laptop. Leslie gave a slight jerk of her head toward the front door and crossed the café.

She heard Bailey's voice behind her. "Be right back, gentlemen."

They met out on the sidewalk, Bailey coatless in the cold air. Without looking, Leslie knew Wilbur and Jake ogled them through the window and would pump Bailey for information when she returned. Not that it would do them any good.

Quickly, Bailey told her about a phone call she'd received from Wilma Redlin. About a pair of shoes. Henry's supposed ghost.

Whoa. Leslie gaped at her friend. Something very weird was going on here. Not that she believed Henry Johnson had come back from the grave to murder his wife, but . . .

How strange that she'd sensed some presence, like fingers touching her neck, before finding Vesta's body. And Chief Edwards's startled expression when she'd mentioned it. Almost as if he knew something was up.

He must have heard about the shoes.

Did he have reason to believe they matched the footprint? Is that why he'd looked so startled?

Tingles kicked down Leslie's back. Vesta's murder was horrible enough, but this ghost stuff made for queasy ground beneath her feet. Like stepping onto quicksand.

"Thanks for telling me," she managed. "I'll ... follow up on it." She knew her voice sounded odd but couldn't bring herself to explain, not even to Bailey. "Keep in touch if you hear anything else, okay?"

Bailey probed her with a look. "You sure you're all right?"

Leslie nodded—a little too hard. "Yes. Really. I need to go now. Thanks again."

She turned toward her rental car, feeling Bailey's eyes on her back. She slid into the driver's seat, stuck her latte in the center cup holder. Turned on the engine to get the heat going. Bailey retreated into the warmth of Java Joint. Leslie would have loved to lie back for a minute against the headrest, seek logic in her thoughts. *Henry's ghost?* But even a moment's quiet loomed as dangerous. She had to keep busy—now more than ever.

Wilma Redlin.

Leslie reached for her cell phone and dialed Information for the woman's number.

NINETEEN

Vince pushed his hands onto his hips and trailed a detail-seeking gaze over Vesta's battered living room.

A devastated house, its items chosen by loving hands and worn from years of use, now stained and dirty and screaming for justice. He felt sick. This could have been his and Nancy's home, or a hundred others in Kanner Lake.

And if they didn't apprehend a suspect soon, in the next few days he could be standing in another crime scene just like it.

Dried blood on the armchair, lots of it. The blue chair with pop-up leg rest was an older model, wings on each side near the top. An uneven circle of blood had soaked into the back, likely where Vesta's head rested. One wing of the chair was also stained—maybe from her slumping against it after the first blow. From there events blurred in Vince's mind. Maybe the perp came around to the front of the chair, hit her again as she slumped over. At some point he—or she—pulled Vesta to the floor, where the largest bloodstain glared against the worn carpet. Vince thought of Vesta's bloodied fingers. She may still have been alive at that point, hands flailing to protect herself . . .

His gaze rose to the ceiling. Distinct blood splatter trailed away, larger circles at first, leading to smaller and smaller dots. Vince pictured Vesta on the floor, someone above her, swinging a heavy object up for another blow, blood flying off the weapon and onto the ceiling.

The ISP techs would have a blood splatter expert who'd make the final call on that scenario.

He stepped past the small wood-manteled fireplace, following the path of blood leading through an arched doorway into the kitchen, across the floor, and to the back door. That door, as Roger had indicated, must have been the perp's entrance point as well as exit. Vince examined a blood smear on the frame. From the killer's hands? Or Vesta's body, as she was carried outside?

No sign of forced entry.

He studied the locks. One was the simple kind that could be popped, but above it sat a dead bolt. Either the intruder had a key—which would mean Vesta knew her killer—or the door had been unlocked. Trusting soul that Vesta was, he couldn't rule out the latter.

He wondered what time she usually went to bed.

Outside the door on the small brick patio sat the red tennis shoes.

Vince inserted a gloved fist inside the right shoe and rotated his arm to turn it over. Roger was right about the mud. And wear on the tread—in the same area of the print he'd found at the other crime scene.

Both shoes appeared to be spattered with dried blood. The right shoe also showed another small purplish stain near the heel.

I felt weird, like something was at my back. Leslie's words filtered through Vince's head. *A kind of presence. It touched my neck . . .*

Vince replaced the shoe. When the techs arrived with their mold of the print, he'd have a better idea if the lab was likely to declare a match.

Inside the house, he worked his way down a hall, checking the two bedrooms and one detached bath. The first was a guest bedroom. Everything in order, closet empty. Window shut and locked.

A green towel hung in the bathroom.

Vince studied the dual silver racks. One contained a green washcloth, with a large empty space where a second towel may have been. The one the killer used? Near the sink, on a circular holder screwed into the wall, hung a hand towel in the same color. He searched for blood on the walls and floor but saw none. Peered into the sink. Had the killer washed his hands here? If so, the techs would find blood traces down the drain. Perp must have fetched the towel after murdering Vesta. Yet the room showed no visible traces of blood.

He opened each drawer and studied its contents. No man's comb. No stray white hairs on the bottom. Each drawer looked very clean.

Mulling possibilities, Vince headed toward the main bedroom at the end of the hall.

Bed made. Lots of knickknacks and photos on the dresser, more pictures on the wall. A large one of Vesta and Henry on their wedding day, standing next to a white tiered cake. Man, they looked young.

Vince examined the walls, the floor, looking for blood or any sign that the killer had been in the room. He saw none.

The dresser drawers held only female clothes. Ditto with the closet. Wilma was right—Henry's possessions had been cleaned out.

Vince lingered in the middle of the room, mind circling through data. His gaze tugged back to the wedding picture. Vesta and Henry looked no older than Tim had been when he died. He stared at the photo, imagining the dreams they'd held at that age. Thinking of their long years together, the jobs worked and kids raised.

Why couldn't Tim have had the same chance?

Vince pivoted and left the room.

He stepped outside onto Vesta's front porch and headed down the short sidewalk to confer with Roger. Yellow crime-scene tape cordoned off the yard, running above Vesta's low white picket fence. Neighbors huddled together across the street, watching, their faces grim. Vince recognized his friend Sam Greene, a Kanner Lake resident for the past ten years and one of the town's volunteer firemen. Good guy. Sam and Henry Johnson had not gotten along, but that was probably true with many of the Johnsons' neighbors. They disliked Henry but loved Vesta.

Sam raised his hand and Vince nodded in return.

Vince's eyes flitted over other faces, noting Bill Gradderling (what was he doing home from work?), Bart and Faith Truman, the Stones, Linda Vandt. And Wilma Redlin. She fluttered her hands, trying to catch his attention.

In a minute, Wilma, in a minute. He raised his fingers in a wave and turned to Roger. "The techs had arrived at Madding Court by the time I left. And the coroner. The two ISP detectives stayed to go over everything with them. They ought to be here within a couple hours. No sign of Jim yet."

Roger grunted. He stood with arms folded, feet apart, watching the cluster of neighbors as if one might break away any minute and make a Red Rover run toward the crime-scene tape. "Not a pretty sight in there." He jerked his head toward the house.

"Yeah."

"You know her well?"

Vince studied the ground. "Since I was a kid. Started mowing their lawn at age twelve. Vesta would give me cookies with my pay. Henry would just frown and inspect my work. Anything not right, I'd hear about it."

Roger nodded slowly. He turned to gaze at Vesta's porch. "Got any idea who did this? Besides Henry's ghost, that is?"

His gaunt face held not the slightest smile. Roger wasn't known for his humor.

"Numerous theories have gone through my mind, all unrelated." Vince told Roger about the towel over Vesta's head. "At first the towel—and the fact that the body was found at Paige's home—made me think *hot tub*. Like somebody out there was picking up from the Edna San case. Now, I'm not so sure. Maybe. But Leslie Brymes's car is well known in this town. Anybody who placed Vesta there would likely know what he was doing. Especially considering that Paige's car sat right next to it, also unlocked."

Roger ran his tongue under his upper lip. "So why Leslie?"

"Exactly. The girls insist there are no new people in their lives. No boyfriends. I'm wondering about Leslie's reporting, if she's getting too close to something. The biggest news around here is Grayson's proposed hotel—and you know how people have taken sides about that. You got the business people and the younger set mostly for it, not to mention Grayson and his investors. Older folks for the most part, and some environmentalist types, don't want to see the area change. I just wonder if there's some idiot out there who thought another murder might sway things one way or another."

Roger absorbed the information, tongue still working under his lip. "Seems to me it'd sway against it. Who'd think another terrible crime would attract more tourists?"

"Maybe. But people can flock to a place out of morbid curiosity." Vince shook his head. "My other thought is, there's more than one person involved. Have to admit it's a lot of running around town for one person." He stepped toward the street. "I need to go talk to Wilma."

When the techs arrived, they'd examine every inch of Vesta's property, long into the coming night. But Vince didn't want to wait for what he sought.

Wilma hurried to meet him in the middle of the road, pulling her coat like a protective mantle around her body. Vince could see the sorrow-filled shine in her gray eyes. Her white hair looked uncombed, wrinkled cheeks pale. A pink turtleneck snugged her throat.

"Mrs. Redlin, I'm real sorry about your friend. She was my friend too."

Wilma nodded. "I know. Thank you." She cast a long look at Vesta's house. "Roger told you about the shoes?"

"Yes." Vince drew a hand along his jaw. "I wanted to talk to you about Henry's things. Do you happen to know if Vesta kept any clothes or toiletries of his? A quick look around her room didn't turn up anything."

"Yes, she did." Wilma gestured toward the left side of the house. "There's a box on a shelf in the garage."

"What's in it?"

Wilma thought a minute. "Two or three of his favorite shirts. A shaver he'd used for years, maybe some other things." She shrugged. "Nothing useful to anyone else. Just sentimental to Vesta."

"Anybody else know about it?" Vince kept his tone nonchalant, but the woman eyed him keenly.

"Don't think so."

"Okay. Thanks." He turned to leave, then glanced back at her. "I'll need to talk to you again soon, all right? I'd like to find out more about Vesta's habits. Who were regular folks in the house, who else might have had a key, what time she went to bed. Think you can help with that?"

"I can help." Her voice softened. "I've either seen or talked to Vesta Johnson on the phone every day for I don't know how many years. Especially after Henry died. She and I didn't agree about a lot of things, like religion, but ..." Wilma's voice caught.

"We were good friends. And I don't know what I'm going to do without her."

She wasn't alone. Most of the town would feel the same way. Vince gave Wilma's arm a slight squeeze. "I'm so sorry. We'll all miss her very much."

She drew herself up straight, a hardness etching her face. "I never did like that Henry Johnson. He comes around here again tonight, he and I are going to have one strong bit of talk, I'll tell you that. I know things about that man."

Vince made no argument—what good would it do? He turned away, moved two steps before she threw after him, "You think he's come back too, don't you? Henry, I mean."

Vince halted, faced her full on. "No." His tone was firm. "I don't."

Sam Greene broke from the small crowd and walked over, extending his hand. Vince shook it.

"Anything I can do?" Sam's eyes flicked from Vince to Wilma.

Vince sighed. "Wish you were on my law enforcement team about now. We're understaffed for something like this. But ISP's on it."

"Yeah, I figured. Good."

"You have any idea who might have done this?"

"None. I can't even ..." Sam swallowed. "I helped her out a lot. After Henry died. You know, fixing things. Whatever she needed."

Vince held Sam's gaze. The man looked downright sick. Fresh anger pierced Vince. That this senseless killing could happen to such a loved woman. In *his* town.

He turned away, mumbling that he needed to get back to the scene. Feeling Sam's and Wilma's eyes follow his abrupt departure, he strode toward Vesta's house and ducked under the crime-scene tape. "Gotta check something out," he said to Roger in passing.

A moment later Vince stood in Vesta's garage, studying a long row of built-in shelving. Assorted sizes of boxes lined the shelf, some with top flaps down and taped, some lacking a top at all. They were labeled on the ends in block lettering with a black felt-tip pen. *Mom's dishes. Tea set. Clothes. Pictures. Movie camera and tapes. Records.*

And one smaller box on the very end, top taped down, no label.

Vince slid the box off the shelf, encouraged by its lightness, and placed it on the floor. He studied the tape, noting its clean edges. No sign anyone had opened it, then resealed it. Vince withdrew a pocketknife from his pants and slit the tape.

On top was a worn blue button-down shirt, neatly folded. A vivid image flashed of Vesta smoothing out the wrinkles—and the searing blade of memory twisted in Vince's chest. The memory of himself, lingering over a box of Tim's clothes after his son's death, love and anguish trembling his fingers.

Vince closed his eyes and dragged in a long breath.

He forced his gaze back to the box. Carefully, he lifted out the blue shirt, then two more beneath it. Without unfolding them, he examined the top of each, lingering on the collar and shoulder areas. He did not find what he sought.

Placing the three shirts on the shelf, he next pulled out a wooden container with hinged top. Inside lay an old electric shaver. Vince examined the blade. It looked clean.

One last item—a red woolen scarf. Again, folded with perfection. Vince lifted it out, feeling a firmness in the center. He lifted away each fold to reveal an old-fashioned, silver man's comb. Unlike the shaver and the shirts, the comb had not been cleaned. Tangled in its teeth lay a few thick, white hairs.

Bingo.

Vince stared at the comb, considering possibilities and providence. To the naked eye, the hairs looked similar to those found on Vesta's body. Who would have guessed, when she wrapped this comb and tucked it away over a year ago, what future purpose it would serve.

From his jacket pocket he withdrew a folded bag and placed the comb inside.

Now—what to do with it.

Most of the discovered evidence would be shipped to the state's main lab in Meridian, near Boise. Only a DNA test in Meridian, which would take a couple weeks, could give a definite answer as to whether the hairs on the comb and those found on Vesta were a match. Even a quick microscopic examination in Meridian, including shipping time, would take a couple days. But he wanted an answer now. Fortunately, there was a much quicker way to see if a match was likely. The less sophisticated lab in Coeur d'Alene, a mere forty minutes' drive away, could perform a cursory comparison of the hairs under a microscope. Such a comparison would indicate if they were consistent. He could send the hairs to Coeur d'Alene first, and if he called the lab and requested priority, he just might hear an answer by the end of the day.

His eyes were deceiving him about the hairs' similarity, that had to be it.

Decision made, Vince left the garage via its side door and walked around to the front. He could send Roger over to the first crime scene to pick up the other hairs, then on to the lab in Coeur d'Alene. Meanwhile, he'd call the lab.

The techs would not need to know the comparison hairs had come from a dead man.

TWENTY

Leslie clutched her cell phone, listening to Wilma Redlin's number ring and ring. After the tenth time, she disconnected.

Doggone the woman. Probably outside, ogling the police work at Vesta's house.

Leslie threw the phone on the passenger seat and backed out of her parking space. Lead-footed—hey, all the cops were busy at the moment—she drove across town toward Hayley Street, which dead-ended at a small public park. At the turn onto Hayley from Clifton, she hit another snag. The stocky and ever-efficient police officer Al Newman, better known as C. B., waved her to a stop.

Great, they've cordoned off this street too. Leslie got out of the car and raised her hands, pleading. "I won't go near Vesta's house; I just want to talk to one of her neighbors."

"So call her."

"She's not answering."

"Sorry, Leslie." C. B. shrugged. "I can't let anybody in but official vehicles and residents."

"Come on, C. B."

"No can do."

With a glare at the officer, Leslie climbed back into her car. Time for a Plan B.

She pulled down Clifton Street about a block and parked. Dialed Jared at the office and asked him for names and numbers of some of Vesta's other neighbors. She jotted them down, then started through the list. The first three didn't answer. *Good grief, the whole neighborhood must be out watching the show.* On the fourth try she connected to Stacy Rawson, a young mother with two children who had better things to do than stand out on a cold street and eagle-eye the police.

"Stacy, this is Leslie Brymes. Could you please do me a *huge* favor? Run outside and look for Wilma Redlin. Ask her to please go back to her house so I can call her. It's *urgent.*"

"No problem," Stacy said. She could spot Wilma through her front window as they spoke. Two minutes later, Leslie had Wilma on the phone.

She got an earful about the shoes. How Wilma had told Officer Roger Waitman about them, then Chief Edwards.

"You're sure those shoes were thrown away?" Leslie asked as she jotted notes.

"Absolutely. I even hauled some of the stuff to the dump myself. One thing, though. I forgot to tell the chief about the spot."

"What spot?"

"On the right shoe, back toward the heel. There was a small purplish stain from when Henry spilled red wine. Vesta never could get it out. The right shoe I saw this morning had that exact same spot. That's how I know for *sure* they're Henry's shoes."

Leslie's pen pulled away from the paper. Okay, maybe this wasn't so productive after all. She wanted evidence to *refute* this ghost business, not support it.

She was starting to sweat. Leslie turned down the heat.

"Something else," Wilma continued. "The chief wanted to know about the box of Henry's things in Vesta's garage."

"What box?"

Wilma told her. "He denied that he believes Henry's come back. But why else would he be interested in a box of a dead man's clothes?"

Leslie thought a moment. "Any chance those shoes could have been saved after all—in that box?"

"No, none. I'm telling you, we threw them away."

All right, enough of this. Next topic. "Mrs. Redlin, did you ever hear Vesta talk about the proposed hotel in downtown Kanner Lake?"

"Sure. Everybody in town talked about it."

"Was she for it or against it?"

"Oh, she supported it. Thought it would bring money and jobs to the town."

Sounded like Vesta, Leslie thought. Not so quick to reject an idea just because it meant change. "She didn't do anything to help support the proposal, did she?"

"Actually, yes. You know the petitions that went around all the neighborhoods for signing? She was the one who walked the forms around our area."

Whoa. Leslie's eyes widened. Vesta *had* been involved in hotel politics.

Had some radical opponent of the project killed her?

When the conversation with Wilma ended, Leslie sat staring at the dashboard, mulling over her next move. The petitions Wilma mentioned were turned into the city council two weeks ago. Everyone in Vesta's neighborhood would have known of her involvement in the campaign. But so could plenty of other people.

Leslie needed to find out exactly who.

She put the car in drive and pulled away from the curb, grateful for this new avenue to pursue. One thing for sure—it beat chasing ghosts any day.

TWENTY-ONE

The note was burning a hole in Ali's backpack.

She shuffled along the lunch line, choosing a hamburger and salad. Feeling the heat of that note. Why couldn't she bring herself to throw it away? If Kristal and her little gang found out she'd lied, they'd *really* be ticked.

Ali put a brownie on her plate and turned away, headed for the door. She forced herself not to look at the table where they all sat. She'd find an empty classroom where she could eat in peace. Who wanted to deal with murderous looks?

She hadn't gone twenty feet down the hall when she heard Chet call her name.

Her steps slowed. She *so* wanted to ignore him. Either that or tell him off. But her stupid heart tugged at the sound of his voice. With a sigh, she turned around. Clutching the plastic tray, smelling ground beef, she faced the guy of her dreams. How obvious she must look, trying to sneak off alone.

Well, fine. If this was beat-up-Ali day, he could just go ahead. 'Cause tomorrow she was *not* coming back here. She wasn't learning anything anyway. If her mom was too sick to teach her at home, she'd just teach herself.

"Hi." Chet walked up to her, arms extended. "Here, let me take that."

Ali meant to hang on to her tray, but somehow it slid from her fingers.

"So." Those eyes of his fastened on her. "Where you headed?"

She shrugged. "Nowhere."

One side of his mouth turned up. "Can I go with you?"

Her chest tightened. She grasped her upper arms, hugging herself. It was dumb to let him have the tray; now she couldn't just walk away. "What do you want, Chet?"

"To apologize. I feel really bad about what happened. I want to make it up to you."

Oh. The swelling in her lungs went down a little. She studied his face. Should she believe him?

Yeah, well, too late for the head to doubt; her heart was already sucking it in.

"Come on." He gestured with his chin toward the nearest classroom. "Let's go in there and sit down."

Ali fell in step beside him, feeling a little light-headed. "Where's your lunch?"

"I ate fast."

They entered the room—where she would sit last hour for Spanish. The blackboard was covered in conjugated Spanish verbs, posters of Mexico and Latin America on the walls. Chet shut the door with his foot. Ali glanced at him, surprised. "You don't mind, do you?" He looked down at her, only her tray between them. Suddenly she knew she couldn't eat a thing. "I just thought we could have a little more privacy this way."

She nodded.

Chet nudged her toward two front desks, where they couldn't be seen through the window in the door. He set down her tray, turned the desks to face each other, and sat down. Ali sat also. The hamburger smelled greasy.

"Go ahead and eat."

Ali lifted a shoulder. "I'm not very hungry."

He held her gaze. Ali felt cut right down the middle. Like he could see inside her, knew everything she was thinking. She straightened. "Okay, we're here. Now what?"

Chet leaned forward over the desk, hands clasped. Ali smelled his scent mixed with the odor of her lunch. She picked up her tray and slid it onto the next desk. Then faced him, trying not to look like she wanted to drink in his every word.

His eyes cut from the lunch tray to her face. "I want to invite you to come with us tomorrow night."

Ali stared, a dozen questions whirling in her head. "Why?"

"Because you found the note. Because I think you were meant to find it."

Maybe the Powers wanted to bring her in. Ali didn't like the tingling in her veins. "You mean like fate?"

"No. More than that."

Ali pressed back in her seat. This must be what having an out-of-body experience felt like. Here she sat with this hot guy, like a dream come true. But all this ... *stuff.* If they could just talk about something else. If only it wasn't that stupid note that brought them together.

"Does Kristal know you're asking me to come?" She couldn't keep the disdain from her voice when she said the name.

Chet gave her a small smile. "She's okay with it. So's everybody else, or I wouldn't be asking."

"Really. That's a switch."

He shook his head. "Kristal's just ... Kristal. She's the one who started this whole thing, so she feels protective. And I know she can be a brat sometimes. But she was just afraid you'd tell somebody. If you get to know her, you'll see how fun she can be. I think that's it—you just need to get to know us."

Uh-huh. "So you're asking me to this ... whatever it is, just so I won't tell? You figure if I'm part of it, I'll keep the secret."

She figured he'd deny it, but he nodded. "That's what the girls first said. But they're coming around." He leaned closer. "Look, I don't want to sound like some stuck-up dude or anything, but we just don't go around asking people to do this. You're the first."

His scent filtered across the desks, his blue eyes on her. If Ali leaned forward, their heads would be so close. "What exactly is it that you're doing?"

Chet's gaze didn't waver. "Calling up the dead."

He said it so seriously, like some actor in a horror movie. Ali might have laughed — if the words hadn't chilled her to the bone. She pressed her lips. "Interesting pastime."

"You don't believe in it?"

"Well, I don't know. I've never tried it."

He smiled. "You have beautiful eyes, you know that?"

She looked down, heat flooding her face. It was probably just flattery, but her heart turned over all the same. Slowly, she leaned forward, laying her arms straight out on the desk. Their hands were just inches apart. "If you want me to join you, you'll answer my questions."

"Fair enough."

His fingers were so close, Ali could almost feel their heat. For a minute she couldn't think where to begin.

"Okay. Where do you do this? At Kristal's house?"

"No. She has a sister who's eight years older. Married. Kathy and her husband have this little hunting cabin in the woods two miles outside of town. Kristal has a key to it."

Ali imagined the forest at night. So dark. She fought a shiver. "Is it near other houses?"

"Not really. It's on about ten acres, first place on the right down Reckless Lane." He smiled at the name. "It's a gravel road. You know where that is?"

"No. Are there lights out there?"

"In the cabin? Sure. But we turn them off and use candles."

Ali nodded. This was sounding way too creepy for her. "How long you been doing this?"

"Just a few weeks."

Chet locked eyes with Ali, waiting for the next question. Irritation bit at her. "Come on, Chet, don't make me drag it all out of you. What's that note talking about?"

He pulled in a long breath. "You sure you're ready to hear it?"

She hesitated, then nodded.

"Okay. Since you asked."

Reaching out to lay his fingertips over hers, Chet told her.

TWENTY-TWO

By the time he was twelve, ghosts roamed the house.

He didn't see them every day, but he knew they were there. Sometimes only in wisps, as the drifting smoke from his mother's ever-present cigarettes. Or an eerie gathered darkness in a certain room. Whatever the form, he sensed their presence constantly.

The house felt heavy.

His parents no longer chanted for Tamara. They'd given up years ago, telling themselves she'd settled into the comforts of eternity. They never spoke of her new home as heaven. How could they, when they didn't believe in God? But *Out There Somewhere* spread a lush garden, a utopia of peace and laughter. There, Tamara played.

They rarely spoke about the ghosts living in their home. The spirits angered his parents. Why should they be hanging around, unsummoned, when their own daughter had refused to show? Besides, they had lives to get on with now, careers to follow. His father had formed his own architectural firm, and money was flowing. Mother had gone back to school and earned a degree in nursing. (All her study of health care did not rid her of her smoking habit.) Flush with their new success, they'd bought a bigger house, complete with swimming pool.

More than once he considered drowning himself in it.

What stopped him was not the pull of life, but the fear of death. What if he became like one of those forms in his house, caught

116

between worlds, ever restless? Or worse, be eaten by his revengeful sister. Whatever his lot in this world — cold, unloving parents, an unsettling home — he would take it over the alternative. He was scared to death of death.

At least he had not seen Tamara again.

Socially, he was a loner. He made a few friends, but they hung out only during school. He sure couldn't bring someone home. One feel of the air, one sight of a spirit, and they'd fly out of there. Then just imagine the stories they'd tell about him at school.

To fill his time, he turned to reading. By twelve he was devouring adult novels. He enjoyed gothics with a supernatural flavor, although he realized the irony of that. As if he needed more ghost stories. But when he read of creepy old haunted houses, he didn't feel so alone. The books were just fiction, but the authors must have based their imagination on *something*. And if a successful author knew about ghosts and still managed to make something of himself, so could he.

The power of writing.

Once in a while, though, spirits would blur the words on a page, and he had to put the book down.

In his midteens he graduated to crime novels, fantasy, and horror. Gothics were for sissies.

During his senior year in high school he fell for a girl. Bethany Anne Francis. Long golden hair, pale blue eyes. Very petite. He dreamt of holding her, but sometimes in those dreams he'd hug too hard, and her ribs would break like a bird's. *Snap, snap*, down her chest, until she dangled in his arms.

Horrifying? Sometimes. But also something else. Alluring. Titillating ...

In college he finally grew up. Developed a quiet sort of charm. Girls were drawn to his sense of mystery, his brooding looks. The girls were sources of both pleasure and pain. Pleasure mostly, because he used them all he wanted. But sometimes he'd look at a face and see Tamara, all grown up and starved for a soul. Whenever that happened he'd never go out with the girl again, despite her tears, and he'd offer no explanation.

As if anyone could understand.

By sophomore year he'd declared a double major in engineering and business. On top of his heavy academic load, he worked part-time so he could share an apartment with two roommates rather than going home during summers and holidays. He and his parents rarely spoke, and that was fine by him. His mother and father had slid into deeper bitterness each passing year. Seeking fulfillment from a world that couldn't give it, they returned to holding séances. In that dark world they claimed to discover meaning in life. (And that meaning would be?) He wanted no part of it, of course. The very thought of a séance whisked him back to when he was six, cowering and shaking beneath his bed.

After college, he threw himself into his job at a real estate development firm. In the next two years he saw his parents just once, a brief visit over Christmas. When his father retired early, his parents moved from the cement-and-freeway lifestyle in California to Kanner Lake, Idaho. There they could live off his father's savings, filling their time with pursuits of their "religion," if you could call it that, and new hobbies. His father learned to hunt and fish. He bought a rustic cabin in the woods for overnight hunting trips.

The son, now grown, worked hard and played hard. Used women as he pleased, stayed single. In the nose-to-grindstone world of building specs and finance, memories of the ghosts and terrors of his childhood retreated to a shadowed and secretive corner of his mind. There they lurked, bound predators of the night.

Until his mother fell sick and called for him, and their chains clanked free.

TWENTY-THREE

One o'clock.

Leslie's stomach grumbled as she made what must have been her twentieth call. She ignored the hunger. No time to eat and no inclination. Had it only been four hours since her bagel breakfast? Seemed like eons.

She finished dialing and heaved back in her chair, eyes roving over the cluttered Kanner Lake Times office. Across from her at his battered gray steel desk, Jared Moore cradled his own phone, talking to Arnie Hawkes, owner of a small fishing-equipment store in town and avid proponent of the proposed Kanner Lake hotel. Jared was betting that Vesta's death was connected to the hotel, and so far his inquiries showed it. He hunched over, thin shoulders rounded, long, bony fingers recording the conversation in his expert shorthand. In all his years, Leslie knew, he'd not seen a murder like this. One of his friends, killed in her own home — so close to his.

The phone rang once, twice, in her ear. *Come on, come on, be home.* Leslie tapped a pen against her notebook. The fourth ring cut short.

"Hello?" The voice sounded out of breath.

Leslie leaned forward to pick up her pen. "Mrs. Westling, this is Leslie Brymes. I've been trying to reach you with a few important questions."

Sandy Westling, a divorcee in her early fifties, was leading the campaign to support the Kanner Lake hotel. Her brother, Trent, owned the used bookstore on Main.

"Oh." She sounded distracted. "I've been out running errands and could hardly get through them because everyone's so ..."

Leslie felt the pierce of the woman's unfinished words. Vesta's battered face flashed before her eyes. She clutched her pen, willing her emotions down. "I know. It's like that with everyone I talk to."

Mrs. Westling took an audible breath. "Are you all right, Leslie?"

"I'm fine. Thank you. I'm just ... focusing on helping to catch whoever did this. Vesta was my friend. This is way more than just a news story for me."

"Same for all of us. What can I do to help you?"

"I understand Vesta walked a petition supporting the Kanner Lake hotel around her neighborhood. Were you aware of that?"

"Oh, yes. I coordinated covering the various neighborhoods, and as the petitions were completed, they were turned in to me. Then I gave them to the city council."

Leslie jotted a note. "Who else besides you and Vesta's neighbors would know she did this? I mean, did you call her to ask for help, or did she volunteer in a meeting?"

"In a meeting. At our initial gathering we must have had fifty people looking to help. A lot of them folks like Trent, who could see what a hotel could do for their businesses. At that time we divided the town into ten neighborhoods so no one would have to cover too much territory. The ten volunteers were given the petition forms."

Fifty people, besides all of Vesta's neighbors. Plus anyone they'd talked to about Vesta's volunteering. Leslie's heart sank as she realized the scope of her task. Half the town could be aware of Vesta's work.

"Mrs. Westling, this may sound strange, but do you know anyone who was at that meeting in order to spy? Someone you later found out supported your opposition?"

The woman paused. "What has this got to do with Vesta's death?"

The sudden edge to her tone—Leslie had heard it before. Everyone was willing to offer information, but at the slightest implication that some activity in which they'd been involved could have ties to Vesta's murder—they balked. No one wanted to think they, too, could be in danger.

"Probably nothing. But we've got to pursue all avenues. Everything that Vesta was involved in, and who those activities would tie her to. It's all we've got right now."

"O-kay." Sandy Westling sounded less than convinced. "Well. I don't think we had any spies at the meeting. Some folks stayed quiet and didn't volunteer to do anything. But I never heard of anyone who later started campaigning for the other side."

The office door opened, letting in chilled air. Leslie turned to see Lucas Mulholland, owner of the leatherworks store up the block, step inside, a mere sweatshirt over his faded jeans. Lucas was in his thirties and accustomed enough to north Idaho weather to not mind the cold. He raised his hand, holding what looked to be a folded piece of paper, and gestured toward her. Leslie held up a forefinger—*Just a minute.*

"Okay, Mrs. Westling. Thank you very much for your time. If you think of anything else, will you call me?"

"Yes. Sure."

Leslie rattled off her cell phone number and disconnected. "Hey, Lucas, what's up?"

"Hi." He strode to her desk, boots quiet against the hardwood floor. Lucas stood about five feet ten, with a lean, graceful frame. This, added to his watchful green eyes and scruffy long brown hair, gave him the look of a streetwise cat. He held out a piece of lined paper, folded twice like a letter and fastened with a single staple. Leslie's name was printed on it in all capital letters.

She took it from him, frowning. "What's this?"

"Don't know. I was walking down the street to get some lunch at Java Joint, and found it on the sidewalk near your door."

"Really? That's strange."

He shrugged. "Somebody probably just dropped it." He glanced over toward Jared, still hunched over his phone, and raised a hand. Jared lifted his chin in return greeting. Lucas looked back to Leslie. "Looks like you two are real busy in here."

She managed a worn smile. "It's not been the quietest day."

He shifted on his feet. "Yeah, I heard the news, of course. Are you doing all right? Must have been a scary thing."

The image of Vesta's beaten body flashed in Leslie's head. "Yes, it was. But I'm ... okay. Thanks."

Lucas gave her a long look as if wanting to ask more, then cleared his throat. "Well, gotta run. Want me to fetch you something from Java Joint?"

"No, thanks. I'll make it down there at some point." She tipped her head toward the piece of paper in her hand. "Thanks for bringing this in."

"No problem."

Leslie waited until he reached the door before turning her attention to the paper. She focused on her name, block printed. *I found it on the sidewalk.*

This did not feel right.

She bit her cheek. Should she even open the thing? She narrowed her eyes, considering. Then eased the folds free from the staple, opened up the sheet. It contained two lines.

Leslie shrieked and shook away the paper like a stinging wasp.

TWENTY-FOUR

The red tennis shoe appeared to match the print.

Vince stood on Vesta Johnson's back patio, two unlikely looking ISP techs at his side. Barry Flenery, a red-haired, freckle-faced man in his thirties, looked more the teenager, but Vince couldn't deny his skills. Tom Prewett, with his wiry hair, intense hazel eyes, and two-day-old beard, could have passed for some rock singer. He even had the gravelly voice.

Barry held the right shoe, bottom up, next to the mold he'd made of the print at the first crime scene. Vince and Tom leaned in to see.

"Pattern's the same." Barry pointed a gloved finger toward the top of the shoe, then its center. "Here and here, see? And on the inside"—he moved his finger—"worn."

Tom extracted two bags from his kit, one for each shoe. "Let's tag 'em." He opened a bag, allowing Barry to slip the shoe inside, then looked to Vince. "Steve said you told him these might belong to the victim's dead husband."

Vince shrugged. "That's the neighbor's story."

"The hairs are definitely weirder, though." Barry closed the bag and labeled it. "If you get a match on them, Edwards ..." He shook his head.

No comment from Vince. He gazed through the open door toward Vesta Johnson's living room, where the two ISP homicide detectives examined the scene. Harrough stood by the

TV, head tilted toward the ceiling. Dyland was not in sight, but Vince could hear him. Their conversation played in the irregular rhythm of crime-scene investigations. Long pauses, short bursts of announcing some discovery, ideas exchanged.

Vince's theory of the hairs had taken the detectives and techs aback. But when they unbagged one from Vesta's knee and one Vince had found, and laid them side by side, none of the five men could deny the striking similarity. All agreed a cursory examination at the Coeur d'Alene lab was a good plan. They kept their poker faces, but Vince knew they were as curious as he.

Roger had left for Coeur d'Alene, bearing the evidence, and was now back in front of Vesta's house. Meanwhile a call to the lab alerted staff as to what was coming. They assured Vince they'd do the examination as soon as possible.

Second shoe bagged, the techs moved on to dust the doorknob for prints. Vince stood back, hands fidgeting. A weak sun, now past its zenith, fumbled a ray through low overcast, spotlighting the patio where the shoes had been. Almost as if nature shouted, *Pay attention here!* Vince stared at it, uneasiness trickling through his veins. Just a random sunbeam, of course. Still, it was ... strange.

How many times had he thought that today?

His cell phone rang, and Vince started. Turning away from the techs, he unclipped the phone from his belt and studied the ID. *Kanner Lake Times.*

He flipped the cell open. "Chief Edwards."

"Hi, it's Leslie." The words shook. "Whoever killed Vesta just sent me a message."

His head jerked up. "What did it say?"

Vince heard a shuddered breath. "It says ..." Her voice cracked. "'Hope you liked my present. I did it for you.'"

124

TWENTY-FIVE

Behind the Simple Pleasures counter, Paige aimed a tight smile at Beth Wagmul. *Here come the questions.*

"Paige, how are you, honey? I just wanted to stop by and make sure you're all right." Beth splayed her short fingers on the Simple Pleasures counter, concern etching her forehead. Her round cheeks were flushed, a short strand of auburn hair teased upward by a puff of wind as she'd entered the shop. Known as one of the best pie bakers in town, Beth was in her early forties, a mother of three rambunctious boys.

By Paige's count, Beth had to be the twentieth person to check on her in the last two hours.

"I'm okay. Thanks." *Except I still can't believe another person close to me is dead.*

This sudden attention, all too reminiscent of her past troubles, unnerved Paige. She felt grateful for the caring, really she did. The people of Kanner Lake had embraced her as one of their own, despite her notorious beginnings in the town. But she hated the limelight. In the last few weeks, the trickle of curious snow-season tourists had been enough to handle. They'd visit Simple Pleasures, browse through the beautiful candles and home decorations, smile at the glitzy bracelets and purses, eyes all the while straying toward Paige. Wanting to inspect in person the young woman who'd made national headlines. Paige adopted a polite but reserved manner toward such people. She would chat as she rang up their items but answer no questions about the events they'd followed on the news.

Beth pushed off the counter and slid both hands into her coat pockets. "This is such a terrible thing to happen. I just can't believe it. Vesta, of all people. And I'm so sorry you and Leslie ... were pulled into it. I want you to know I'm praying for you." Her eyes glistened. "I'm praying for the whole town."

"Thank you."

Sarah Wray, Paige's boss, appeared from her office at the back of the store, bustling over to exchange hugs with Beth. Sarah's orange and yellow pants outfit seemed all the more colorful against her bleak expression. Her typically sunny outlook was nowhere in sight today.

Paige was content to fade to the background as the two women talked about the murder. She'd told Sarah minimal details of what she and Leslie had seen, but every person who'd stopped by had added their two cents—some rumor, some fact. Amazing how fast information got around Kanner Lake.

"And all this stuff about Henry Johnson's ghost!" Beth shook her head.

Sarah's eyes opened wide. "What are you *talking* about?"

"You haven't heard? Wilma Redlin said Henry's old shoes were on Vesta's back patio—and they had blood on them. Shoes Vesta threw away a year ago."

Paige's body went cold.

"Oh, my." Sarah thrust a hand into her gray curls. "That's crazy. There has to be some explanation."

"And then your neighbor across the street"—Beth turned to Paige—"was watching when the van from Idaho State Police came. She saw them pouring stuff on the grass, then lift it up when it hardened. They were making a mold of a footprint, that's what she said. She's seen it on TV."

The footprint. Chief Edwards had told Leslie about it. Did Leslie know about this ghost rumor?

"So ..." Sarah studied Beth's face.

"So the question is, does the shoe match the footprint?"

Sarah's mouth gaped. "You trying to tell me you believe Henry Johnson came back from the grave to kill his own wife? That's preposterous!"

"Of course it is." Beth looked at Sarah from the corner of her eye. "But tell me this. Where did those shoes *come* from?"

Sudden heaviness descended on Paige, as if a woolen blanket had fallen on her shoulders. She sank onto the counter stool. She no more believed in ghosts than in space aliens; living people had dealt her enough tragedy. But just this morning Leslie had felt something. And now ... Paige felt it. A darkness, some *thing* just beyond her human senses, a glimpse of shadow in peripheral vision.

"Honey, you okay?"

Beth's voice barely registered. Paige stared out the window at Main Street. A blue truck drove by. Two men entered Java Joint. A woman passed on the sidewalk. Normal occurrences, colors the same, buildings the same. But something about the town—something even above and beyond the horrible crime just committed—was *wrong*.

"Paige?"

She blinked. Turned toward the women and shook her head. "Sorry. I was just ... thinking."

Beth and Sarah eyed her furtively, as if afraid they'd upset her, and ended their conversation. A minute later Beth left the shop, and Sarah retreated to her office, nervously rearranging a vase of silk flowers on the way. As soon as she disappeared, Paige reached for the phone to call Leslie.

Before she could pick up the receiver, it rang.

Paige jumped, heaved a sigh at her nerves, then answered. "Simple Pleasures, this is Paige."

"Hi. It's Frank West."

Oh. Not *Officer West*. Just *Frank*.

"Hi."

"Uh. Just wanted to check on you. I'm out here on your street still, logging people in and out. But I had a minute and thought I'd make sure you're okay."

What did she hear in his voice? Nervousness? It didn't sound like the Officer West of a few hours ago, authoritative and determined to protect her and Leslie from the gruesome sight they'd already seen.

"I'm fine." She sounded less than convincing. "Thank you for asking."

"Sure."

An awkward silence.

"Have you called to check on Leslie?" Paige asked.

"Oh. No. Guess I've been kind of busy."

"Sure, I know. But if you get a chance, I'm sure she'd appreciate it."

An understatement, to say the least. Leslie was crazy about Frank. Had been as long as Paige had known her.

"Okay, I will." Frank paused. "Well, here comes a car, so I'd better go. Just ... Paige? Know that I'm thinking about you."

Paige stilled. *I'm thinking about you.* It wasn't the words so much, but the way he said them. Kind of hesitant and self-conscious. Not like a cop would talk to a witness of a horrible crime, but like a man would say to a woman ...

Understanding spattered down on Paige like sudden rain. She straightened her back, gaze darting around the shop, not finding a safe place to land. She thought of this morning—his protectiveness, his focus on her over Leslie. Of running into him at Java Joint last week, and the way he'd lingered to talk.

Oh, wow.

Oh, *no.*

Leslie would feel terrible if she knew.

Paige's eyes fell on the display of blue wine glasses across the room, a reflection of overhead track lighting in their stems. She fixed upon the color, brain churning for a response. She could almost feel Frank's anxiety as he waited for her reply. He'd put himself out there, made himself vulnerable. That could so easily lead to hurt.

She pulled in a breath. Then whispered the only thing she could think to say. "Thank you."

They clicked off the line. Slowly, Paige pulled the phone from her ear and stared at it.

TWENTY-SIX

Vince sat behind his desk, forearms on the wood and fingers laced. His gut told him Lucas Mulholland was telling the truth, but it wasn't time to let up just yet.

"I'm telling you all I know." Lucas pitched forward in his chair, hands spread. "I picked the thing up off the sidewalk outside the *Times* office, saw it was addressed to Leslie, and took it inside. That's *it*."

Vince studied Lucas's face. "Are you sure no one saw you pick it up?"

"Like I said, I don't know. I wasn't looking around." Lucas's tone implied this should be of no consequence. "If I had something to do with that murder, why would I walk in and deliver my own note, huh? That's crazy!"

Maybe, maybe not.

One thing for sure—Vince would not be returning to work with the ISP detectives at Vesta's house anytime soon. First, he or another officer would have to visit every store on Main, see if anyone had witnessed someone leaving the note. It probably hadn't been on the sidewalk very long, but Vince couldn't be sure, given the lack of much wind today. Second, as with the message left on the victim's body, techs would need to determine what kind of paper was used—the brand, where it was manufactured. Armed with that information he and the detectives could track where the paper had been sold, maybe leading to a list of purchasers.

But before they sent the note to the Meridian lab, Vince could do some investigating on his own. There were obvious differences between Leslie's note and the one left on Vesta. The circled number one was drawn in black felt-tip pen on plain white typing paper. No watermark or other distinguishing elements on the paper, at least not to the naked eye. But this note was on blue-lined paper, written with blue ink. A faint rough edge at the top of the paper showed it had been torn off from a pad. Three close vertical red lines formed a left margin, measuring an inch and a quarter. When Vince held the paper up to light he could see patterns of gray and white pulp.

The perp was in Kanner Lake, right here, right now. Or at least very close by. This note left on Leslie's doorstep proved it. If he—or she—was a resident of Kanner Lake, he may have bought the pad of paper in a town store.

Interesting that two different kinds of paper were used. Was the killer aware of paper and pen tracking? Had he chosen different ones to confuse the investigation? Or had the note been an impulse, the nearest items used?

"Lucas, thanks for coming in." Vince rose. "Let me know if you think of anything else."

Lucas pushed to his feet. "No problem." He dragged a hand through his hair as he made for the door. "Man. This town is just too weird these days."

No argument there.

Vince watched Lucas slip out of the station and veer left through the parking lot, his hair lifting with each catlike stride. His shop, All That's Leather, was a mere half block away. Vince would keep an eye on the man. Lucas was single and had no alibi for the previous night. *I was home alone. Sleeping.*

Right now Vince wished he had a ten-man police force instead of five. Too many possibilities to cover and not enough live bodies. Fortunately Jim Tentley had been reached and would soon report in. "Sorry, Chief," he'd said. "I was running errands in Spokane and forgot to take my phone."

Vince didn't care where the man had been. He was just glad for Jim's help. Now he needed it more than ever.

He left the station, carrying the bagged note, ticking off the stores he and Jim would need to visit. *Just one hit's all I need, God. And I need it today.*

TWENTY-SEVEN

Leslie slumped on a stool at Java Joint, elbows on the counter, fingers thrust at her temples. The note had taken a wrecking ball to her wall of self-defense. Any minute now she was going to lose it.

The killer, whoever he was, knew her. *Knew* her! And all too well. He'd pierced to her soul, plucked out an ugly truth, and rammed it in her face.

Thank heaven Lucas Mulholland hadn't read that note, or its horrible words might be all over town by now.

Absently, Leslie watched Bailey make her latte—her second today. Her emotions bounced from grief and guilt to fright to near limb-shaking anger. Her one solace was the café's post-lunch slack. She was in no mood to face a bunch of people and their questions. Only S-Man remained at his table near the wall, and he was buried in Sauria. How Leslie envied Ted's alternate world. Might be fiction, but it gave him an escape.

Bailey poured the latte into a biggie cup and slid on a protective holder. She set the drink on the counter, then walked around and slipped onto the stool beside Leslie. Laid an empathetic hand on her shoulder. Tears welled in Leslie's eyes. She lowered her chin and watched one drop on the Formica, then another.

"Leslie, this is *not* your fault." Bailey rubbed the back of her neck. "This is the work of a very sick mind, and for some reason he's dragging you into it."

Same thing Paige had said over the phone not five minutes ago.

"I know he's sick, but why me?" Leslie kept her head down. "First Vesta's put in my car, then Chief Edwards asks me questions like maybe something I wrote ticked off the wrong person. Now this. Why would Vesta's killer think he was giving me a present? I must have done *something*."

But of course, she knew what she had done. And it was *awful*. Her ambition had cost Vesta's life. Hadn't she relished every ounce of attention she'd received from the Edna San case? Her newspaper articles, the interviews on local and national TV. To think that every time she preened before some microphone, this killer had been out there, watching. Seeing the satisfaction on her face over landing in the center of a big story.

Now he'd handed her another one.

"You're giving him too much credit." Bailey's voice was firm. "Whoever is doing this isn't thinking rationally. If he's focused on you, it's not because of anything you did. You just happened to be in the limelight, which made you an easy target. Anyone in the country could have seen you on TV, and there are some mighty crazy people out there."

Leslie sniffed. Bailey rose to fetch her a paper napkin and returned. "Here." She thrust it into Leslie's hands.

"Thanks."

Leslie wiped her eyes and nose, then lifted her chin. Bailey stared at the back wall. The muted *tap-tap* of keys emanated from S-Man's computer. After a moment, Leslie realized the sound had stopped. She turned toward him. He sat back in his chair, watching her with the body language of a male wondering if he dare intrude on woman-talk.

She managed a meager smile. "Hi, Ted."

"Hey. You're back."

"Yeah, well. Can't keep me away for long."

He pushed his chair from the table and stood up, flexing his shoulders. His gaze fell on her coffee cup. "You had anything to eat with all that caffeine?"

Like she'd even thought about food. "No."

"Leslie, that's not good." Bailey's tone slipped into her chiding-mother mode. She headed around the counter. "I'm fixing you a sandwich. Last thing you need is to faint from hunger."

"But I really—"

"I'll pay for it, Bailey." Ted made his way across the café, boots scuffing the floor.

Leslie shook her head. "You don't have to do that."

Ted leaned against the counter, gave her a shrug. "I know."

"I'll put it on a sourdough roll, okay?" Bailey started pulling out meats and cheeses.

Leslie sighed. "Okay then. Thanks. Next lunch of yours is on me."

His mouth slipped in and out of a smile. Leslie and Paige had once agreed that Ted was kind of cute when he smiled. He just didn't do it very often.

"Keep yourself safe. That's enough payback for me."

Leslie's gaze dropped to her lap. The kindness in his tone brought fresh tears to her eyes. She swallowed hard, blinked them back. "Ted, do you believe in ghosts?"

Bailey's hands slowed, slices of roast beef in her fingers. She glanced at Leslie long enough to catch her eye, then returned to making the sandwich.

Ted's focus wandered toward Java Joint's front windows, and he shifted on his feet. "Can't say I've thought much about it. Never met one, personally."

Surprising that he hadn't said no. For all his imagination, Ted was a pretty down-to-earth guy. "So ... you think they're possible?"

"I don't know. But you don't really believe a ghost left you that note, do you?"

Ah. Ted heard more than they thought he did. "No. And I don't believe one killed Vesta, either."

His shoulders lifted. "Then there you go."

Leslie nodded slowly. But what had she felt this morning? She *had not* imagined that. And what about Henry Johnson's shoes and the footprint? And how had that note ended up in front of her office—and *nobody* saw how it got there? At least that's the last she'd heard from Chief Edwards.

Bailey set the roast-beef sandwich before her. "Here now. Eat."

Leslie glanced at her watch. Two forty. She'd better get herself together. She had rescheduled her interview with Myra Hodgkid for three fifteen. After that stupid note, she *had* to draw information from Myra that pointed toward some radical in the "Give Kanner Lake a Break" crowd. If Vesta had died because of that hotel, then Leslie couldn't blame herself. Like Bailey said, it was just the work of a sick mind. Leslie so wanted to believe that.

Then why did the killer send me that note?

Bailey tapped a finger on the edge of her plate. "Eat."

Leslie picked up the sandwich, stealing another look at her watch. Twenty minutes max before she headed over to her appointment.

God, please let Myra give me something. Please.

TWENTY-EIGHT

He was bent over a long table with a colleague, studying initial concepts for a residential/shopping division when it happened. He reached out to tap a finger on a problematic section of the development — and the blue lines of the plan shifted.

Tamara's putrid face glared up at him.

His breath caught, hand frozen midair. Cold fear encased him like an icy grave.

The spirit vanished.

"You okay?" Jack Shaghlin's voice drifted into his ears. "Wrench your back or something?"

Seconds passed before he could speak.

"Yeah, I'm fine. I just—"

The phone on his desk rang. He stared at it blankly. Then, with robotic movements, answered it.

"Hi, it's Dad."

Dad.

His first thought was to slam down the phone. With the timing of Tamara's appearance — he should have known. His parents rarely called. Whatever his father wanted, whatever had happened, it couldn't be good. "Hold on a minute, please." His voice sounded hollow. He turned to Jack, pointed to the phone and mouthed, "It's my father."

Jack left the room, closing the door.

He sank onto the corner of his desk. Took a deep breath. "Okay, I'm here."

Silence. Then the words, flat toned: "You're mother's been diagnosed with lung cancer. She'll need surgery followed by radiation treatments. We think she can beat it. But she wants to see you soon. It's been a long time since you visited." The last sentence accused, as if his absence had somehow caused the illness.

His first reaction was shock. Followed by sarcasm. *Maybe she'll finally stop smoking.*

On second thought — no. His mother was nothing if not stubborn. And bitter. A toxic combination. She'd do what she pleased till the day she died.

A month passed before he found the time to take a few days off and fly north.

His parents no longer lived in their Idaho home. They had leased a small furnished house for six months outside Seattle, "trying out" the neighborhood, as his mother put it. Now with her diagnosis, they would stay longer, seeking treatment from Seattle doctors. In time they planned to put the Idaho house and their hunting cabin up for sale and buy a home in Washington.

"Kanner Lake's just too quiet," his mother complained the first day he arrived. "Thought I wouldn't miss the city, but I was wrong. I need more civilization than some little Idaho town." She made a sound of disgust.

He pictured Kanner Lake, where he'd once visited them. Beautiful area, with forests and water, open spaces. How like his mother to close herself to it.

She looked gray and hard, her eyes cynical. Life had dealt another blow, the spirit world unable to console her. She lay around on the couch a lot, spewing caustic remarks about everything and everyone — and smoked.

He hated being there. At least it wasn't the house of his childhood. Still, the place felt heavy, oppressive.

He'd brought a night light for his bedroom.

His father was restless. The man had lived fifty-eight years, seen success, yet seemed to have lost all focus. He drank a lot at night. Scotch, straight up, multiple glasses. He'd finally stagger to bed, mumbling curses. In the mornings he'd drink three cups of coffee, then disappear for the day, scouring the area for a house to buy. In his own home he could remodel. Tear down dysfunctional rooms and build them up again, fresh, new. Maybe then … something. Maybe then.

"We fixed those people, you know," Mother said idly on the second morning after his father had banged out the door. They were in the living room, he in a padded brown armchair and she lying on the matching couch. A cigarette lay smoldering in a glass ashtray on the coffee table, pulled close within her reach.

"What people?"

"The town of Kanner Lake in general. Place was full of holier-than-thou types. Didn't like our séances."

The begged question balanced on the tip of his tongue. He fought it at first, afraid of the answer. He had enjoyed Kanner Lake, and his mother knew it. She took a long drag on her cigarette, a sly look stealing his way. She knew him too well. He'd be more anxious not to know.

He crossed his legs in male fashion, ankle resting on the opposite knee. Smoothed a wrinkle from his khakis. "So what did you do?"

Her lips spread in a satisfied smile. She knocked ashes onto the glass dish with three taps of a rough-nailed finger. "It was after midnight one weekend, and we were fed up with the place. The moon was a crescent that night, a weird coral color. We took it as a sign. So we drove around, stopped on various streets. Under that coral moon, we called the Powers to put curses on the town."

Curses? A shiver ran up his spine. After all he'd seen in his life, he had no doubt in such power. How could his parents do that to such a nice town? They were even more detestable than he'd realized.

He gave a slow nod, no expression, as if his mother had just remarked on the weather. "What will happen?" His voice dropped, and he hated that she saw his fear.

She smirked. "Don't know. But it'll be good. Too bad I won't be around to see it. But make no mistake — those people will pay."

TWENTY-NINE

"Leslie Brymes, I can't *believe* your implications. Are you accusing one of my 'Give Kanner Lake a Break' workers of killing Vesta Johnson?"

Myra Hodgkid perched on the edge of her flower-chintz sofa, gray eyes blazing. A blue-veined hand clutched the armrest, her loose-skinned jaw set.

Leslie's muscles throbbed. How had this interview gone so wrong so fast? It started with the fits of a gas-choked engine, and the ride had gone downhill from there. *Please, just give me something.*

She forced her tone to sound even. Lose her temper now, and no way she'd get what she needed. "Mrs. Hodgkid, I'm so sorry. I can assure you that's not what I'm implying. I just wondered if you could think of anyone who showed a little too much enthusiasm for the cause. If it makes you feel any better, I asked the same questions of Sandy Westling a few hours ago."

The woman huffed. "There's no question our campaign against the hotel stirred the hearts of many residents, but to imply that someone would descend to *murder*—"

"I *didn't* imply it. I just asked for your thoughts."

Myra Hodgkid gave a long look down her nose at Leslie, as if examining a dog sniffing her front lawn. "My *thoughts* are that no one in this town would kill another resident in some insane scheme to scare off the developers. Period. No matter how strongly they felt against the hotel. And I highly resent the insinuation."

"No one even talked a little too loudly, or made—"

"Absolutely not! Now stop it."

Frustration kicked up Leslie's spine. She had to get this interview under control. Myra was known for her querulous nature, but this was over the top. "Okay, no need to argue." She raised her left hand palm out, a sign of truce. "I'm just doing my job here."

"Oh, no, you're doing much more than that."

Leslie stilled. Carefully placed her pen on top of her notebook. "What is that supposed to mean?"

Myra tightened her mouth. "You're not just a reporter on this story, are you now. You're part of it. Vesta was found in *your* car. Now I hear you received a note from her murderer. Seems to me you should be looking to *yourself* for answers, not me."

The words slammed Leslie. She stared at Myra, anger welling within her so strong and acidic, it scared her. The woman knew she'd hit home, was gloating over it.

Leslie reached for her purse, threw the pen inside, and pushed to her feet. "Thank you for your time." The words dropped like pebbles on asphalt. "I have no more questions."

Not now, not *ever*.

Myra rose, the very languidness of her movements signaling smug pleasure. "I'm sure you don't."

Grabbing her coat, Leslie turned on her heel and headed for the door. Myra made no move to see her out. At the hallway's threshold, Leslie swiveled around to face her. Elder or not, this woman deserved no respect.

"Vesta Johnson was my friend." Leslie's voice squeezed. Tears scratched her eyes, but she blinked them back. She would not cry in front of this woman. "I'd give anything to have her alive and well. And I'll do everything I can to find the person who killed her."

She pivoted into the hall. It took every ounce of discipline she possessed not to slam the door on the way out.

Leslie ran to her rental car, threw her coat and purse and herself inside. She gunned the engine and pulled into the street, imagining Myra at the window, watching her hasty exit with ultimate satisfaction.

Please, God, I didn't do anything! Tell me this isn't my fault!

A block away, Leslie could hold herself together no longer. She pulled over to the curb and put the car in park, lowered her head to the steering wheel, and sobbed.

THIRTY

"All right, Jim, what names you got?" Vince sat at his desk, paper before him and pen in hand. Raring to go.

"Quite a few, but hang on a minute." Jim tossed down his notebook and settled into the chair across from Vince. Then picked up the pad and starting flipping pages.

When Jim finally reported for work, Vince's first order of business was to fill him in on all that had occurred. Then they split up to visit downtown shops. Now it was three thirty, and they'd met back at the station to compare notes.

The news wasn't good. Jim reported that no owner on the second block, where the *Kanner Lake Times* office was located, had seen anyone dropping a note outside the newspaper's door. And neither of them could report a sighting of anything suspicious by any customer who'd been in the area around the time the note was found.

Jim, a big guy in his late forties, carried a laid-back attitude and a slow, easy smile. He'd been a Kanner Lake officer for over five years, and his service had earned the trust of the town. If anyone could coax information out of a resident, it was Jim. But no such luck today. Vince had to believe that no one, in truth, had seen anything.

Of course, one of those customers, or even a business owner, might be covering his own tracks.

The clock on Vince's wall ticked away relentless minutes. In less than three hours darkness would fall over Kanner Lake. Vince did not want to think about what could happen tonight.

And he couldn't stop thinking about it.

"Okay." Jim flicked his finger at the top of a page. "First, Java Joint. Bailey Truitt reported four people in the café around the time in question. Ted Dawson—S-Man—was there as usual. But he happened to leave his computer and the café for a brief walk to stretch his legs."

Vince pulled down the sides of his mouth. "Really."

"Yeah. I talked to him. He said he walked down the street toward the lake rather than up, so he wasn't even facing the *Times* office."

Vince jotted down the information. "Okay. Who else in Java Joint?"

Three more—IGA owner Ralph Bednershack, city council-man Jerry Taply, and realtor Carla Radling. Other folks in and out of various shops were Myra Hodgkid and Beth Wagmul. Beth had made numerous stops, the last one being Simple Pleasures.

Vince's short list of people in the area began with Lucas Mulholland. Then on to Peter Levinson, a local civil engineer working on the hotel project, and Ira Benson, a retired fireman who'd stopped in at Wilson's Hamburgers for lunch. Tanner Crayl was also in Wilson's. Tanner was in his thirties, a fast-talking guy who sold cars down in Post Falls. Final three on the list were Mary Bruntz and her four-year-old twins.

Vince counted the names. "Eleven adults."

They exchanged a look. A day ago none of these names would have caused them an inkling of alarm. Today, no one was above suspicion. Some of them had alibis for the previous night: they were asleep in bed, with their spouses. But Peter Levinson, Tanner Crayl, and Ted Dawson were single. Ergo, no alibi. And alibis from the rest of the folks had not yet been 100 percent confirmed.

"Eleven we know about." Jim lifted a shoulder. "But for all we know the perp avoided being seen altogether."

"Yeah. Or maybe perps, plural—one keeping a lookout while the other left the note. We can't rule out the possibility that more than one person's involved."

"True. Course, there's always the ghost."

"That's a big help."

Jim shrugged. "It's where the evidence points at the moment."

Vince shook his head. He knew Jim didn't believe the ghost theory any more than he did. All the same, he hoped to hear from the Coeur d'Alene lab in the next hour or so. Surely their findings would at least put the matter of the hairs to rest.

They perused their individual lists, thinking. The clock's ticking had never sounded so loud. Vince rubbed his face, his gaze falling on the photo of Nancy and Tim. *Nancy.* With a start he realized she would be home from work by now. He needed to check in with her, insist that she get out of town. He would probably work through the night. No way she was staying there alone.

He pushed back his chair. "All right." His words clipped. "Let's do the store rounds. Call my cell and let me know what you find."

Only five possible stores in town could have sold the paper they sought. Vince would visit two of them; Jim, three.

But Vince would stop home first.

Jim left the station; Vince took a minute to go over his notes. Just as he reached his car in the parking lot, his cell phone rang. The ID noted the lab in Coeur d'Alene. *All right.* He flipped the phone open. "Chief Edwards."

"Hi, Chief, Lester Sullivan at the lab. I've been working on those white hairs for you. Roger Waitman told me to call you directly."

"Absolutely, thanks. What did you find?"

"The hairs are consistent."

Vince stilled. "You sure?"

"As sure as I can be without the DNA. I took a good gander at 'em under the microscope, then had two other techs do the same. We all agree they're consistent. A real unusual thickness and shape in the shaft. You just don't see hairs like this very often. My bet is the DNA'll clinch it."

The news wedged a two-by-four between Vince's ribs. He stared at the pavement, thoughts scrambling. If the tech was right, where could the hairs on Vesta have come from? That box he'd found in her garage had not been opened. Her house looked clean.

I felt something at my back. It touched my neck. Leslie's words rang in his head.

The air around Vince chilled. Thickened.

Something pulsed on his left, his right. Behind him. The distinct, undeniable sense of evil.

What ... ?

Sweat popped up the back of his neck.

He jerked his head this way and that, searching for the source.

The feeling vanished.

Vince's limbs slacked. He leaned against the door of his car, pulling in air. Stabilizing himself. The whole thing couldn't have lasted more than two seconds, yet he felt so drained. What *was* that?

He'd just gone off for a moment, that's all. Too much stress.

"Chief Edwards, you there?"

Vince, snap out of it.

"Chief?"

"Yeah. I'm here."

That heaviness. Even the memory of it filtered dread through his veins.

"Thanks, Lester," he managed. "For doing this so quickly." Whatever that presence was, he had *not* imagined it.

"No problem," Lester replied. "Glad you've found your suspect already. Keep safe when you arrest that maniac, you hear?"

Yeah, right. How do you keep safe from a ghost?

THIRTY-ONE

Leslie drove toward Pastor Hank's office, tears dried but face still hot. She'd called him as soon as she stopped bawling, asking to talk—*now*. If anyone could help sort out her feelings, it was Hank Detcher.

During the short drive to the church, she spotted two news vans from Spokane. Oh, great. Reporters were no doubt running all over town, interviewing residents, filming on site for their evening programs. Jared said three had called the office, seeking her comment. She wouldn't give one, of course. Finding Vesta's killer was more important than getting herself on TV again.

Still, even dredged in guilt, Leslie had to admit that the sight of those vans punched jealousy through her heart.

No doubt about it. She was a rotten person.

Leslie turned a corner, New Community Church sliding into view. The sight of its white wooden exterior offered little comfort. It seemed to scream her sins. Leslie pulled into the church parking lot, checked her face in the rearview mirror, and took a deep breath. She would not allow herself to appear too bedraggled, even to her pastor.

As she stepped through a side door into the office hallway, Leslie heard muffled voices emanating from the sanctuary. She turned left toward Pastor Hank's office, away from the sound, grateful she didn't have to pass by it. No doubt people had gathered to pray and comfort one another after hearing of Vesta's death. If anyone saw her, they'd fall all over her with concern. No way could she handle that now. At the first hug she'd crumble.

Leslie hurried down the hall, ducking by the kitchen, on past the nursery, and up to Pastor Hank's open door. She stepped into the small wood-paneled office, saw him seated at his desk, head down. Kneading his forehead with both hands. The sight stabbed her. At the moment he didn't look like the pastor who could handle about anything. He just looked tired.

Leslie rapped on the door.

Pastor pulled up his chin, his sagging expression creasing into a smile. "Hi, Leslie." He pushed back from his desk and walked around to meet her with a quick hug. "You didn't sound very good on the phone. How are you doing?"

Instant tears bit her eyes. "Having my moments."

"I'll bet. I can imagine the day you've had."

She blinked a few times. "Yeah, well, you can't be having a great one yourself. I'll bet you've been counseling grief-stricken people nonstop. And I know how much you loved Vesta."

Sadness swept over his face. "Yeah. This is ... such a tragedy. I still can't believe it."

Leslie nodded, not trusting herself to speak.

Pastor Hank gestured to a chair before his desk. "Please. Have a seat."

As she slipped into the chair, Leslie's gaze roved over his book-cluttered desk, then bounced up to the back wall, filled with photos of events in the church. Dinners, Easter services, weddings, Christmas plays. Normal life. How far away that felt now.

Pastor resettled in his own chair, leaning his red-sweatered arms on his desk. "So. Tell me what you're feeling."

Where to begin ...

Halting at first, Leslie told him—more than she'd planned. She knew the information would be safe with him, and once she started talking, it all just spilled out. The presence she'd felt in the hallway. The message pinned to Vesta's chest. Rumors of Henry Johnson's shoes—which Pastor had no doubt heard. Then the footprint Chief Edwards had found. The note left on her office doorstep. The horrible guilt that her ambition and selfishness had led to Vesta's death.

Pastor Hank listened, empathy deepening the lines on his face. When her words trickled away, he leaned back and shook his head. "Leslie, that is a lot to deal with. First, let me say you're in no way responsible for Vesta's death, regardless of what that note said. Her murderer most likely targeted you for the immediate publicity he would get, since you've already been on the news. As for his message ..." Pastor's gaze drifted across the room. "What's troubling you is your interpretation of the note. It's a sick person who thinks a murder victim would be a present for anyone. But those words triggered something in you that probably already existed deep down. You might want to examine it later. Now, though, is not the time. You have enough to deal with, and you couldn't see it clearly anyway." He offered her a small smile. "Does that make any sense?"

Leslie flicked a piece of lint from her jeans. His words sounded right, but she couldn't comprehend it all right now. Which, she supposed, proved his point. "Yeah, it does."

Maybe she never really liked the ambition within herself. But it was her *life*. What would she do without it?

Weariness swept through her. She wished she could lie down and take a very long nap. Like for about a month.

"Okay. I guess I'll ... look at that later, like you suggest." Even saying the words made her feel a little lighter. One problem at a time. Leslie ran a hand through her hair. "What do you think about all this ghost stuff?"

"Now there's a topic." Pastor Hank rubbed his jaw, considering. "Do you know there's a ghost story in the Bible?"

Leslie blinked. "No."

"Let me first say it's not a 'ghost' as people think of them today—tormented spirits unable to find rest. But it is a story of God allowing the spirit of someone who died and now dwells with Him to return to earth for a short time to accomplish a specific purpose. The story's in 1 Samuel, chapter 28. God forbade the Israelites to go to mediums. But King Saul disobeyed and asked a medium to call up the spirit of the prophet Samuel. The king wanted to know what to do about the Philistines, who were threatening him with war." Pastor smiled. "Apparently the medium didn't expect Samuel to appear, because she screamed when she saw him. And Samuel wasn't too happy about being disturbed. But he did come. And he answered Saul's question."

Wow. "What did he say?"

"Samuel, you mean? Not quite what Saul wanted to hear. He told the king he and his two sons were going to die in battle the following day."

"Did they?"

"Yup."

Leslie's eyes drifted to the wall of photos behind Pastor Hank. She obviously should read the Bible more.

"There's also the transfiguration in the New Testament," Pastor Hank continued. "When Jesus was on the mountain with three of His disciples, and Moses and Elijah appeared, and spoke with Him."

Leslie gave him a long look. "So ... what? You can't be telling me you believe Vesta was killed by her dead husband."

Pastor Hank shifted in his seat. "No, I'm not saying that. There's no indication in the Bible that spirits linger in this world. The stories of Samuel, and Elijah and Moses—I think they're anomalies. Rare occasions when God, for a specific reason, allowed the spirits to come back to earth—and then they left again."

Okay. She could buy that much. Leslie crossed her arms. "So when we hear about ghosts haunting places, are all those stories just made up? Or somebody's imagination?"

That presence she'd felt this morning—that was *real*.

Pastor Hank drew a breath. "No. I don't believe they're all just stories or imagination. Some no doubt are. But the rest? I think they're demonic presences."

"Demonic?"

He inclined his head. "I know it's not an easy subject. But let me ask you this. Do you believe in angels?"

"Sure. I know they're in the Bible."

"Yes. But the Bible also talks about fallen angels. They were tossed out of heaven along with Satan. These are demons—his followers. They are as present on this earth, although usually unseen, as angels. If you believe that angels exist, it's pretty hard to deny the existence of demons, because the Bible says they're both very real."

Leslie pondered that. "Okay. So ... is that what I felt this morning?"

"Possibly."

"Why? I mean, why would one bother *me*?"

Pastor Hank shook his head. "I don't know, but there's a darkness over this town. Well, obviously—we've just had a terrible murder. But I've felt it for some time. And just today four different people have phoned to tell me how God called them to intense prayer this morning. One of them was Helen Communs. I know she called you. The other three found themselves praying against an unknown evil. And I'll tell you, that scares me. When God calls His people to pray like that, something's definitely up."

Okay, this was scaring her too. "I wish I understood all this."

"Same here. I sure don't have all the answers." Pastor laced his fingers. "Ultimately, I think God's creation is more awesome and mysterious than we can know. Some things just won't be explained this side of heaven. But one thing I do know—Jesus's name is stronger than any evil. That's why we have to keep praying, Leslie. You especially, since you've been bothered. Ask for protection in Jesus's name, and He will give it."

"Yeah. You can count me in on that." Even if she didn't know how to do it very well.

She looked at her watch. After five. Paige would be getting off work at six o'clock, and she'd need to be picked up. Leslie smiled at Pastor Hank. "Thank you so much for your time. I should be going soon."

He held up a hand. "Let me pray for you before you go."

"Okay."

They bowed their heads, and he prayed. For God's grace and mercy to be loosed over the town. For Vesta's killer to be brought to justice. For special protection over Leslie. By the time he finished, fresh tears brimmed in her eyes.

He stood to see her out. Offered her a tired smile as they stood in the doorway. "Call anytime you need me, hear?"

"I will. Thanks."

Leslie slipped down the hall, not sure if she felt better or worse. *Something's definitely up . . .*

The image of Vesta's bloodied face pulsed before her.

She hurried to her car. Night would be here soon. The thought of darkness chilled her to the core. She couldn't wait to get to her parents' house and lock herself inside.

As she slid into the car, her cell phone rang. The ID indicated a Spokane reporter.

Leslie made a face and threw the phone in her purse.

THIRTY-TWO

He awoke with a start.

For a moment he trembled in the house of his childhood.

His eyes popped open to a dark room, dimly lit by his night light. He saw a plain wall, no pictures. Closed blinds at the window. Small dresser in the right corner, round candles scattered on it. Open doorway to attached bathroom.

Reality flooded his brain. His parents' rented house in Washington. He'd come to bed, swallowing down his fear. Feeling spirits everywhere. Wondering if his parents had placed a curse on *him*.

He stared at the ceiling, longing for his California apartment, his job. His life there wasn't exactly happy, but it was solid. Predictable. After his horrible childhood, he'd made something of himself. Grown strong. Or so he thought. Now, after just two days with his parents, he felt the ground roll under him, like a sailor ashore.

How was he going to stand another day and night in this place?

The room was hot. He sat up, pushed the bedspread past his feet. With a *shoosh* it fell to the floor.

A ghost rose up.

He froze.

Tamara.

His heart stuttered into a hard beat. He felt the kiss of air against his bare back, and hair rose on his arms. The wall. He had to touch the wall.

155

He dug both heels into the mattress, shoved himself backward. His shoulder blades slammed first. His head flew back, hitting next. He clutched the bedsheet, pulled it up to his chin.

The spirit hovered. A short, squat form. Disheveled.

Not Tamara.

A man?

It felt vaguely male, but not quite human. Exuding evil. An evil thick and fat, as tangible as a swaying serpent. Understanding flooded him as strongly as the night he'd faced his sister at the age of six. This thing wanted him. Every inch of his flesh, every hair on his head. His arms, his legs, his heart. His *soul.*

He needed light. Just reach over and snap on the table lamp to his right — and the thing would disappear.

Move!

His muscles hardened to concrete.

The spirit swelled.

His arm lashed out, banged into the lamp. It crashed to the floor.

He leapt from bed, mind shrieking, feet stumbling. After an eternity he rammed into the wall by the door, hands scrambling for the light switch. Terrified sounds fell from his lips.

A looming behind him. Malevolence breathed ice down his neck. The skin on his back crinkled.

He felt the switch, smacked it on. Light flooded the room. He collapsed to his knees, snapped his head around, eyes squinted in the glare.

Nothing.

Nothing.

He slid onto his rear, legs bent and elbows on his knees, and slumped against the wall. Trying to breathe.

Time passed. He didn't know how long.

Something cracked inside. Jagged down the length of him like ground in an earthquake.

He hung there, shivering and spent and waiting for dawn. Two things he vowed.

To leave his parents' house that day.

And never return.

But it was already too late. He couldn't deny it. The ghosts had fixed their greedy eyes on him again, and even after he left this place, they would find him. Earthly distance meant nothing to a spirit. His own apartment would no longer be safe. Not as long as his parents continued to lure these lecherous things through their séances.

He couldn't go back to that kind of life again. Couldn't live with the fear. It would drive him insane.

What if he begged his parents to make the spirits leave? They had called them here; they could send them back. A séance in reverse. He would take part in it, showing the ghosts he was strong. Unafraid. They'd let him alone then.

Wouldn't they?

He dug both hands into his scalp. What was he thinking? He was totally losing it. One minute of his parents' chanting would dredge up all the petrifying childhood memories. One minute of that sound, and he'd fold.

The room grew cold. He shivered. Leaving the light on, he crawled onto the bed, sitting up with back pressed against the wall. Drew the sheet over his shoulders. He longed for the bedspread, but would not lift it from the floor. Its movement had disturbed a ghost once. No need to tempt fate again, even in a lighted room.

He slept no more that night.

THIRTY-THREE

Vince stepped through the front door of his house, closed and bolted it behind him. "Nancy? I'm home."

She appeared from the kitchen, phone in hand, blue eyes red-rimmed. The mere sight of her, alive, safe, weakened his limbs.

"Vince! I was just going to call you." Her voice hitched. "I didn't hear about Vesta until I got home, then the phone started ringing off the hook. Now I just heard about some note sent to Leslie Brymes." She clattered the receiver down on an end table, and pressed against his chest. "What's happening? This is so terrible."

Vince held her tightly. "I know." He buried his face in her hair, smelling the familiar citrusy shampoo. "I know."

They stood for a moment, Nancy shivering as she cried. Anger and fear thrummed in Vince's chest. They'd seen too much death in the last few years. He hated to see his wife go through any more trauma.

She took a deep breath and pulled away. Vince placed a palm against her cheek. "You know I'm going to be working night and day on this case."

She nodded. Laid her hand over his.

"We have some information that we haven't let out." He told her about the message pinned to Vesta's chest. Nancy's face paled. "I want you to stay with Heather until this is over."

Her eyes widened. "But I don't want to leave you—"

Vince slid his finger to her lips. "No arguments, Nancy. First, I'm not going to leave you in danger. Second, I've got far more than I can handle right now, and I can't possibly concentrate if I'm worrying about your safety. No way am I letting you stay here by yourself."

"But what about you? How will I know you're safe?"

"I'll call as often as I can. And you know my cell's always on. But I'm not the one in danger. I'm worried about people in their homes tonight—especially women alone."

Nancy stared at the floor. Resignation fluttered across her face. She led him by the hand to the couch, beckoned him to sit beside her. "What is going on with these ghost rumors?"

The memory of that feeling prickled down his limbs.

He smoothed her hair. "Just rumors, that's all. The shoes are real, but I can't say for sure they belonged to Henry Johnson. Either way, the perp's gone to a lot of trouble to set up the story. Good way to try keeping us off track."

Yeah, Vince, but what about the hairs?

Time was ticking. Responsibilities pulled at him, and night was approaching. He needed to get back to work.

He dreaded the dark.

Vince stood. "Go get packed now, okay? I'm not leaving until you're on your way."

Ten minutes later he stood on the front porch, waving her off. Heaviness weighted his body. What if he couldn't solve this crime anytime soon? How long could he insist that Nancy stay away from her own home?

How could he let her return as long as a killer roamed the streets?

God, please help me. Help us all.

Vince turned to double-check the lock on his front door—and his cell phone rang. He glanced at the ID, flipped open the phone. "Hey, Jim."

"Chief, good news. I just stopped by my third store, Quick-Mart. I think they've got our paper."

THIRTY-FOUR

Ali was washing dishes when the news came on. "Gruesome murder in Kanner Lake, details after these messages."

She stilled, eyes turning toward the television.

After school her mom had told her about Vesta Johnson's murder. Ali started crying right off. Vesta, one of the sweetest ladies she'd ever met. When she and her parents moved to Kanner Lake, Vesta had come across town to bring them a casserole and cake. Ali just couldn't believe the news. Who would hurt somebody like Vesta?

Now, standing at the sink, Ali had all kinds of mixed-up thoughts. Her day at school—wonderful because of Chet, scary because of that note and the curse. Then hearing about Vesta. It was too much. Ali felt like she'd been abandoned on some unknown road at night, left to find her way home. No way could she tell her mom what had happened at school.

Much less what she planned to do tomorrow.

"I met some girls," Ali had told her mom when she finally quit crying. "They're hanging out tomorrow at one of their houses and invited me to come."

Her mom's face brightened. "That's great, honey. I'm so glad you're making friends."

Guilt pricked at Ali. Her mom didn't deserve a half-truth. Not at all.

And if Mom found out what she was up to, she'd never let Ali go anywhere ever again.

From where she stood, Ali could only see half the TV through the living room doorway. Mom and Dad sat on the couch in profile, light showing the thinning patches of Mom's brown hair. Mom had managed to make dinner, which tired her out. She used to have so much energy, but now spent most of the day resting and taking naps. In a few hours she'd drag herself to bed. Somehow—and Ali's heart squeezed whenever she thought about it—her mom managed to stay cheerful, even if her smiles sagged. She seemed far more worried about Ali's happiness at school than her own problems.

Ali set a plate in the dishwasher, picked up another one to rinse. The TV flipped through commercials—some new hybrid car, a sleeping pill, a telephone service. When the news came back on, Ali turned off the water and hurried to the living room doorway to watch.

Cindy Brewster, a Spokane reporter, stood in front of a street marked off by yellow crime-scene tape. Ali listened to details about the murder—and nearly freaked. Vesta had been left in Leslie Brymes's car—the reporter who wrote for the *Kanner Lake Times*. The killer left some note for Leslie, right outside her office. A man named Lucas something-or-other was interviewed, saying how he'd found the note but saw only Leslie Brymes's name written on it in capital letters. "Police have not released the contents of the note," Cindy added. "And Miss Brymes has refused comment on the case."

Another scary note found by somebody. Two in one day.

Ali felt a connection to Leslie Brymes. Ali knew who she was. Saw her on TV back in Montana. Leslie was young and really pretty. And famous because of the Edna San case. She had it all.

"In a bizarre twist," the Spokane reporter continued, "the only evidence so far points to the victim's late husband, Henry Johnson, who passed away over a year ago ... "

Ali froze. For a minute she thought she'd fall to the floor. She steadied herself against the doorway, Chet's voice filling her head.

"We were trying to call up Edna San's spirit, just for kicks. But last week something happened. This presence came into the room. We all felt it at the same time. The thing brushed my shoulder. Touched Kristal's and Nate's necks. Then we saw *it across the room, Ali. It was* for real. *An old man with white hair. He had a blue sweater on and beige pants. He looked at us, and we all felt like this evil smacked us in the face. Then he just disappeared. Right through the wall ..."*

Cindy Brewster cut to an interview with one of Vesta's friends, who talked about the dead man's shoes on Vesta's doorstep—with blood on them. And a wine stain, which *proved* they were his shoes. Then some neighbor of Leslie's told how she'd seen the police making a mold of a footprint.

"The question the whole town is wondering tonight is"—Cindy's tone lowered—"will the footprint match the shoes of the deceased Henry Johnson?"

"What in the *world*?" Ali's mom leaned against her husband as the television flashed to commercials. "This is *crazy*."

Ali's mind reeled. She pushed off the doorway, walked on weak legs to the sink to finish the dishes. This couldn't be right. There had to be an explanation. Somebody staged the footprint and those shoes—forget that Vesta's friend insisted they'd been thrown out. So what if Kristal's gang just happened to call up a ghost last week.

Coincidence, that was all. Had to be.

An old man with white hair ...

What did Henry Johnson look like?

"I gotta do homework." She banged the dishwasher shut and fled upstairs.

Ali locked her door and collapsed on the bed, next to her backpack. She could barely breathe. If only she could call

Chet, but she didn't have his number. Didn't even know his last name. He must have heard about this by now. What did he think about it?

She stuck her hand deep into her backpack, searching for the note. *There.* She pulled it up and unfolded it, praying the words would somehow be different than she remembered. Because somehow, some way, she had to get out of this thing.

Meeting with the dead tomorrow night, same time, same place. Let's see what the ghost does this time. Same group, and nobody tell!
P.S. If anyone outside our group reads this note, that person is cursed by the Powers!

Ali slumped. Same words, same coral moon at the bottom— whatever that meant. She forgot to ask.

She couldn't go to the séance now. It had been sort of cool in a scary way to think she might see a ghost. But now the thought petrified her.

Maybe Chet and Kristal and everybody would be scared too. Maybe they'd want to call the thing off.

What if they didn't? How would she get out of it? The group would *really* be freaked after the murder. They'd make sure nobody told. Now that Ali knew everything, if she tried to get out of going tomorrow, they'd think she was going to snitch. Maybe tell the police.

Should she should tell the police?

Ali threw the note on the bed, hugged her arms to her chest. She imagined calling the Kanner Lake police station. *Hello, you know that story about the shoes of a dead man? I know how his ghost got here . . .*

She dropped her head in her hands. Yeah, right. They'd throw her in the loony bin. And her parents might find out. Or worse, the police would go question Kristal and everybody, and the

163

group would know who told. Forget ever making friends then. Forget talking to Chet for the rest of her life.

Ali squeezed her eyes shut. She *couldn't* go to the séance.

She *had* to go.

Maybe she could just pull out and swear she'd never tell anybody. Which she wouldn't.

But then she wouldn't be one of the group. Plus she'd be cursed.

That's stupid, Ali, do you really believe in a curse?

How could she not believe it? A person had been *killed*.

Ali's eyes filled with tears. *Why* did she ever pick up that note? She snatched the stupid thing up, ready to tear it to pieces. But her hands stopped.

Ali stared at the note. *Rip it up! Flush it down the toilet.* But she couldn't. Her fingers just ... wouldn't move.

Minutes ticked by. She sat there like a zombie.

Finally, with a shudder, not knowing what on earth was wrong with her, she folded it twice—and buried it in the bottom of her backpack.

THIRTY-FIVE

He froze in the chair in his living room, fingers hooked into the armrests. Staring at the television long after the news segment concluded. The station blitzed to loud commercials, but he barely heard a word.

Shoes from the victim's dead husband ... a footprint on the grass ... a note. His whirling thoughts didn't know where to land first.

The footprint.

How had it gotten there? *He* hadn't left it.

Had he?

He couldn't have been that clumsy. Didn't remember stepping off the driveway at all.

The note.

His fingers curled deeper into the chair. He had. Not. Left. A note.

Right? Was he losing his *mind*?

No. *They* had done it. They were messing with his head—and the police. Raising the stakes so he would be all the more careful tonight.

Every nerve began to tingle, hair rising up on his arms. His eyes widened, darted around the room.

The house was growing dark. Corners glooming.

He shoved to his feet and strode over to smack the light switch. Flicked on the lamp beside the couch, then hurried into the kitchen to turn on every light he could find. In the ceiling. Over the stove. Above the sink.

His head swiveled to the kitchen table. Even from across the room he could make out the letters of the message they'd left that morning.

His heart pumped fear and wild excitement. Part of him wanted to do the deed *now*. Get it over with and go on with life. Flee Kanner Lake if he had to. As much as he loved the town, he should never have set foot in this house. How could he believe he'd be safe here?

The other part of him wanted to fly in the face of his tormentors, peck out their eyes. Let them kill their own victims. Already they played with him, invading his house, wreaking havoc around Kanner Lake. Who was to say they'd leave him alone after tonight?

He fell into a kitchen chair, breathing hard. Jerked out a hand and swept the newspaper and the ugly message on it to the floor. He blinked down at them, eyes blurring. Desperate ideas crowded his head. What if he disappeared—left everything behind? Cashed out his money and lost himself in some foreign country? Kanner Lake was just a little town in northern Idaho. Who'd find him across the ocean?

They would.

You have no place to hide.

He stared at the papers on the floor—until his breathing evened and his vision cleared.

Resolutely, he bent over to pick them up. He laid them back on the table, smoothed them out. *There. Happy now? Don't be mad at me. I didn't mean it.*

His gaze strayed out the window to the backyard, where shadows lengthened amid the trees.

Welcome the darkness, a voice whispered inside his head, *welcome it.*

Yeah. He'd do that. What choice did he have?

One more assignment, that was it. Tomorrow this would all be over. Hit fast, hit hard.

And hope no dead man's shoeprint was left behind.

THIRTY-SIX

QuickMart was on Travis Street, one block up from the three-hundred stretch of Main. The place smelled of bleach, its floors just mopped.

"Careful where you step"—Ray Whittlen nodded to Vince—"it's slippery."

Vince watched his feet as he walked toward the counter. The Whittlens closed up at five thirty—a little early for a convenience-sized grocery store. But they had kids at home, and Mary had to prepare dinner and oversee homework. Theirs were busy lives.

Vince had the note, bagged for protection. Mary hovered behind the counter, watching with rounded eyes. She was a short and soft-spoken woman with a polite, almost formal way of speaking. Vince guessed she'd never had the slightest tie to crime in her life, much less a heinous murder, and the mere thought left her trembling. Ray, a foot taller than Mary, loomed beside her, hands on his hips, large mouth pursed with indigna-tion at the idea that the killer might have set foot in *his* store. "We'll do whatever we can to help," he'd declared in his parking lot the minute Vince climbed from the patrol car. "You just tell us what you need."

When they'd stepped inside the store, Ray had locked the door behind them and turned his red-lettered sign over to "Closed."

An unused pad of the paper in question now lay on the coun-ter. Jim stood next to Vince, arms crossed, as he picked up the pad to examine it. *Yeah, absolutely.* Same type of paper, same color of horizontal lines, three red vertical lines forming the left margin. Vince tore off a sheet, held it up to the light, noting the patterns of gray and white pulp. Wordlessly, he pulled on gloves and extracted the note from its bag. Held it up to light in one hand and the torn sheet in the other, comparing the two. Definite continuity.

He slid the note back into its bag, slipped off his gloves and stuffed them in his coat pocket. "How long have you stocked this paper?"

Ray lifted a shoulder. "Long time. It's a staple brand."

Vince focused on the pad. "Happen to remember anyone buying it lately?"

Ray shook his head. "Mary and I talked about that while you were on the way over here. We can't think of anyone. We do have a security camera covering the counter." He pointed up to the left corner of the store. "That would have tape for the last three days, then it recycles itself. But you might want to look at it."

Vince exchanged a glance with Jim. They would definitely do that. "Anyone else work for you, Ray?"

"No, just Mary and me. We're trying to save all the pennies, you know. Make ends meet with three kids."

Mary started to lean a hand on the counter, then snatched it back, as if afraid to share the same space with the bagged note. "Tommy, our twelve-year-old, was here in the store today. He has been recuperating from a cold, and I didn't want him infecting his friends at school. He spent most of the day in our office, down that hall and by the rear entrance." She gestured toward an open doorway in the same corner as the security camera. "He was out here a few times, but I don't think he ever waited on a customer alone, did he, Ray?"

"No."

"He still here now?" Vince asked.

"Yes." Mary's eyes flicked from Vince to Jim. "Do you want to see him?"

Vince said he would, although he doubted the boy could add any information.

Tommy, small like his mother, shuffled through the door, eyes lowered and clearly uncomfortable with being questioned by police. His brown hair was cropped short, light freckles across his nose. Kid looked young for his age. Vince gentled his tone. "Hi, Tommy. Hear you're not feeling well today."

The boy gave a quick nod.

Vince asked about the paper. Did Tommy remember anyone buying it today, or any other day he might have been in the store?

"No, sir." He raised his eyes to Vince, then looked down again.

"Okay." Vince studied him for a moment. "Were you here all day in the store? Happen to go downtown at any time?"

Tommy blinked twice at the counter.

"Son, straighten up!" Ray's voice turned sharp. "Look at Chief Edwards when he's talking to you."

Tommy's chin rose. His eyes met Vince's, one small twitch in his left cheek. "No."

Vince catalogued the troubled gaze, his hesitation. Nervousness? Or had this boy seen something? "You sure about that? I need you to tell me the truth now."

"I'm sure."

Vince held the kid's eyes for a long moment. He didn't know Tommy well enough to gauge whether he was lying. But one thing seemed clear—if the kid had slipped from the store today, he wouldn't admit it in front of his parents. "All right, son. Thanks for your time."

He watched Tommy disappear into the hallway leading to the office, waited for the click of a closed door. Then looked to Ray, voice lowered. "Seems a little skittish."

"He's not usually," Mary cut in, one hand finding the base of her throat. "But all this talk today. Since this morning people have been coming in here with news of the murder. He probably heard more than we realized."

Vince nodded. "Yeah. Understood. Whole town's upset." He looked over his shoulder. "Where do you keep these pads of paper?"

Ray angled his forefinger toward the right. "Aisle one, down toward the end."

Jim headed in that direction, Vince following. They discovered five pads of the paper on a lower shelf. Jim stooped down, reached for the top one.

"Wait." Vince put a hand on his shoulder. Jim looked up questioningly. "Maybe you ought to put on gloves." He extracted a pair from his pocket and held them out. Jim slipped them on. Pulled off the top pad of paper and examined it. Then perused the others one by one. At the bottom pad he paused, brought it nearer to his eyes. Turned it sideways. He stood up. "Look here." He held the pad before Vince's face, using a gloved finger to nudge up the white border at the top. Underneath it lay the edge of a missing piece of paper. "A page has been torn off."

Vince leaned over and peered at it. Jim was right.

A rock sank in his stomach. Terrific. Their search had just widened dramatically. Forget who bought the paper; now it could be anyone who'd entered the store.

"How did you know?" Jim asked.

Vince stared at the pad, trying to decipher the subconscious nudge that had urged him to pull out the gloves. Being a cop had taught him to go with his gut. You followed a rabbit trail on a hunch; sometimes it worked out, sometimes not.

He shook his head. "I didn't."

Fifteen minutes later he and Jim stepped out of QuickMart into the dusk, bearing the bagged pad with missing page plus two security videotapes—one from the camera covering the rear-aisle section where the paper was shelved, and, just in case, one from the front counter. Some lucky officer would get to watch up to six total days of footage.

Darkness approached. Vince itched with uneasiness. The memory of those seconds in the station parking lot haunted him. What he'd felt could not be real.

But he *knew* what he'd felt.

And soon, night. Would it bring another victim? Vince flashed to Nancy, sending a prayer of thanks that she had fled town. Still, hundreds of innocent residents remained.

A circled number one.

Hope you liked my present, Leslie.

In the next twelve hours, not one of his officers would see his own bed.

Vince backed out of the QuickMart parking lot and headed around the corner toward Main, Jim following in his own car. At the police station they would reconnoiter to work out a patrol plan for the night. One officer would have to remain at the crime scene of Vesta's house as ISP detectives continued their work. (Which, by the way, had better yield some evidence pointing to a *living* person.) Leslie's and Paige's rented home had been cleared, so no officer need be stationed there.

Vince sighed. He didn't like running his whole force all night. Left a full crew of tired officers in the morning. He'd have to let them rotate getting some sleep tomorrow.

As they entered the station, the phone rang. Jim picked up the call. Vince got on his cell to Roger, checking to see what was happening at Vesta's house. The detectives and techs were still working—no surprise there. It would take hours yet to go over every inch of that house. Dust for prints, vacuum the carpets, take photos, check the blood splatter. Then days more to process all the evidence at the lab.

"Chief," Jim said when Vince hung up, "it's Sam Greene. He wants to talk to you."

Vince took the receiver. "Yeah, Sam, got something for me?"

"Hi. Look, I know you're busy, but I thought you'd want to know this. I've been hearing rumors this afternoon—that Vesta's death could be connected to the hotel issue. I know that's probably preliminary, but it reminded me of something. Last week I was talking to Tanner Crayle about buying a car, and we got on the subject of the hotel. Tanner doesn't like the idea any more than I do. I'm no idiot about it, but Tanner got all worked up about people trying to shove the hotel project through. He told me, 'Before this is over, I'm going to strangle somebody.' "

Vince processed the information. Tanner Crayl—one of the eleven adults spotted on Main around noon. They'd phoned him at the car dealership where he worked. He said he knew nothing about the note. Hadn't even heard Vesta was dead.

A name coming up once—you do a routine follow-up. A name coming up twice ...

"Okay." Vince buffed his forehead. "Sam, thanks for telling me."

"Sure. I hope it's nothing. I'd be ... I mean, Tanner's a good enough guy. Still, I couldn't sit on it."

"No, you did the right thing. Thanks, Sam."

"Okay. Take care, Vince."

Vince hung up and turned to Jim. *I'm going to strangle somebody* ... "Change of plan. After we're done here, looks like we need to have ourselves another talk with Tanner Crayl."

THIRTY-SEVEN

As the cold night wore on in his parents' house, he shook with chills. The bedspread, taunting with the warmth it could bring, lay on the floor.

A ghost hid underneath. He *knew* it.

Time dragged by.

Long before sunrise he slid from bed, showered, and dressed. His limbs felt tattered. Surely as the coming dawn he balanced on a cliff between life and hell — or were they the same? Every sense was heightened, yet the line between sanity and insanity blurred.

In the kitchen he made coffee. His hands trembled.

Shuffling footsteps scuffed carpet in the hallway. Mom was up. His muscles tensed.

Memories from childhood jerked through his brain. Snuffing the life of a worm in his hand — and killing his sister. Sniveling under his bed. Running panic-stricken from Tamara. Pressing his feet against the floor of his parents' car to keep the ghosts from coming —

His mother appeared in the doorway, wrapped in a blue cotton robe. Her short hair stuck out in all directions, eyes puffy from sleep. She looked old and exhausted. Stopping on the threshold, she leaned a narrow wrist against the wood. Eyed him, mouth hard. "What're you doing up at this hour? And what on earth was all the noise about last night? Thumping and bumping. You woke us both up."

Oppression throbbed the air. And he knew—the spirit from the bedroom now lurked in the kitchen. Watching, waiting. Summoned by the mere whine of her voice.

Terror seared his veins.

Calm down, man.

But he couldn't. Not now that the ghosts had come back. No way could he live like this. Day after day, wondering what lurked behind him. Never knowing what he would see when he woke up. The chill of evil forever in his apartment.

Whatever it took, whatever he had to go through, he had to put his life back on track. "Sorry I woke you. I ... saw something."

She lifted a shoulder. "Is *that* all. Well, next time see something a little more quietly, do you mind?"

Her blithe attitude pierced his gut. Did she really not know what she and his father had done to him? What he'd lived with since the age of six? He stood before her, a little boy forced to kiss his dead sister, now grown into a warped and broken adult.

Right now he couldn't even call himself a man.

He drew himself up, hiding his fear. "I've decided to leave today. I want you to do something for me before I go."

Long-sufferance moved across her face. She pursed her mouth with the disgust of a sick woman put upon by a healthy son. "What?"

He ignored her tone. Somehow he had to get through this.

"Those candles in my bedroom? I want you to use them for a chanting."

THIRTY-EIGHT

Shortly before six o'clock Leslie pulled up outside Simple Pleasures to wait for Paige. She gazed down Main Street toward the west, where an orange sun dipped beneath the distant hills. Darkness would soon draw wings over Kanner Lake.

Vesta's beaten face throbbed in her head.

Leslie punched the auto button to lock her doors.

Paige and Sarah appeared at the front windows of the store. The overhead track lighting flicked off, and they stepped outside, Sarah bolting the door with a key. Leslie hit the lock button again to let Paige in the car. As Paige slid inside, Sarah bustled around the front to Leslie's window. Leslie rolled it down. Evening air brushed chilled fingers across her cheeks.

Sarah leaned over, pushing her round face close. "You okay, hon?"

"I'm fine."

Sarah reached in and grasped Leslie's shoulder. "You two go straight home to your parents' house, you hear? No going out anywhere. I've made Paige promise."

Like we'd want to be running around on a night like this. Leslie held up a hand. "Don't worry. We're homebodies."

Sarah nodded, as if she'd saved them from destruction, then stepped back with a final wave. Leslie rolled up the window. She and Paige kept watch as the woman walked half a block down to her own vehicle and slipped inside.

"Look." Paige pointed across the street toward Java Joint. "Bailey's closing up."

Leslie rolled down her window again. "Bailey! Where's your car?"

Bailey swung around and waved. She pocketed her keys, then hurried across the street, her blue coat and jeaned legs melding into the dusk. "Leslie, you go see Pastor Hank?"

"Uh-huh."

Bailey studied her. "And? Did it help?"

"Yeah. Sure." Leslie tried to smile, knowing she hid little from Bailey. "We'll talk tomorrow, okay?"

"Okay." Bailey stooped down, head tilting to view the passenger seat. "Hi, Paige. I'm praying for you both tonight."

"Thanks."

"Bailey," Leslie pressed, "where's your car?"

"Around the corner." She pointed up the street.

"Get in. I'll pull a U-ey and take you there."

Bailey climbed in.

Up the rest of their block and the next, as far as Leslie could see, shop owners were closing their stores. All would be heading straight home, double-locking their doors and windows. A Hitchcockian picture flashed into Leslie's head: blackbirds gathering in silent, menacing anticipation ...

She turned the corner and stopped behind Bailey's car. Waited until Bailey was inside, engine running, before she drove on.

"My Explorer's been cleared," Paige said. "Chief Edwards called hours ago. But let's just pick it up in the morning." She drew in her shoulders. "I don't want to go to the house right now. You know?"

"Yeah. Me neither."

Paige sank into quiet. Leslie glanced at her, registering the upturn of her brows, the tightening of her mouth. "Hey. What's wrong?"

Paige pressed her hands between her knees. "You mean other than Vesta's murder, and the note you got, and some killer being right here in Kanner Lake?"

That edge in her voice. Almost self-defensive. "Yeah, other than that."

"Like that's not enough."

Leslie braked at a stop sign. Turned to look long and hard at her friend. Paige stared straight ahead. *Fine, then, Paige, be that way.*

They drove on in silence.

Two minutes later Leslie pulled into her parents' driveway and killed the engine. This was going to be one fun night.

As they got out of the car, darkness pulled a suffocating blanket over Kanner Lake.

THIRTY-NINE

Seven o'clock. Vince and Jim drew their cars up to the curb outside Tanner Crayl's house. His property covered three acres set in forest near the eastern border of town, the closest neighbor a couple tenths of a mile away.

The slam of their two car doors shocked the quiet evening.

They'd phoned the car dealership in Post Falls, only to be told that Tanner had left work at three o'clock. And tomorrow was his day off. Vince had opted not to call Tanner's cell. Better to drop by unannounced.

Vince's gaze moved over the ranch-style house. A low gleam through draped windows on the left side. Living room? No porch lights. Closed double-garage door on the right.

He didn't like the feeling in his gut. Anxious. Unsteady. Dark pessimism whispered that no matter his efforts, no matter how thinly he spread himself, he would not be where he was most needed in the hour that mattered.

And that could cost someone's life.

He glanced to the sky, seeking stars, something that twinkled in this heavy night. All had fled.

Vince led the way up a sidewalk toward the house, his breath fogging the air. The temperature would dip to freezing tonight. Vince thought of Vesta's body left for hours in a frigid car, and fresh indignation knocked up his spine.

179

The doorbell rang two tones—*ding dong*. The two men waited. In the darkness Vince could barely see Jim's face.

No sound from inside. Vince punched the bell again. Thirty seconds passed.

Jim cleared his throat. "Looks like he's out."

"Yeah."

A single man could be all sorts of places after a day's work. Out to dinner. Over at a friend's. On a date.

"I'll cruise back by here later," Vince said.

He and Jim had worked out the patrol schedule, dividing the town into five sections, one for each man. Roger was pulled off from guarding the crime scene at Vesta's house. The ISP detectives and techs would be there through the night anyway, and Roger was needed on the streets. Frank asked for the section that included Leslie's parents' house, and Vince said okay. The kid would keep extra close watch on those girls, and that's the way Vince wanted it.

He stepped off Crayl's porch, his unease doubling. He sure wished he knew where Tanner was—now. Vince looked at Jim. "On second thought, we'd better call his cell. I want to talk to this guy as soon as possible."

They walked back to their vehicles. The night seemed to swallow the sound of their footsteps. *Spooked*, thought Vince. It felt just plain spooked.

The door handle of his car bit cold into his fingers. He thought again of Vesta, beaten and abandoned in Leslie's VW. *Dear Lord, don't let that happen to anyone else tonight.*

Vince pulled open the door for some light to read by, drew his notebook from his jacket pocket. Flipped to Tanner's number.

Tanner's phone rang once, then went straight to voice message. Vince glanced at Jim. Wasn't like a car salesman to turn his phone off.

"Tanner, this is Chief Edwards." Vince kept his tone even, friendly. "I have a few follow-up questions for you, and would like you to call me as soon as possible." He stated the number to his own cell, said "thank you," then hung up.

Before sliding into his car, Vince looked long and hard at Tanner Crayl's house. If ever he wished for laser vision, it was now. What he'd give to see through those walls.

He started the engine and headed back to his unsettled town, wondering what the night would bring.

FORTY

Past midnight. He was on the move.

Black-gloved hands gripping the wheel, he went over the plans he'd laid. Tonight's circumstances demanded total skill. He knew police roamed the streets. Would have guessed it even before he spotted a patrol car crossing the intersection two blocks ahead. He rolled slowly, close to the curb when possible, lights off. Eyes flicking from road to rearview mirror. At the first sign of headlights he would park, kill the engine, and duck down in his seat.

A narrow alley, fenced on one side, ran behind the Tiny Tots Preschool and right up to his target. He pulled into it, inching forward in the darkness. There were no streetlights here. Gradually his eyes accustomed to the gloom. He could make out the play yard of the school, white lines marking off three employee parking spaces.

He flicked the switch so his interior lights wouldn't turn on when he got out of the car. On the pavement, he clicked the door shut.

The rubber soles of his black shoes made no noise as he crept down the alley. Sounds of his own breathing filled his ears. His heart didn't pound as it had last night.

The target's house was a good forty years old. One story, wood. Painted blue. Navy shutters. Its side yard bordered the end of the alley—very convenient. He slipped around the end of the alley's fence and into the target's side yard. Sidled down the fence until even with the rear of the house, then cut across to the small stoop. No lights on inside. He tipped back his head and breathed the chilly air. He could practically *smell* the stillness of the house, the vulnerable, sleeping form of his victim.

His heart danced and his veins zinged, every sense pulsing with awareness. What was the chemical that exercise released in the body? Endorphins? Apparently killing had the same effect.

He forced the back door lock open, using a cloth he'd stuffed in his black jacket to smother the metal *pop*. Holding his breath, he eased inside. Cocked his head, listening. His gaze cruised the kitchen, registering objects as his eyes grew accustomed. Table, refrigerator. Doorway leading into a hall.

His movement through the house barely whispered the air.

He heard her light snoring before reaching her room.

She lay on her side in bed, facing away from him, covers drawn to her chin. He paused in the doorway, checking the room. No clothes on the carpet to trip him up. Good. Phone on a bedside table. No matter. He would hit far too fast for her to reach it. On that table ... something else. He leaned forward, frowning, willing his brain to catalog the shape.

A billy club.

He almost laughed. *This* was supposed to stop him?

For a moment he was tempted to use it. What black justice that would be.

He rounded the bottom of the bed on cat feet. Approached her head. She inhaled in her sleep, and he smiled.

It would be her last calm breath this side of the grave.

FORTY-ONE

Leslie broke the surface of consciousness like a body pulled from water.

What had awakened her?

Her eyes opened to the familiarity of her old room. Double bed, blue walls, dimly washed in the penumbra of a streetlight. Flowered curtains. Immediate memories jumbled her brain— telling her parents over dinner of her conversation with Pastor Hank, Paige's quietness, locked doors rechecked at bedtime—

Something was in the room.

The knowledge lanced Leslie's every pore. Her eyes darted, seeking. Her heart slammed into double beat.

Nothing.

Vesta's battered head.

A sense of pure malice sprayed over Leslie's body. Sweat sprang to her forehead. She clutched the bedspread, breath gagged in her throat.

Her eyes roamed left, right. Still she saw no one. She looked up, down, at every corner.

What was it? What did she—

Something loomed on her right.

She gasped, jerked away to her left, gaze jabbing the darkness. What could it be? The house was locked, her bedroom door too.

She saw only the wall, the faint outline of a framed print.

"Lesslie."

Her name hissed. Through her ears, or straight into her head?

She didn't know, couldn't decide, couldn't see anything but the walls of her room, and furniture, and her open suitcase in the corner chair. She only knew that *something* was there, something vindictive that enjoyed her terror.

"Leslie."

Prickles ran down her face. Tears? She needed to *run*. Get out of the room!

Jesus, help me!

A shadow moved. Wavering, amorphous. Leslie focused on it with popping eyes, her body gluing to the sheets. This was it, she was going to die right here, right now, and her limbs would do nothing to save her. The shadow undulated, shaped into vaguely human. Leslie choked out a cry. Pieces of her life, good and bad, jammed through her head like electricity volts. Her vision blurred, and she saw Vesta's beaten body, and Frank West's face, Paige's troubled eyes, and Bailey's smile, and heard Pastor Hank's voice: *I sense a darkness over this town.*

Leslie, move.

Her skin heated up, melted, and ran like wax.

The darkened *thing* formed a distinct head. Shoulders. Arms and torso.

A man.

His hands floated before him, waist high. Coming together, one thumb on top of the other, fingers spread and greedy. He leaned over the bed. Down. Reaching for her throat.

Leslie shot out of the covers and across the bed. Her feet hit the floor, and she fell—hard. Palms scraping against carpet, knees crawling, her body lifting up, fingers scrambling for the doorknob. Where was the man? Still on the other side of the bed? Behind her? She couldn't stop to look, couldn't see through her tears, only felt him and his closeness, evil breathing down her neck.

Time jumbled, and somebody started screaming, (was that her?), and her hand banged the door, and the knob wouldn't turn and then finally it did, and her legs thrust her up, and she fell again and up again, and into the hallway, stumbling for the light switch, whacking it on, the sudden glare squinting her eyes, and her mouth was still screaming, doors opening, her mother and father and Paige running toward her—

Leslie collapsed in her father's arms.

FORTY-TWO

I want you to use them for a chanting.

The words rang in his ears. How would he ever do this?

His mother looked at him as if he'd gone mad. She pushed away from the kitchen door, stuffed both hands into the pockets of her robe. "A chanting? Whatever are you talking about?"

Why was she playing so *dumb*? "Okay, a séance, or a session, or whatever it is you call it. Only one in reverse."

A slow smile claimed her face. A condescending smile. "A reverse séance, how quaint. First a 'chanting,' now a 'reverse séance.'"

She was enjoying this. As if she'd gotten out of bed at five a.m. just to seek him out, anticipating his request. As if she reveled in his fear.

She sighed her way over to the coffeemaker. Withdrew a mug from the cabinet. "And what exactly is it that you want me to do?"

You know.

"I want you to make them go away."

She turned, coffeepot poised above the mug, her expression one of complete innocence. "Who?"

His fingernails dug into his palms. "Your ghosts."

"My ghosts." She poured the coffee, set the pot back in its machine. "*Mine.* As if I control them."

"Of course you do. You held séances, they came. Didn't you tell me just yesterday that you 'called curses' down on people in Kanner

187

Lake? Obviously you can summon these things as you please. And if you can call them here, you can send them back."

"Why do you want them gone?"

"They … scare me."

She withered him with a look. "Really."

Anger rose in a flood tide. He despised this woman. His father too. For the first time he realized the depth of his hatred. Using every ounce of willpower he possessed, he leaned against the counter, folded his arms. Trying, trying to appear casual. "Are you going to do it or not?"

She clacked her coffee mug down on the tile. "You don't have a clue what you're talking about. I can't *make* spirits do anything. They have wills of their own. Oh, I can give them some fun ideas, like cursing someone. But even then, what happens is out of my hands. As for telling them to go back …" She gave a little snort. "Doesn't work that way."

If that was true, he was doomed.

"Why are you afraid, anyway?"

As if he should have to explain.

She shook her head in disgust. Picked up her coffee mug and headed toward the living room. "Just go back to bed. Maybe that'll straighten your head out a little."

He listened to the sound of porcelain hitting wood as she placed her cup on the coffee table. Her deep sigh as she settled on the couch. *Flick, flick* went her lighter, the slow suck on the day's first cigarette, the long exhale. She did not turn on a light.

Hatred bubbled out his pores.

He turned and made his way down the hall, dimly lit from light spilling out of the kitchen. In his bedroom he packed his small carry-on, scraped the keys to his rental car off the dresser. He would not spend another minute in this house.

His footsteps and the wheels of his suitcase muffled on the hallway carpet. He headed toward the living room to say good-bye, no further explanation. Not that she would care.

The house lay dead quiet. Its silence unnerved him.

He turned the corner, gaze cruising the semidarkness. His mother was a vague shape on the couch. Leaving his suitcase, he walked farther into the room, waiting for his eyes to adjust. Through the front window, the first fingers of dawn turned the sky a faint, sickly coral.

Her mug of coffee sat on the table, still full. A cigarette butt was smashed into the ashtray. His mother slept, one hand resting on her chest, the other near the opening between two sofa cushions, stretched wide by the press of her body.

In that crevasse, a glow. He focused on it, frowning. Pulled closer.

It was the tip of her second smoke of the day. Just lit.

The cigarette had fallen tip first. His eyes could just make out the long, vertical shaft, caught half an inch from the sofa bottom. Much remained to burn.

His mother slept on. He stared at the cigarette …

An ember of fantasy glowed in his head.

FORTY-THREE

Two twenty a.m.

Paige slumped on the living room couch with Leslie, both of them in robes. Mrs. Brymes was on Leslie's other side, a hand on her daughter's knee.

A loud rap sounded on the front door, and Mrs. Brymes rose. "There he is."

Frank. Paige ran a hand through her hair. If only she could finger comb her messy thoughts as well. Sadness over Vesta, and fear and protectiveness over Leslie scattered like windblown leaves in her head.

Mr. Brymes's slippered footsteps sounded in the hall. The door opened and closed. "Hi, thanks for coming so quickly."

"No problem." Frank's voice. "I was in the neighborhood. I radioed the chief. He should be here in a minute."

"Like I said, we know no one was really here. She probably just had a dream. But we'd all feel better if you just checked around the property."

"It wasn't a dream." Leslie threw Paige a look of weariness and fear. "It was *not* a dream."

Frank strode into the living room, and Paige's heart lurched at the intensity of concern on his face, the strong cut of his jaw. Why hadn't she noticed before how well he filled out his uniform? He looked capable and authoritative and ... good.

His dark eyes grazed hers, then landed on Leslie. "You all right?"

She nodded and slipped off the couch. Walked to him in silence and leaned her forehead on his shoulder. Surprise etched his face. He brought up one hand, patted her on the head. Then eased away.

Chief Edwards arrived. Together, he and Frank checked every door, every window. Mr. Brymes walked around with them. Mrs. Brymes brought Leslie tea, and they resettled on the couch. Paige declined the offer of a cup. She felt numb. And she ached for Leslie. Paige knew what real fear and mortal danger felt like. It was a feeling she wouldn't wish on her worst enemy, much less her best friend.

God, please let this end.

The men's footsteps left the dining room, entered the kitchen. Paige glanced at Frank through the pass-through window. He did not look at her, but she felt the pull of his awareness.

A dozen times since yesterday afternoon—no, more—she'd relived their telephone conversation. Now every past contact she'd had with Frank colored itself in new light. His fleeting smiles, his eyes searching hers whenever they "happened" to meet. She hadn't understood before, in part because he hid his emotions well, and in part because she didn't know *what* to look for. The men in her life had either used or abused her, and she'd certainly had no modeling of a healthy male-female relationship from her mother.

The door to the back deck opened. The men stepped outside. Chilly air swirled into the living room, nipped at Paige's feet.

Leslie sighed and listed toward her mother. Their heads tilted together, touching.

Paige reached over and squeezed Leslie's leg, her heart twisting. Never, ever would she do anything to hurt Leslie. This was the friend, the sister, she'd longed for all her life. That she'd prayed for.

So what to do with that new feeling within her? The part of her that quivered with each mental replay of Frank's phone call?

She had no choice.

Ignore it.

A vague sound from out front penetrated Paige's thoughts. A car driving off? She turned to look out the window.

No headlights. And no more sound.

She pulled in her shoulders, thrust her hands between her knees. How would anybody in this house sleep anymore tonight?

The men reentered the kitchen. Mrs. Brymes eased from Leslie and pushed to her feet. Chief Edwards walked into the living room, his badge gleaming in the overhead light. He gave Mrs. Brymes a grim nod, then approached the couch. The gear on his utility belt squeaked as he leaned toward Leslie. "We've checked everything. Your house is clear, and there's no indication that anyone's been here. I want you to know Frank will continue patrolling the neighborhood the rest of the night. Okay?"

Leslie looked up at him and nodded, a stray piece of hair stuck to her cheek.

Chief Edwards regarded her as if deciding whether to say more. Then straightened, hands resting on his belt, and turned to Mr. Brymes. "Don't hesitate to call us again if you need anything."

"Thanks. We will."

Frank's gaze flicked to Paige and hung for a second before he turned to leave.

Leslie's parents walked the officers to the door. Leslie did not move. Paige rose from the couch and sidled toward the front window to watch Frank go. A streetlamp spilled yellow light over the two patrol cars, washing them a muddy brown and white. The Brymeses' blue mailbox tinged a pea green.

Paige's gaze fell on a lump nearby, on the curb.

What was that?

She frowned, looking harder. The lump took shape—even as her heart denied it.

Paige gasped. Swiveled and ran toward the front door. The men were stepping out on the porch. "What's wrong?" Mrs. Brymes demanded as she trotted by.

Paige hit the hallway, her heart in her throat. *"Chief!"* She flung up her hand, pointed toward the street, but Frank was already staring at the still form.

The chief looked around, and his face paled. "Oh, Lord, *no.*"

He and Frank raced down the steps and across the lawn, Mr. Brymes close behind.

PART THREE

Descent

FORTY-FOUR

He stumbled through his back door, heart banging. His legs felt rubbery, and his hands shook. Had anyone spotted his car? Had he made too much noise? The cops had been *everywhere*, at all the wrong moments. No time to carry out his tasks as planned. Every ounce of calmness had come crashing down as he drove away from Sandy Westling's house.

What was he *doing*, killing for them? They were going to ruin him. Had already ruined him.

His head throbbed. He needed water. And sleep. Peace ... he longed for peace ...

And knew he'd never see it again.

This. Had. To stop.

It *had* stopped. Tonight was his second and last time. They would ask no more of him. They wouldn't. They *couldn't*.

The house pulsed with threatening darkness, but he dared not turn on a light.

In the kitchen, he filled a glass of water and guzzled it. Clanked the glass on the counter—too close to the edge. It teetered, fell to the linoleum floor, and shattered. He cursed, jumped away as if the broken shards were striking snakes. Then leaned against the counter, panting.

His nerves thrummed.

He couldn't see well enough to clean up the mess tonight. In the morning. He would do it then.

A picture of himself, barefoot and bleary-eyed from lack of sleep, flashed in his head.

The dim outline of the folded newspaper showed white against the green tile of the counter. He swept it up, unfolded its pages, and dropped them over the area where the glass had landed. There. That would remind him.

Now, a shower. He would have no blood on him this time. But cold trembled his muscles. He needed the comfort of hot water, warming his body if not his soul. Then, sleep.

Blessed, blessed sleep.

FORTY-FIVE

Four a.m.

Vince rubbed his eyes as the coroner's wagon loaded Kanner Lake's second murder victim in twenty-four hours. Sandy Westling, lying half on the sidewalk near the Brymeses' house, half on the street. Apparently shoved from a car. She'd been strangled.

Pinned to her chest—a piece of paper with a circled number three.

Houses up and down the street were lighted, neighbors at their windows, on their porches, watching in horror. If only they knew how much worse it would become.

A circled number three.

Where—and who—was victim number two?

Anxiety wound tentacles around Vince's gut. At that moment he was tempted to send his officers banging on every door in town. Somebody out there, somewhere, had to be lying dead. And he wouldn't be surprised to learn that person was a part of the hotel-welcoming campaign. Sandy Westling made the second known victim who had openly supported the project.

His thoughts flashed to Tanner Crayl. The man never called back. Vince drove by his home twice before midnight and saw no lights. Where *was* he?

Two new ISP detectives worked the scene. Dyland and Harrough were just closing up at Vesta's and would need some sleep.

Vince had sent C. B. and Roger to secure Sandy Westling's house. They reported a jimmied backdoor lock, tumbled covers on her bed.

Thank God Nancy was safe in Spokane.

Vince lowered his head, pressed thumb and fingers against his temples. *What* was happening to his town?

"Chief?"

A female voice called from the Brymeses' front porch. Vince turned to see Leslie, clad in jeans and a sweatshirt, no coat. Hair uncombed. Shivering.

"Yeah." His voice sounded hoarse.

"I need to talk to you a minute."

Vince walked up the Brymeses' front sidewalk, one hand at the back of his neck. Vaguely, he wondered when he would ever see his own bed again. He stepped up the two stairs, stopped in front of Leslie. "Why don't we go inside? It's too cold for you out here."

She shook her head. Her cheeks looked pale, her eyes round as a terrified child's. "I don't want my mom to hear. She's upset enough already."

Vince gave her a wan smile. Girl was getting some spunk back. As much as she'd gone through, she was worried about her mother.

A shudder racked Leslie's shoulders. She folded her arms and pressed them against her chest. "Sandy was strangled." Leslie's voice flattened. "Probably right before she was ... left here. That's what you said."

"Yes."

She held his gaze, her mouth firming. "I *felt* something in my room tonight. At first it was just a shape. Then—a man. Reaching out for me. Reaching to strangle me. Just about the same time Sandy was killed."

Vince struggled to keep his poker face. He'd been down this road in his own mind already, and he didn't want to go there again. Forget what Leslie had felt—twice now. Forget what he'd experienced. And the shoes, and the hairs. Catching a flesh-and-blood killer cunning enough to strike two nights in a row was challenging enough. But to focus on things that defied explanation ...

"Do you hear me? You have to believe what I'm saying."

"I do believe you, Leslie." *But what can I do about it?*

Her expression hardened. "Something's going on in this town. I talked to Pastor Hank yesterday. Whatever it is, it's evil. It's more than even"—she gestured toward the coroner's wagon—"this."

"Chief?" One of the ISP detectives called from the street.

"Yeah, be there in a minute."

Vince turned back to Leslie. "I don't know if this will make you feel better or worse. But I've felt something too."

Leslie blinked at him, the creases in her forehead flattening. The unexpected information seemed to give her new resolve. She straightened her back. "That footprint. Does it match Henry's shoes?"

He hesitated. "Can't know for certain yet. But it looks likely."

Slowly, she nodded. Another shiver gripped her, and she rubbed her arms. "Is there anything ... else?"

"I can't tell you that, Leslie, not while this whole thing's under investigation."

She drew herself up. "No, huh-uh. That doesn't work this time. If there's something else that points to Henry Johnson, I want to know."

"Leslie. A dead man did not kill these two women."

"What is it?"

"No, Leslie."

"*What* is it?"

"*No.*"

Her eyes glistened. She jabbed a finger against his chest. "I am not a reporter right now, Vince Edwards! I don't know if I'll ever be again. I'm Leslie Brymes, the one this killer keeps leaving *presents* for." Her voice trembled. "I'm a witness to this. I'm *in* this. A body was left in my car. Now on my lawn. There was something in my room tonight. *And I want to know what's going on.*"

Vince passed a hand over his jaw. His eyes felt sandpapered. "I wish I knew, Leslie. Really I do."

"*What* other evidence did you find?"

Energy leaked from his veins, draining his determination to win this battle. He heaved a sigh. "Hairs. Okay? Two hairs on Vesta's body. White. Thick. They're consistent with Henry Johnson's."

She gaped at him. "How could they have gotten there?"

"I have no idea. Now look, I'm needed down there. I've just given you confidential information, and I expect you to keep it quiet. Is that clear?"

His voice had honed an edge, and he expected self-defense in her reply. But she merely nodded. Then whispered, "Thank you. You can trust me"—and turned away.

As he trudged down the sidewalk toward the detectives, Vince heard the Brymeses' door open, then shut.

Where is body number two?

FORTY-SIX

He awoke curved into a fetal position, muscles cramped.

Nauseating memories flooded his brain. The feel of skin beneath his choking hands ... last gasps of breath ... lugging the body ... a police car ... sweat-popping fear—

He groaned. Pressed his hands to his temples.

Slowly, the memories eddied ... pooled into quieter waters.

That's better. His strength was returning. He unwound his limbs.

Today he would not be victimized.

This day would be different. Had to be. Today he would fight. Spit in their faces, wrestle back control of his life.

Don't believe me? Just watch.

He pressed his heels on the floor, tried his unsteady legs. Stumbled to the bathroom, slapped on the shower.

Wait. Hadn't he taken one last night?

He turned the shower off. At the sink, splashed cold water on his face. He dressed by rote. He must think clearly, sweep away the cobwebs in his mind.

The police would be increasing their efforts today. Probably bring in more Idaho State guys. He would have to lie low. Have an answer ready for any suspicious questions. After a time, this would pass.

He unlocked his bedroom door, stepped into the hall, eyes roving for sign of their presence. Saw nothing out of order. He walked into the kitchen, headed for the coffeemaker. Spotted the unfolded newspaper on the floor.

Oh. The glass he'd broken last night.

For the moment he ignored the mess, shuffling to the sink in slippered feet to fill the coffee urn with water. Wondering at his illogical thinking the previous night that he might enter the kitchen in bare feet. He always wore his slippers on cold mornings. He turned from sink to coffeemaker, poured in the water, dumped grounds into a white filter, flipped the switch. Stared a long, mindless moment at the red *on* light.

The machine hissed and gurgled. Dark liquid dripped into the urn.

He blinked, shook his head to clear it. Turned away to clean up the broken glass.

As he leaned down to pick up the newspaper, he froze.

No. No no no …

Another message.

He stared at it, head tilting, unable to comprehend the jumble of words. Then, like blurred vision clearing, the meaning materialized. Names. One after another. A whole long list of them. And the very last word—

kill

He hacked out a laugh of pure disbelief. Straightened and backed up, hands thrusting into his scalp. Were they insane? How could they possibly expect *this*? What did they want him to do, kill half the town?

Hysterics rose in him. He slumped against the counter, spitting hoarse chuckles and guffaws. He clawed fingers against the tile … crossed his arms and leaned over … covered his mouth with both hands. He laughed and laughed, hoping they heard— laughed until his chest burned, and his head throbbed, and he knew he sounded like a madman.

Finally, he forced back the sounds. Took a deep breath. Pushed away from the counter, eyes fixing on the paper. Slobber trickled from his lips. He smeared it away.

In the dirt of his soul, anger punched to the surface, then grew as ferociously as the fairy tale beanstalk.

They'd done it now. Gone too far, way too far. They'd pushed and pushed; now he'd push back. He'd said he was going to fight, right? They'd just see what he could do. He had no *choice* but to fight, because he finally understood.

Their demands would never stop.

Did they really think he would walk into his kitchen like a lamb to slaughter every morning and find another order? And why, by the way, did they always leave their notes on the *Kanner Lake Times*?

With a growl, he snatched up the newspaper and message, bunched it into a ball, and stuffed it into the trash under the sink. Banged the cabinet door shut.

There. That would stop them. At least for today. At least he wouldn't have to stare at their new list of names, memorizing, pulled toward them with the inevitability of the damned. And he would never bring another *Kanner Lake Times* into this house. Not that it would help. If they wanted a copy here, they'd bring it. Or start leaving their notes on any one of the newspaper copies proliferating the streets.

What had happened to his quiet town? First Edna San's death and all its repercussions, then the hotel controversy—

All fueled by the pages of the *Kanner Lake Times.*

The realization hit hard. He stilled, fists at his chin, caught in the epiphany. He'd never liked Leslie Brymes to begin with, but to see how they used her . . .

The anger grew, filling him up. He stalked to the pantry to fetch broom and dustpan, attacked the broken glass with fury.

Even now they used her writing, and she couldn't see it. Or *wouldn't*.

He pushed glass into the rubber dustpan, flung it into the trash.

How long before her ambition destroyed the whole town? Even if they could no longer force his obedience, even if they killed him—would they find some other poor soul to carry out their tasks?

He swept a second round of glass into the catcher. Dumped it into the wastebasket.

Always, always, they left their notes on the newspaper. Of course. What other publication found its way into every Kanner Lake home?

He bent down farther, held the broom low, and smacked up the last fragments of glass.

What other paper wielded so much persuasion with the town's residents?

Into the garbage flew the final pieces of his mess. He thwacked shut the cabinet door, thrust the broom and dustpan back into the pantry.

If that newspaper hadn't been around, if Leslie Brymes hadn't been around to write its articles and stir up the hotel mess, they wouldn't have bothered him in the first place.

He paced through the house, looking for something to do with his hands, energized by his own building rage. A tiny voice in his head whispered that the last thought was a lie. That they would have come to extract their payment from him someday, with or without the help of some yapping reporter. But he gave it no heed. The need to blame sizzled inside him like a downed live wire. It felt good. Empowering.

No more victim mentality—hadn't he suffered that enough?

No more. From now on, only the guilty would pay.

FORTY-SEVEN

Ali didn't see Chet at school before first period, didn't see anybody in the group. All through geometry class she stared at her desk, trying to figure out how to get out of going to the séance. She'd hardly slept last night, worrying about it—and thinking she was hearing things. The dark felt like it wanted to crush her. She kept thinking about a ghost roaming the town. She knew it couldn't be true, but . . .

Even after turning her lamp on, she tossed and turned. When she got up this morning, she'd felt like weights were strapped to her chest.

Finally, after geometry, Chet slid up beside Ali at her locker, Eddie and Kristal at his side. "Did you hear?" He looked grim, and Kristal's face was pale.

Ali nodded. "Did you know Henry Johnson?"

"No. But his picture was in our Spokane newspaper this morning, with the article about the murder." Chet reached into his binder and pulled out a small black and white photo cut from the paper. "It's him. It's the ghost we saw."

Ali's eyes went wide. For a minute she couldn't even talk. "Are you *sure*?"

"It's him." Kristal's voice shook. "And now he's done it again."

Again? Cold trickled through Ali's veins. "What do you mean?"

"A second murder." Kristal clutched her books to her chest. She didn't look anything like usual. Superior. Smug. She just looked scared out of her mind. "I just got a call from Kathy, my sister. She was in Java Joint and heard them talking about it. Sandy Westling was killed last night and left on the street in front of Leslie Brymes's parents' house. Leslie was staying there. I *knew* Sandy Westling; we all did. She's the mom of one of Kathy's good friends."

Ali's hand went to her mouth. She stared from Kristal to Eddie to Chet. Somebody else murdered? Left for Leslie Brymes to find— again? How *awful*. How terrible for Leslie too. This couldn't be real. It was some horror movie. Time for the lights to come up.

"We figure they have to be connected." Eddie shook hair from his eyes. "Both bodies were left where Leslie Brymes would see them. Why, I don't know, but if that ghost killed the first one, he did the second one too."

"But ... how?" Ali whispered. "Why?"

Kristal's eyes filled with tears. "I don't know. I don't understand any of this. We were just fooling around. We didn't mean to hurt anybody. But *I'm* the one who started it, and now Sandy's *dead*." The tears spilled down her cheeks.

Ali touched her shoulder. "I'm so sorry. I didn't know Sandy, but I knew Vesta. I really liked her."

Kristal nodded. Flung her head back and sniffed, swiping at her face. "Anyway, you have to come tonight. We *all* have to be there. We have to call this ... *thing* in. Make it go back to wherever it came from."

Eddie shook his head. "I don't know, man. What if it doesn't work?"

"It *has* to." Kristal started to cry again. "We have to try. We can't let it just be out there and kill people we know!"

Ali's eyes cut from Kristal to Eddie. She still didn't want to believe this. "Can a ghost really kill somebody?"

Chet ran his hand over his jaw. "A week ago I'd have said no. Now..." He looked up and down the hall, as if afraid one floated right there.

Ali shuddered. She remembered last night and the darkness — how scared she'd felt. She couldn't imagine turning off the lights and calling up some murderous ghost. Then she thought of the note's curse. Between the two, she didn't know which was worse — to risk the curse of this evil power, or be in the same room with it.

Except that the first was a maybe, and the second was a sure thing.

She pulled in a breath. "I don't think I can go with you."

Kristal blinked at her. "You *have* to go. You're in this now."

"I'm not 'in this.' Just because I found some note. I had nothing to do with what you all did."

Kristal's expression hardened. "*You* read the note. That makes you a part of it."

"But really, I don't want to be. Especially now."

"Look." Kristal's face flushed. "I don't want to be part of it either. But we've got to *do* something. I don't know if we can help; I don't know much of anything anymore. None of this makes any sense to me, and it's all scaring me to death. But we've got to meet just one more time — tonight. And you're coming. We all agreed something led you to that note. You're *supposed* to be a part of this."

Ali pressed her shoulder against her locker, forcing herself not to look away from Kristal. Fact is, she couldn't deny it. She had felt really pulled to pick up that note. The thing had practically called her name.

Which frightened her all the more.

"I can't come. Really. But I won't tell anybody what you're doing, I promise."

"Look, you're one more person." Eddie leaned toward her. "That's more human energy and strength, and we need all we can get."

One more person. Right. Ali knew the truth. They were in this too far, and if she didn't join them, they were afraid she'd tell. It was as simple as that. The only way to shut her up was to put her in the middle of it.

"Ali, it's okay." Chet gave her a small smile, his gaze lowering to her fingers as if to remind her of their touch yesterday. Like she could forget. "Kristal and Kim and I are going to pick you up tonight at seven. We'll meet the others at the cabin. We'll all stick together, and everything will be fine. Tell your parents we won't be out late."

Her parents. How stupid she was! They were her way out. They wouldn't let her go out after dark with friends they didn't know, not with some killer walking around. By the time she got home from school, her mom would have heard about this second murder.

"Okay." Ali managed a little smile. "I'll give you my home number and address, Chet. You give me your cell number, just in case I need to call."

Suspicion flicked across Kristal's face. "You won't need to call. You *are* coming."

"Okay. Yeah. Sure." Ali pushed from her locker. "I'll be there."

No way, ever, she thought as she walked down the hall. *No way.*

FORTY-EIGHT

He stood riveted in his parents' living room, eyeing his sleeping mother.

Between the couch cushions, the cigarette tip glowed.

Childhood memories ran through his mind, one horrifying scene after another. The ghosts, the tears, his fears. Lonely days spent reading for escape. The awkwardness of high school years.

A muffled snore from his mother. She stirred.

"Hey," he said. "Mom. You're tired. Go back to bed."

A stuttered breath. She cleared her throat with a hack. "Yeah, okay." She ran a hand over her face, swung her legs to the floor, and pushed upright. Stiff-legged, she stumbled toward the hall.

He darted before her, pulling his suitcase from her path.

After a long moment he heard the door to the master bedroom open, click shut.

He flicked on the living room light. His eyes fastened on the cigarette. Still burning.

His parents would sleep for hours, thanks to having their night disturbed. During those hours, that slow-burning tobacco could become a very dangerous thing.

He really should remove it.

With your parents gone, the ghosts will leave you alone.

Hope surged. Could that be true? He had no proof, of course, but he believed it. He clung to it. There were plenty of crazy people in this world who séanced the night away. The spirits would float toward them. He would be free.

He ran his tongue over his lips. Narrowed his eyes at the smoldering cigarette.

Reading crime novels had taught him a few things. The fabric could take hours to ignite, and might not catch at all. Too much coaxing paper could be detected by investigators. But one tissue, placed just right ...

He found himself moving to the front bathroom. There he fetched an upright Kleenex box. Took it into the living room and placed it on the table near the couch. His eyes fell on the full coffee mug. He blinked at it, considering. Then carried it into the kitchen and dumped its contents into the sink. Next he poured out the coffee in the pot, punched off the machine. Back in the living room he pulled a tissue from the box. Tapped the cigarette down until its tip rested on the sofa bottom, then worked the flattened tissue between its unburned portion and one of the cushions.

He stood back, eyeing his work. Willing power into that glowing stick. Already he could see a blackening circle in the fabric beneath its tip.

His hand fumbled in his pants pocket, assuring that the rental car keys were there.

Suitcase in hand, he stepped through the front door. It locked behind him.

As he drove away he glanced in the rearview mirror—and imagined the house in flames. For the first time since he'd arrived in Washington, he smiled.

FORTY-NINE

Breakfast, great. As if I can eat.

Leslie slumped at the table in her bathrobe, eyes gritty, hair uncombed, battling rage mixed with helplessness. Outside, the police cars and other official vehicles had gone. Sandy Westling's body had been carted off to the morgue, the crime scene cleared. Apparently there had been little to see. No footprints, no tire tracks.

At least no new evidence pointed to Henry Johnson's ghost.

Leslie's father reached for a piece of toast on a center plate. "I think you should stay here today, Leslie. Just lock the door and don't go anywhere. Jared will understand if you don't go in to work."

She sighed. "Dad, come on. You're at work, Mom's at work, Paige is at work. You want me here all by myself?"

"That's true." Her mother poured coffee into a mug, set it before her. "Really, I don't know where you can go to be safe. I just—"

"I should be with people, that's where. Like downtown, at the office." Leslie knew she sounded peevish. Which wasn't fair; her parents were just frightened for her. She lightened her tone. "Obviously, this maniac isn't after *me* anyhow." She dumped sugar into her coffee and slammed it around with a spoon. To make her mother happy, she would drink a little. But what she really wanted was her latte from Java Joint. "He just wants to leave me his 'presents.' Like some idiot cat leaving dead birds on the carpet."

Her mother shuddered.

Leslie got her way in the end—after her father called Jared Moore and extracted a promise that the man would not leave her in the office alone. They did persuade her to wait for Paige, who didn't have to report to Simple Pleasures until ten. Besides, there was the matter of Paige's car being parked at their rental house. Leslie would need to take her over to get it.

"Call Chief Edwards or some officer first," her mother insisted. "I don't want you two driving over to that house, even in daylight, by yourselves."

A valid point. For all they knew, the missing body awaited them on the back porch.

Leslie's parents left before eight o'clock, driving their own cars. Leslie was to report in with her father at least three times that day. "You don't call me, I'm calling you, understand?" He pointed a finger at her, trying to pull an authoritative expression over his haggard face. None of them had slept much.

"Yes, okay. Promise." She kissed them both, and they took turns hugging her long and hard.

Paige materialized from the guest room after nine, wordlessly wrapping her arms around Leslie. When they were ready to leave the house, Leslie dialed Frank's cell phone. "No need to bother the chief," she said at Paige's surprised expression. "He's got enough to do."

Paige nodded.

Frank drove up to the house at a quarter before ten. Like the gentleman he was, he rang the doorbell and escorted them to the rental car, even though it sat right on the driveway. His shoulders drooped. Leslie was pretty sure he'd never been to bed last night. Her heart panged for him. "Will you get a chance to sleep for a while?"

He took a long, deep breath. "Just got a couple hours." His eyes slid from her to Paige. "Wasn't enough, but there's so much work to be done."

"I can help." Leslie forced her voice into a chipper tone. "Just tell this li'l ol' reporter everything you know, and I'll run down all kinds of stuff."

He gazed at her, forehead creasing. "Leslie, you know I can't do that."

Good grief, why did this guy take everything so seriously? "For heaven's sake, Frank, I was just kidding."

"Oh." His brief smile didn't reach his eyes.

Leslie turned away, a stab piercing her chest. Was he ever going to get her?

She and Paige slid into the car. Leslie waited until Frank started his own vehicle and pulled from the curb before backing out to follow. The way he looked, even from the back, just driving his car. The shape of his head, his thick, dark hair. The size of his shoulders . . .

Leslie's heart twinged. She banged her palm against the steering wheel. "Paige, this is beginning to hurt. *When* is he ever going to start paying attention to me?"

"I don't know." Paige's voice sounded tight. "But maybe you shouldn't be thinking about that right now. I mean, there's other stuff going on at the moment."

"Which is exactly why I *am* thinking about it." Leslie threw her a hard glance. "I can't think about everything else, Paige, or I'm going to go crazy. Two nights of this, and I can't take any more." Her throat clinched. "How can you judge me, anyhow? You know me better than that. How do you think I'm going to sleep tonight, wondering who'll show up dead on my doorstep tomorrow?"

"I'm not judging you."

"Yes, you are."

"No, I'm *not*." Paige made a frustrated sound, then play-punched Leslie's shoulder. "Stop it. I'm too shaky this morning, and you're just going to make me cry. And then you'll start to cry and you'll have to pull over and we'll both just sit here and sob. And Frank will park his car and come back here and think we're both idiots."

"Well, if he doesn't understand two girls crying after two deaths in a row, *he's* the idiot. So there."

Paige drew a quick breath and blew it out. "Yeah." She folded her arms. "So there."

They drove the rest of the way in silence.

The front lawn of their house lay empty. *Well, one thing to be thankful for.* Frank walked around the premises and checked in Paige's Explorer, declaring them all safe.

"Bye." Paige threw Leslie a smile before sliding out of the rental car. "Call me today—lots. Or just cross the street and come see me. Or we can meet at Java Joint."

"Yeah, or maybe all three."

Paige hesitated. "You're going to be okay, right? Not do anything stupid?"

Leslie's head drew back. "Me? I'm ace reporter, remember? Miss Tough Girl."

A wan smile curved Paige's lips. "Yeah. Real tough."

She got out and headed for her own car. Frank followed both their vehicles until they pulled into parking spaces on Main. Leslie waved to him as he drove past.

Someday, Frank West. Someday.

For now, she just hoped to live through the next twenty-four hours without stumbling across the missing body of victim number two.

FIFTY

Almost noon on day two. Had the world been normal just forty-eight hours ago?

Vince sank into a chair in Sandy Westling's kitchen and bent over, massaging his forehead. Muted voices and shufflings of ISP detectives and techs—replacements to those he'd used yesterday, who now slept—filtered from Sandy's bedroom. As with Vesta's house, they'd started at the back of Sandy's home— obvious point of entry—and worked their way down. Taking photographs, seeking infinitesimal pieces of evidence. Later they'd vacuum the place, sort through in the lab what they'd sucked up. *Déjà vu.*

A circled number three. Where was the second body? When would they find it?

This afternoon he would release details about the circled number messages to the media for the sake of public safety. People needed to understand what was going on—and everyone should be checking on their friends and family members. For this reason, and to deal with the overwhelming number of calls from the media in general, he'd scheduled a press conference for three o'clock. Reporters were descending upon Kanner Lake again, whether he liked it or not, and his best move would be to use them to his advantage.

Now all he needed was the energy to deal with their questions.

Vince couldn't remember when he'd felt more worn. His nerves were quivery, a million details frazzling his sleep-deprived brain. He'd taken to writing everything down just so he could remember what avenues he'd pursued, and what to do next. He'd phoned Nancy at the hospital, made sure of her safety. Told her what happened. *Check.* Sent Roger and Frank home to sleep for a few hours, after which they'd switched off with C. B. and Jim. *Check.* Tonight they'd all be patrolling again.

Sleep for himself? No check.

Back on duty since nine-thirty, Frank was now out front protecting the crime scene, logging people in and out. Although it demanded the full attention of one of his few officers on duty, protection of the scene reigned top priority. These days, with legal technicalities and crafty defense lawyers, the merest hint of a tainted scene could spell disaster in a trial—or even before a case got to trial. Every person who entered that site, and when, and why his/her presence was needed, had to be registered.

Roger had been assigned his own task, equally important, given the growing velocity of this case. He was ensconced at the station, fielding phone calls and tips, and watching the video from QuickMart. Hoping to spot the film sequence of someone ripping a piece of paper from that pad.

Vince had caught up with Tanner Crayl, who finally answered his cell phone this morning. Tanner was full of apologies for having left the phone at home by mistake (how he managed that, he couldn't say) while he went out on a date, then ended up spending the night at the woman's house. Or so went his story. The woman—a Melissa Golinsky from Spirit Lake—confirmed it. However, she admitted drinking too much at dinner, which made her "sleep like a rock." Tanner could have slipped from her bed and returned without her knowing. And, of course, the previous night, when Vesta was murdered, Tanner had been in his own bed. Alone.

Alibi for the first night? No. For the second? Yes, with a possible hole. Not good enough for Vince. Not with two dead bodies on his watch.

Before going off duty, Roger had questioned Lucas Mulholland regarding his whereabouts the previous evening. Again, no alibi. He was home, alone, Lucas insisted. He slept through the night.

Vince flexed his shoulders, inhaled three deep breaths. One thing was settling in his mind: the murders tied into the hotel controversy. Two women who lived alone—dead. Both had worked to push the hotel through. Both left on the premises of the reporter who'd covered the story. As a "present."

Vince wanted to believe he was right about the connection. It was logical. Gave him a scenario. Problem was, it didn't begin to explain the other weirdness. What he'd felt. What Leslie had felt—twice. Second time apparently when Sandy was being strangled. The footprint and hairs he could chalk up to coincidence that would be disproved by further lab work. But he'd felt a presence yesterday. He *knew* it, and nobody could convince him otherwise.

"Chief Edwards!" The sound of his name drifted from Sandy Westling's bedroom. "You might want to see this."

He pushed to his feet, alert despite his exhaustion. "Coming." He trudged through the kitchen and toward the master bedroom. As he entered the room, Terrance O'Malley, one of the ISP techs, held up a pair of tweezers.

The sight punched Vince in the gut. Even before he saw the evidence, he knew.

"Found this on her pillow," O'Malley said. "Didn't I hear they bagged similar ones yesterday?"

Vince drew near—and saw a single coarse white hair.

FIFTY-ONE

At lunch, Kristal invited Ali to sit at the table with their group. Just like that. A snap of fingers, and Ali was with the *in* crowd.

The cafeteria air hung heavy with the smell of sloppy joes and french fries as Ali sat down beside Chet. Kristal was at the end of the table, to Ali's right. Trays clicked down, silverware clanked, voices resounded. Some girl three tables over screamed in laughter.

"You sure Kathy and her husband won't be at the cabin tonight?" Nate dragged three french fries through ketchup and shoved them in his mouth.

"Yes, I'm sure." Kristal waved a hand. "It's not hunting season, you dork."

"Well, excuse *me*. Testy, testy."

"Shut up, Nate." Kim jabbed his shoulder.

"I am not testy!" Kristal closed her eyes. "I just can't believe what's happening, that's all. I feel like I'm going to blow apart or something."

Ali couldn't believe it all either, including the fact that she was sitting at this table. Was it only yesterday she'd wanted to eat lunch in a classroom? Now look at her—surrounded by . . . she wasn't sure she could call them friends yet. Maybe more like accomplices.

She winced. Making friends wasn't supposed to feel like this. Even sitting next to Chet, feeling him close, she couldn't exactly tell herself she was living her daydream. But would she want to return to yesterday, being all alone?

Face it, Ali, that's what's going to happen next week, after you stand them up tonight.

She'd go back to being a nobody, all right. No, worse. She'd be a traitor. Somebody kicked out of the club.

Chet brushed her arm as he reached for his glass. Her skin tingled. He glanced at her and smiled. She smiled back, feeling her lips waver. Did he like her? She wanted that *so bad*. How incredible it would be. She wanted all of this, no use denying it—friends, acceptance, a place to sit at lunch.

How could she ever go back?

"... used by the Powers." Eddie's voice snagged Ali's attention.

The Powers. Ali jerked her head toward him. "Sorry, what did you say?"

He leaned forward, lowering his voice. "I'm just trying to figure it out. The note Kristal found talked about the Powers and a curse on the town. Back then we thought the curse was the whole Edna San murder, remember?" He glanced at Kristal. "Either that, or it was just talk. Now I'm thinking we walked right into something. We started doing this séance stuff, which somehow really did release the Powers, and now the town's definitely cursed. It's like we've been used."

"Yeah. We were set up." Kim looked sick.

Eddie's words banged around Ali's head. What was he talking about? There was more history here than she knew. She wasn't sure she *wanted* to know. She bit her lower lip, looking from Eddie to Kim. "What do you mean, a curse on the town?"

Kristal sighed. "It was in this note I found in my sister's cabin last summer, soon after she and her husband bought it. I was helping them put stuff in the kitchen drawers, and I felt something at the top of one. I bent down to look, and saw a piece of paper taped to the bottom of the drawer above." Kristal shivered. "I pulled it off real careful-like—and I couldn't believe it. Somebody had written this letter about how mad she was at people in the town, and how she and her husband drove around one night when the moon was a weird color and cursed Kanner Lake. At the bottom she drew a picture of a coral crescent moon."

Ali pulled her head back. "Who wrote it?"

"I don't know. My sister bought the cabin from some man, so it must have been the owners before that. The paper looked yellow, like it had been there for a while, but I don't know how long."

"Did you tell your sister?"

"No ..." Kristal hesitated. "I don't know how to explain it, but the note made me feel strange. It was kinda spooky, but exciting too. Like going to a scary movie. And I didn't want my sister to ruin it. I thought she'd just laugh." She sighed. "So I hid it. And then, first time Kathy said I could hang out with my friends there, I thought we should have a séance. Call on those Powers, whatever they were." Kristal's eyes clouded. "But I didn't think it was true, really I didn't. We were all just having fun. Right?" She looked around the table.

Heads nodded. Chet said, "Yeah."

The smell of sloppy joes twisted Ali's stomach. She pushed her tray away. *If anyone outside our group reads this note, that person is cursed by the Powers!* The words echoed in her head. *Anyone outside our group ...* She felt cold all over. "And now you've cursed *me*. With your note."

Kristal blinked, then looked at Kim. "Not really. I was just ... you know. Playing the game."

"But it's not a game."

"Look, it doesn't matter." Kim balled her napkin and tossed it on her tray. "That was only if you weren't part of the group, and now you are."

"It doesn't matter *anyway*." Chet touched Ali's hand. "Don't be worried about that."

Ali focused on the table. How could she not worry? The curse worked on the town, right? And if she didn't go tonight …

Maybe she should. Maybe getting out of this was just too risky all the way around.

But it wasn't up to her. Ali couldn't see her parents letting her out the door.

"Hey. You okay?" Chet leaned toward her a little. She could see the flecks in his eyes, the scar beneath his chin.

She managed a smile and nodded.

He looked away and said something to Nate. Ali shut out their conversation, too worried about the coming night. Did she really want to sit home alone and wonder what was happening at that cabin?

She took a long drink, feeling the water slide down her throat.

Which was scarier—to be with them and know, or not know? And that curse …

She sipped more water.

If she introduced her parents to Chet and Kristal and Kim … If she told them they were just going to Kristal's house and would all stick together, and wouldn't be running around town … Ali lowered the plastic glass, heard it tap against the table. And besides, everybody had cell phones. If she gave her parents some numbers …

Ali leaned back in her seat, looking around the cafeteria. Everyone was sitting around, talking and laughing. Everybody had somebody, even if they were with just one other person. She pictured herself yesterday, carrying her tray alone. Ali closed her eyes. She might as well have been carrying a sign: Pathetic. No Friends Here.

Chet hit the table with his hand, and Ali jumped. He pushed back his chair. "You done?" He smiled at her, and the crinkle around his eyes nearly snatched her breath away. "I'll walk you to your next class."

She nodded.

As they picked up their backpacks, Ali's mouth opened. "Chet? When you come tonight, could you all take a minute and meet my parents? Otherwise they might not let me go ..."

FIFTY-TWO

Vince pulled in deep breaths, filling his lungs with oxygen as he drove away from Sandy Westling's house. The call he'd just received had yanked him from the crime scene as fast as he could make an exit. He wouldn't have a lot of time to follow it up. The press conference was less than ninety minutes away.

"Chief," Roger had said over his cell phone, "we got lucky on the QuickMart film. The three days of tape started just yesterday morning..."

Vince spotted four news vans parked down near the city beach as he turned onto Main. More would soon arrive. Reporters, both local and national, were rolling into town for the press conference. National reporters in nearby states had probably made plans to come yesterday after Vesta's murder. Leslie's involvement in the Edna San case—televised across the country—and the fact that Vesta's body had been left in her car would have pricked their ears. With the Spokane stations needing their own vans to cover this story, it would take the national folks a while to procure a rented van from Seattle and make the five- to six-hour trip across Washington state. By now they knew they'd be hearing even more of a story than they'd expected.

Vince pulled into the station parking lot and hurried from his car.

"Hi. That was fast." Roger sat at a central desk surrounded by the equipment brought in to view the tapes. The man looked as bad as Vince felt: cheeks washed pale, eyes blinking and red.

"Yeah." Vince grabbed a chair and brought it over to the desk. Roger ran a hand down his face and pushed his chair aside to give Vince room.

He punched a button, and the two men watched the silent film.

Tommy Whittlen ambled down the aisle. Furtively glanced over his shoulder. Stooped at the stack of paper, picked up a pad and tore off the top sheet. He replaced the pad at the bottom of the stack, folded the paper twice, like a letter, and hid it beneath his shirt. Then he returned up the aisle ...

The whole sequence lasted less than thirty seconds.

Roger paused the tape.

"Oh, boy." Vince lowered his head and rubbed his eyes. Roger had told him the culprit's identity. Still, seeing the tape for himself ...

Yesterday Vince wondered if Tommy was telling the truth— had the boy sneaked outside and seen someone leave the note near the Kanner Lake Times office? But this, Vince had not expected.

Slowly, he straightened.

Roger shifted in his chair. "Think he just played a dumb joke?"

Vince focused on the grainy frozen image of Tommy in the store aisle. "Either that, or he got that paper *for* somebody."

"His father?"

Vince pictured Ray Whittlen's face as the man pointed to the security camera. He shook his head. "He wouldn't have led us to the tape so quickly."

"Maybe. But you'd think Tommy would know about that security camera too."

"Yeah. Just like window-breakers in the snow ought to know not to take a three-legged dog along." Vince shook his head. "Kids can just be stupid. Especially twelve-year-old boys."

With a sigh, Vince rose. "I've got little more than an hour before the press conference. I'll head over to QuickMart. If we luck out, Tommy will be there again, and I can talk to him. Otherwise we'll have to pull him out of school." He clamped Roger on the shoulder. "You might as well keep watching until I get back to you, just in case something else turns up."

As he slid into his vehicle, Vince realized he could thank the heavens for one thing about the tape.

He hadn't seen a white-haired ghost with red tennis shoes pulling off that piece of paper.

FIFTY-THREE

The day after he returned to California, he received a visit at the office from a local policeman, bearing bad news from Washington. His mother and father had both been killed in a fire in their rental home.

Four days later he sat in a Washington police station, the grief-stricken son answering a detective's questions. He'd been visiting his parents on the day of their death, had he not? His original flight back to California was scheduled for the following day, yet he left early. Why had he changed his mind?

The lies came fluidly. He'd needed to get back to work, he told the detective, and in fact had hit the office directly from the airport. But he had questions of his own. Did anybody know what started the fire?

Investigators had determined the cause: a cigarette in the couch cushions.

"Odd timing, though." The detective, a portly man with keen blue eyes, leaned back in his chair with utmost casualness. "You'd expect the cigarette would have been dropped there the night before, but the burn time doesn't fit. It must have been left in the morning."

He felt his face drain of color. A moment passed before he allowed himself to speak. "It probably was." His troubled gaze wandered from the detective's face toward the window. He focused outside on a gray, accusing sky, then brought a hand to his forehead, closed his eyes. "Mom and I were up talking early in the morning." The words scraped with remorse. "Neither of us had slept well. Which was fine for me, but she was sick and really needed rest. I had already dressed, but Mom was in her robe. I don't think she ever meant to stay up. When I left the house, she went back to bed." He shoved from his chair, paced an aimless three steps. "I should have checked. Somehow I should have known. If I'd only found that cigarette. If I'd only taken longer to leave the house ..."

In the end, his answers satisfied the cynical detective. Or maybe, if suspicion remained, no proof existed to fan it into flame.

He inherited his parents' stocks and savings — over three million dollars' worth. Plus the house in Kanner Lake, fully furnished. And their hunting cabin.

No ghosts bothered him. He was free.

Two months later, feeling cocky and strong for the first time in his life, he quit his job and headed to Idaho. There he could live on his investments. In time he might find another job — maybe in a completely different field — but no hurry. He loved the beauty of the land; he enjoyed the town. Most of all he reveled in his freedom, made all the sweeter because he chose to live in his parents' house — and saw no spirits. It was a final nose-thumbing to his mother and father. Justice accomplished. The abused son now ruled.

He couldn't help gloating.

But once in a while, from deep within him a voice would whisper: *It's only a matter of time.*

He had not really killed his sister through the death of a worm, yet she'd haunted him. Now after what he had done to his parents, how could he believe they'd let him be?

Sometimes he could almost feel them hovering beyond the grave, calculating, biding their time. Waiting for just the right moment ...

FIFTY-FOUR

Vince sat in Ray Whittlen's office across from one pale-faced twelve-year-old. Tommy pitched forward in his chair, head down, hands clasped and rubbing together until the skin on his knuckles whitened. Ray glowered at Tommy from behind his desk, his elbows shoved against the wood hard enough to sink dent marks into it. Tension crackled the air. At first Ray wouldn't believe Tommy had anything to do with the note to Leslie Brymes. Now he watched as his son melted, guilt written all over the kid.

"Tommy." Vince edged his voice. "Answer me. *Did* you write that note?"

A long pause. Then a slow nod. Tommy wouldn't raise his gaze from his own sneakers.

Ray Whittlen pulled in a long, hard breath. His face reddened, mouth opening. Vince shook his head at the man—*Let me handle it*. Ray's jaws snapped shut.

"Tommy," Vince said. "Look at me."

The boy's chin rose. Tears stood in his gray eyes.

Vince held his gaze with a look that threatened dire consequences if Tommy chose to tell further lies. "Did you write it by yourself?"

Tommy nodded.

"No one helped you?"

"No." The boy's voice was barely audible.

"Did someone ask you to do this, or give you the idea in any way?"

"No."

Another loud inhale from Ray. He pressed back in his chair, arms folded, eyes narrowed.

Vince rubbed his jaw as his tired mind chugged to work through the logic of this. A twelve-year-old, acting alone, for a mere hoax. All the investigative trails Vince had followed as a result of that note—now meaningless. It no longer mattered who had been spotted on Main Street yesterday around the time the note was found. Nor did it matter who had found it. Lucas Mulholland now should garner no more suspicion than anyone else in town. Even Tanner Crayl, with his "I could strangle someone" remark and his less-than-airtight alibi for the previous night, couldn't be viewed in as suspicious a light as before.

The *wasted* hours. Vince's exhaustion prickled his nerves. He had to fight to keep from yelling at the kid. Vince cleared his throat. "I want you to tell me what the note said—exact words."

Tommy seemed to shrink within himself. He threw a glance at his dad, the freckles on his face darkening against his color-drained skin. He looked back to Vince with pleading eyes, but Vince simply waited. The question had not been posed to increase Ray Whittlen's anger. "I'm listening."

The boy swallowed. "It said, 'Hope you like my present. I did it for you.'"

Ray's eyes slipped shut, as if he could not imagine his son being so cruel.

Fresh anger bubbled in Vince. "*Why* did you do this?"

Tommy hitched a shoulder. "I don't know."

"What do you mean you don't know?" Ray leaned forward and smacked his palms on the desk. "There has to be a *reason*!"

Tommy pulled his top lip between his teeth. His focus returned to the floor. "I just … thought it would be cool to see words I wrote on the news, that's all. I didn't mean anything by it. Didn't know it would hurt anything."

"It's hurt a lot." Vince tapped two fingers below Tommy's chin, forcing his head up. "That note took me and one of my men away from other things we could have been investigating—*important* things that could lead to the murderer. Do you understand that police hours are valuable, especially when we're investigating a homicide? They're costly both in time and money. Do you know I could charge you for this and make you go to court? I could also fine your parents for the hours we spent running down your little trick."

Tears spilled out of Tommy's eyes, down his cheeks.

"You also hurt Leslie Brymes a lot, because she believed the note was true. Don't you see how your words could make her think she was to blame for what happened?"

Tommy shook his head. "I didn't mean that. I didn't mean to hurt her."

Vince shifted in his chair, eyes locked on Tommy. Silence pulsed. Vince let the moment drag out, as if deciding what fate to declare for the criminal sitting before him. Vince had little time—the press conference started soon—and he wanted to wring all the terror out of each second that he could. The kid deserved so much more than a little fear.

When Vince spoke again, he honed in on details. When had Tommy written the note? How had he left it near the door of the newspaper office? Had he told anyone what he had done? Vince heard no earthshaking revelations in the answers, not that he expected any. It was enough to put this maddening matter to rest. He had two homicides and a killer loose in his town—and darkness was coming.

He glanced at his watch. Two forty. Time to move. Vince pushed to his feet to tower over Tommy. "I've got to be somewhere in a few minutes. And beyond that I've got a double homicide to investigate. I don't need *you* causing me any more trouble, is that clear?"

Tommy's head jiggled up and down.

Vince looked to Ray, his voice tight. "I'm going to take some time to decide what to do about this. We'll talk later."

Ray rolled his chair back and stood. "Okay. Understood." His eyes cut to his son, as if he had no doubt of the punishment he would inflict. "I can guarantee you he'll keep out of trouble from now on."

On his way out of the store, Vince passed Tommy's nervous mother. She locked on to him with round, questioning eyes, but he barely slowed. "Let Ray tell you what happened. I've got to get to the press conference."

He stepped through the door, still fighting his anger. At Tommy—and himself. Given Tommy's demeanor yesterday, he should have looked more closely at the kid. He couldn't help adding up all the wasted man-hours. If they'd been better used, would he have found his suspect by now? Would his town now be safe?

As Vince slid into his car, worn and sickened, a desperate prayer ran through his head.

God, don't let my mistakes cost a life.

FIFTY-FIVE

Leslie Brymes, ace reporter. Yeah, right.

Chief Edwards's press conference would begin in ten minutes. Leslie knew reporters were gathering outside near the city beach, milling around in their coats, microphones set up, notebooks clutched in their anticipating fingers. Another nationally watched murder case on her own doorstep and what was she doing?

Hiding.

She hadn't gotten a thing done since hitting the office almost five hours ago. She went around and around in a vicious cycle, emotions and thoughts all over the place. Couldn't concentrate. And she sure didn't want to *feel*.

Tears and terror eddied behind her wall, threatening and swirling more with each hour that led toward night. All she could do was keep slapping down bricks. The best way to accomplish that was to stay busy, but her brain wouldn't work. Sleep would help, but no way could she rest either.

Leslie shoved aside papers and banged her elbows on the desk, let her head fall in her hands. She could hear Jared shuffling around in the back room. Any minute now he'd be leaving for the press conference, performing what would normally be her job. But the thought of all those story-greedy reporters hounding her with questions made her nauseous.

So much for doing anything to get her face on TV again. Had she really lived that dream just thirty hours ago?

Footsteps approached. "Leslie, you all right?" The words sounded clenched.

She raised her head to see Jared shoving a thin arm into his worn brown jacket, pencil in his teeth and notebook in his bony fingers. The pad switched hands, and he pushed in the other arm.

"Yeah, sure. Fast-pedaling, like I've been all day."

Empathy creased his wizened face. The big-story sparkle that should have lit his eyes glowed not the slightest. "I'd tell you to go home, but I don't want you there alone. And now I've got to kick you out of here. I promised your dad."

Leslie straightened. "I know. It's okay, I'm not getting anything done anyway. I'll go grace Java Joint with my uplifting presence."

She pushed to her feet, gathered her coat and purse. This spinning-wheels-in-the-mud could not go on much longer. She needed something tangible to pursue and accomplish. Some way to fight her own madness.

Jared gestured *You first* toward the street. She crossed the office and stepped outside to the clouded-over, cold day, Jared behind her. He locked the door. They started down the sidewalk in silence. No need for Jared to drive to the press conference; it was a block over from the beginning of Main.

As they reached Java Joint, Leslie's cell rang. She pulled it from her purse. *Chief Edwards.* She flipped open the phone. "Hi, Chief."

Jared stopped to listen.

"Leslie, hi." The chief's voice sounded gravelly from lack of sleep. "Have some news I'm going to announce, and I wanted you to hear it first."

Please make it good. "Okay."

Quickly, he told her. The note she'd received yesterday was a hoax. A bored Tommy Whittlen had written it and sneaked down to leave it near her doorstep. How no one saw him the chief couldn't say. Then again, crimes in broad daylight often happened without witnesses. The luck of fools.

The news gusted through Leslie, scattering her thoughts like dried leaves. At first she couldn't speak. Jared gestured with impatience—*what happened, what happened*? She sank against the Java Joint window, dropped her head back. "I can't believe this. I absolutely just ... He put me through all that guilt? Made me think Vesta's death was *my* fault? How could he do that?" Anger bounced up her spine, pushed her upright. She paced a step. "How *could* he?"

"I know. I'm sorry. Just a kid prank, nothing more. He had no idea how it would make you feel. He just thought it would be cool to see his own words in the news."

Leslie's eyes narrowed. "Ha-ha, fooled him; they didn't know what it said."

"Yeah. Good thing. When Tommy told me the words, I knew he wrote the note. Little reason for him to lie about that with his dad standing right there, face red as a beet. That boy's in for some serious punishment."

"You going to charge him?"

Vince sighed. "I don't know yet. I got more important things to handle right now. I think Ray Whittlen will take care of his son."

Leslie thrust a hand into her hair. "So you're going to announce this at the press conference?"

"Yeah, I have to, without naming him, of course. You'll need to keep that part off the record. They'll be asking about the note anyway, and we need to put that piece of false evidence aside."

"Sure, I'll keep it off the record. But I wish I could *fry* him in public!" Leslie locked eyes with Jared, who stood with hands on his hips, watching her like a hawk. She paced two steps, then stopped herself, knowing if she went any farther she'd just continue right up the street, hang a left, stomp into QuickMart, and *strangle* one stupid, sneaky, idiot little twelve-year-old. She threw a grimace in the general direction of the store. The Whittlens had better make it up to her. Like give her free food for the rest of her life.

She gritted her teeth. "Thanks, Chief, for calling. I know you're busy."

"Sure. Thought it would make you feel better."

Oh, yeah, for sure. In more ways than one. On the sudden fire of this news, her guilt boiled away, anger pouring in and sizzling. The burn felt good, *good.* Popping with energy.

"Chief." She walked away from Jared, lowering her voice. "What did you find at Sandy's house?"

"They're still looking. I need to go now."

Oh, no. Huh-uh. That tone change—he knew something. Leslie hunched over, her eyes finding a tiny crack in the sidewalk. "They found some piece of evidence, didn't they? What was it? Something else leading to Henry Johnson?"

A sigh leaked over the phone line. "Leslie, you need to drop this thing."

"Drop it! I'll drop it when it drops me! Did they find another footprint?"

"No."

"Hair?"

A hesitation.

Leslie's head came up, her fingers tightening on the phone. "Chief." She hadn't expected this, not really. "Are you telling me they found more white hairs?"

Another pause. Leslie could almost hear the cogs grinding in Chief Edwards's head as he debated how to answer. "Just one. On her pillow."

One. That was enough. More than enough.

"Oh." Leslie's energy drained away as quickly as it had come. So what if the note had been a hoax? The rest of this—the evidence of a dead man, that presence in her room last night—would not be so easily explained. And the renewed thought of fighting something outside this world, something she couldn't begin to understand, frightened her far more.

"Thanks for telling me, Chief." Her voice sounded so small.

She lowered the phone and folded it shut.

FIFTY-SIX

Chaos—in *his* town.

His anger had grown to a live and sizzling thing. Just look at what the murders had done to Kanner Lake. How ironic! To think that the hotel controversy had once been the biggest divider in the town. To think how he and his friends hated the thought of a hotel built right here near the city beach, where people now swarmed to hear details about gruesome deaths. That determined, heart-driven fight to keep the quiet atmosphere of the town—now shattered by this.

He hunched at the back of the crowd, hands shoved in his pockets, shoulders up to guard his neck from the cold. Listening to Chief Edwards tell what the police knew, what they suspected, how residents needed to be on guard as long as this killer roamed the streets. Reporters shouted questions, townsfolk milled and whispered, fear on their faces. Mothers held small children tighter, men stood with their legs planted apart, warriors set to protect their families. Even nature was struck. In the background, Kanner Lake lapped weakly at its beach, and clouds hung low and gray.

He lowered his head, closed his eyes. Nausea rolled through him as he thought of what he'd been forced to do. How everyone around him now paid.

Well, no more. No matter their threats, no matter the price he would have to pay, he was done with it.

He couldn't walk through town without feeling haunted. Everywhere—the *Kanner Lake Times* newspaper. In shops, in the grocery store, selling in a white steel cage on the street. *Step right up, folks, deposit your fifty cents and open the door to more controversy and argument! We got it right here!* The paper that fed its readership the daily bread of dissension and anger. No wonder they chose that paper to leave their demands to kill. At sight of a *Kanner Lake Times* paper, he had to tear his eyes away. Who knew which copy harbored their next note?

He opened his eyes, sickness and rage entwining within him until he thought he would burst. A small pebble lay by his foot. He stepped on it, ground it against pavement, wanting to feel the thing crush to dust, but it would not give. His fingers fisted in both pockets, his right hand pressing against the warning note to Leslie Brymes. This *would* stop. He alone would save this town. And if that meant playing the sacrificial lamb, if that meant their threats and the worst fear of his life come true—so be it.

So be it.

The press conference ended. Reporters called more questions, but Chief Edwards walked away. The crowd rippled with movement and the buzz of voices, its edges eaten as people fanned out toward their cars.

He turned toward town, forcing calm into his expression. His next step to freedom lay before him. He'd need every ounce of control.

Such a gamble he was taking to give Leslie Brymes this chance. Proved what a good man he was at heart. Surely, for the sake of her own life, she would heed his warning. Surely she would understand what she had done—and obey.

Crossing the street, he headed up Main.

FIFTY-SEVEN

Ali paced her room, feeling more scared by the minute. For the hundredth time since supper she wished she wasn't going to the séance. But she'd committed herself and no way could she back out now.

It was surprising how easily she'd convinced her mother to let her be out with new friends. Mom had picked her up from school, full of horrible details about the latest murder. Wondering aloud why they'd ever moved to "safe" Kanner Lake. But Ali made all the promises a mother needed to hear. She would be with a group of people. Three would pick her up, and they'd go straight to Kristal's house. No running around town. Her friends would have cell phones on. Mom and Dad could check on her anytime.

"Really, Mom." Ali turned to her as they slowed at a stop sign. "Do you want me sitting home by myself, listening to TV news about people being killed, or do you want me having fun and making friends?"

She had never given her parents reason not to trust her. Ali knew, watching her mother's face, that Mom believed every word.

"Okay, Ali." Mom sighed, then gave her a sad smile. "I know what it's like, needing friends."

The pain in her mother's eyes shot right through Ali. She'd been so wrapped up in her own world, she hadn't noticed her mom was just as lonely. Mom had lost her friends too when they moved. And on top of that, she was sick most of the time.

Ali had turned away to stare out the windshield, a rock sinking in her stomach.

You lied to her, and she doesn't deserve it. Now there's no backing out.

Ali ran her hands through her hair. Her eyes fell on her backpack, lying on the bed. She could almost Superman-see the note inside it, glowing like kryptonite. If she hadn't picked it up, she'd be in her room tonight, dreaming about being out with Chet.

Now she'd be with him.

Heat flushed through her. She kicked her shoes off, yanked out of her hoodie, and threw it on the floor. Everything would be fine tonight. It would. So what if she'd soon be sitting in a pitch-black cabin in the woods, calling for some ghost who was supposedly killing people. The thing probably wouldn't even show up.

If it did ... who were they to tell it what to do?

Ali closed her eyes, imagining the darkness. Cold fingers on the back of her neck.

She would totally *freak out.*

Her eyes popped open. Already her heart was beating overtime. She had to stop thinking about this. Chet would be with her. Maybe he'd hold her hand. As long as he was close, she could handle it.

If she told herself that enough times, maybe she'd believe it.

"Ali!" Her mother's voice came from downstairs.

She pushed off her bed, opened the door, and stepped into the hallway. Her mom stood at the bottom of the stairs, phone in hand. She held it out. "It's for you. Chet." She raised an eyebrow.

Chet!

Ali slipped down the stairs, avoiding her mother's eyes. "Thanks."

Clutching the phone, she hurried back to her room and closed the door. "Hi." Her voice sounded too airy and excited. She took a breath. "Sorry, just ran up the stairs."

"Guess where I've been." Chet sounded grim. "Downtown. At a press conference about the murders. Somebody told me about it just as we were leaving school. I hurried over and caught most of it. Lots of reporters here. The police chief was answering questions. This is going to be on the news all over the country."

Ali sank down on her bed. The country? Maybe she should have realized how big a story it was, but . . .

Now she was *in* it. Right in the middle. "Did you hear anything new?"

"Yeah. Get this. The guy's a serial killer who's planning on doing it again. He's leaving numbers on the bodies."

"Numbers?"

"Yeah. A one and a three so far. Think what that means, Ali. There's a 'two' out there somewhere, and they haven't found the body yet."

Her fingers curled into her leg. *"Another* one?"

"Yeah. And nobody knows who it is yet."

This can't be happening. Ali licked her lips, her eyes pulling to the backpack. "Did he say any more about the ghost stuff?"

"No. Reporters asked a lot about it, but he wouldn't answer. Except to say that they were hunting for a real person, not 'something in the spirit world.'"

Ali closed her eyes. *How* did she get messed up in this? "That's true, Chet, it has to be. Even if they're real, how could a ghost kill somebody? If we really believed that's possible, would we be going to that cabin tonight?"

"Ali, we *saw* the ghost of that old man. I swear. The police don't know about that. Imagine if they did. I don't *know* how a ghost kills somebody. I only know that people are dead. But it looks like they're killed when they're alone, not together in a group. Anyway, *we* brought that thing here. We have to try to send it back."

"What makes you think we can?"

"I don't *know* if we can, but we have to try." Chet sounded impatient. "We can't just sit back and watch more people die."

"Maybe we should go to the police."

"No way." His tone hardened. "You're not thinking of doing that, are you?"

"Of course not."

"Yeah, well, make sure you don't. Last thing we need is to be linked to all this on national TV."

Ali shuddered to think of it. Her parents would come unglued. And the last thing her mother needed was more stress. "I won't, don't worry."

"Okay. So. We'll be there at seven."

"I'll be ready."

Ali clicked off the line and heaved herself down on the bed, staring at the ceiling. *The police don't know. Imagine if they did.*

Suddenly the full reality of her situation slammed Ali. If she hadn't been lying down, she'd have fallen over. What on earth was she *doing*? A killer lurked out there somewhere, and here she was, planning on sneaking off to the forest for a séance. This was *insane*. The whole thing was just ...

Terrifying.

She rolled over and buried her face in the covers. If only someone at least knew where she was going. Because for all the insisting that nothing could go wrong tonight, if something did—no one outside their group would even know where she was. Besides, she didn't even know Kristal and everybody that well. Why should she trust *them*? Even Chet. Yeah, he was hot, and she couldn't wait to be with him, but still ...

And really, didn't she have a *responsibility* to tell someone? She knew something about a murder. Like inside information.

Even if it turned out not true, even if she looked stupid for tell-ing it (dumb girl believes in ghosts!), at least she'd have done the right thing. Could she really keep this a secret while the police ran around trying to find clues?

You're not thinking of doing that, are you?

Of course not.

But if she told, the police would probably start questioning Kristal and Chet and everybody. The group would know she told. And would never forgive her. She'd never be their friend again.

Leslie Brymes.

From nowhere the name floated into her head. Leslie was a reporter. Reporters had secret sources. They weren't supposed to tell. They *couldn't* tell. Hadn't Ali seen reporters go to jail on the news because they wouldn't give some source's name?

Leslie Brymes. Another thing—she wasn't old. She'd be more likely to understand how Ali got into all this. And she could investigate about the Powers and the ghost ...

Besides, didn't Leslie deserve to know? The bodies were being left for her to find.

Ali sat up. The phone lay beside her, face down on the blue cover. Waiting.

If anybody outside our group reads this note, that person is cursed by the Powers!

Fine, then. Leslie would never see the note.

Should she do this?

Ali reached out and touched the phone. Then pulled her hand back.

Touched it once more. Changed her mind.

The third time, she picked it up.

FIFTY-EIGHT

The phone was ringing as Leslie shoved open the office door. Her stomach felt warm from one of Java Joint's biggie lattes, but her nerves had not settled. Bailey wanted to close the café temporarily, join everyone else down at the press conference, so Leslie ended up taking her coffee across the street into Simple Pleasures to visit with Paige. No customers in that store either; half the town was down by the beach, soaking up details about the murders from Chief Edwards.

If they only knew the whole story.

At three forty-five she'd glanced through the window to see tangles of people walking up Main, Jared included. Conference apparently over, she headed back across the street to meet up with her boss at the office door. Maybe, just maybe she'd manage to get some work done. Make a few calls based on information Jared had heard. Do *something*.

"I'll get it," Leslie told Jared on the second ring. Better not be some fancy TV reporter, pestering her with questions. She hurried to her cluttered desk, shoes tapping across the worn wood floor, and plucked up the receiver. "Kanner Lake Times, Leslie."

Silence.

Oh, great, who was this? "Hel-*lo*?"

"Hi." Another hesitation. A female voice, young. "Um. Miss Brymes, I live in Kanner Lake. And I sort of … know something about the murders. Well, not really the murders themselves, but I know, um ... There's this group ..."

The words trickled away. Leslie was already walking around her desk, reaching for paper and pen, ears pricked by the tenuous tone of voice. Whoever it was sounded hesitant and scared, capable of ending the call at any moment.

Coat still on, Leslie slid into her chair and poised herself over the desk. "A group?"

"Yeah. But ... first, you can't tell anyone I told you this."

"No problem there."

"Really, because my parents don't know, and I don't want to lose my friends."

"This is not a problem." Leslie softened her voice. "You can trust me. It's part of my job to keep unnamed sources to myself."

"Okay."

The caller began to talk. Leslie sensed Jared at his desk, shuffling papers, clacking his keyboard. But as the words flowed into her ear, her world narrowed to focus only on the young voice, its startling story, and the scratch of her pen. She listened without interruption, the blood in her veins percolating higher with each new revelation. A note, a curse on the town. *Henry Johnson's ghost.* A séance—tonight. Leslie's body heated, felt the *pop-pop* of increasing dread. Sweat itched her forehead. She wished she could take off her coat but didn't dare stop the conversation.

When the words ran out, Leslie asked questions to fill in the holes, working to keep her voice even and calm. Finally, she wheedled the caller's name. *Ali Frederick.*

"Ali? Is that short for something?"

"Alison."

"How old are you?"

"Sixteen."

Sixteen. The poor girl was in way over her head. And playing with dangerous stuff. How could this connect to the murders? Did it at all?

Pastor Hank's voice ran through Leslie's brain: *I don't know what's going on, Leslie. But I sense a darkness over this town . . .*

Leslie glanced at Jared, who aimed her a piercing look under drawn eyebrows. She nodded, unsmiling—*I've got it under control.*

"Ali, the number you called me from. Is it your cell phone?"

"No. It's our home phone. Please don't call it. I wouldn't know how to explain that to my parents."

"What about a number for one of your friends? Could I use that to reach you?"

"No, because the only people I know are in this group." Panic tinged Ali's voice. "Nobody can know I called you. *Nobody.*"

"Okay, don't worry, I won't call you." Leslie closed her eyes. *This is not good.*

A rogue wave of memories from the previous night surged. The evil, that paralyzing fear. "Look, Ali. I don't think you should go tonight. You're playing with some serious stuff. I'm grateful you called, and I will follow up on this. But now I'm concerned about *you.* Is there any way I can talk you out of going?"

As it turned out, nothing Leslie said could move the girl—and she didn't want to say too much. She couldn't tell Ali about the white hairs, didn't want to frighten her more with tales of her own experiences. And on the spiritual side, Leslie only had a vague notion of what to warn Ali about.

"Will you call me tomorrow and let me know what happened? Call me tonight on my cell phone if you need me. Really. Anytime."

"I want to call you tonight after I get home, if that's okay. Just in case. I mean, I'm sure everything will be fine. But I kind of wanted someone to check in with. Because you'll know where I am."

"I get it, Ali. That's absolutely okay. Please do call. Because now I'm going to be expecting to hear from you, and if I don't, I'll think something is wrong."

"I will. Promise."

Leslie gave Ali her cell number and hung up.

Jared pounced immediately—what was happening, what had she heard?

She stared at him, trying to gather her thoughts. "Just a scared kid. It's really nothing, but she needed someone to talk to." She related the barest details, something urging her to omit the kids' purported ghost sighting. Without that, there wasn't much of a connection with the case. Jared processed the information, then shrugged and turned back to his keyboard, pulled by the priority of writing his story about the press conference while his notes were fresh in his mind.

Leslie folded the pages of notes from the phone call and placed them in her purse. She'd kept so much from Jared about this case— the white hairs, her own strange experiences. Now this. Even with the latest hair being found, Leslie couldn't bring herself to tell Jared about that evidence, stunning as it was. The chief had entrusted her with the information because of her own involvement in the case. She took that trust seriously. She could not let him down.

Man, had she changed since yesterday morning.

She stared at her desk, fingers drumming. Ali's young voice pulsed in her ears. She'd placed herself in an untenable position—promising she wouldn't tell anyone, yet feeling unable to handle the situation. Could she just sit back and let this young girl go to that séance?

Ten minutes passed as Leslie considered the situation. Then she pushed back her chair. "Jared, I'm going to go get something to eat. Should have when I got coffee, but Bailey was closing the shop. After that, I might go back to my parents' house. Mom's home from school now, and I'm doing no good here anyway."

"All right, kid." Jared pointed a finger at her. "Lock those doors tonight."

If only that were enough. She gave him a wan smile. "Yeah."

Instead of heading down toward Java Joint, Leslie walked up the street and around the corner to her rental car. She slid inside, locked the doors, and turned on the engine and heat. Then opened her phone to call Pastor Hank.

She couldn't tell him Ali's name or any specifics. She did end up telling him about the note found in a "cabin nearby" and the teenagers' séances.

He pulled in a long breath.

"Pastor Hank, do you think all this has anything to do with what's going on?" A Spokane news van drove by. Leslie swiveled her head in the opposite direction. "That darkness you felt? And the murders?"

"The murders, I have no idea. The darkness, absolutely." His tone was grim. "One thing the Bible makes very clear—we're not to hold séances or have anything to do with calling up the dead. These are practices that demons love, Leslie. They're drawn by those behaviors. I don't doubt those kids saw something, but I bet it was a demon, not a ghost." He paused. Leslie waited him out. "No wonder I've felt darkness over this town for some time. It could have been released as a result of that curse, regardless of how long ago that was. Now these kids are stirring the pot. This is true spiritual warfare, and what we need to do is pray."

"But if this is 'spiritual warfare,' as you call it, how does that explain hard evidence—in *this* world—that points to Henry Johnson?"

"I don't know, Leslie, I really don't. But I have to rest on what I *do* know: God's power is stronger than any darkness. And that power is released through prayer."

Leslie rubbed her forehead. So much here she could not understand. All the ominous colors and textures and unknowns.

What had happened to the normal world? Her brain flashed a startling picture of terrified boat captives ferried over boiling waters to the gates of hell. Had she seen that in a painting somewhere? Now she'd fallen into it.

"I tried to talk this girl out of going tonight. It did no good."

"That's bad news. I sure wish we could stop the séance from happening. It's the last thing the town needs right now. And those kids have no idea the fire they're playing with. They think it's all just fun and games, but it isn't. Not at all."

Just fun and games.

The phrase echoed in Leslie's head after she ended the call. She slumped over, forehead on the steering wheel, an ache in her heart. Confusion and fear and dread of the coming night thickened the air. Vesta dead, Sandy dead, a "number two" out there somewhere, not yet found. (Where could that body *be*?) Ghosts and séances, and a lonely young girl trying to make new friends. Where was the truth in all this?

God, help us figure this all out. Let the murders stop. Please.

Leslie straightened, tossed back her hair, and focused on the cloudy sky. One thing she did know: she could not survive another night of this. Nor could Kanner Lake. How could she—or any of them—ever turn off the light in her room this evening and hope for sleep, knowing she might awake to the terror of last night? Even worse, knowing another victim was likely being killed?

Her stomach grumbled. Stubborn nature lived on.

Leslie turned off the engine and slid from the car, purse in hand.

As she approached the corner of Main, a stunning realization hit. No one knew more about this case than she did. Chief Edwards knew the investigation. Ali and her friends knew about the curse. Pastor understood the spiritual side. Only she, Leslie Brymes, had gathered all these pieces.

If only she knew what to do with them.

Her steps slowed. She folded her arms for warmth, focusing up the street as far as she could see. Two blocks up, a woman walked down the sidewalk, holding a little girl by the hand. A blue vehicle passed them, and the woman waved.

Would she be dead tomorrow?

Leslie's mind churned, her feet rooted to the pavement. Vague thoughts wafted, misted away, then materialized into a throbbing form. She couldn't catch the killer. Couldn't erase some crazy person's curse on the town. But she had to do whatever she could to stop this insanity. Hadn't she known that since finding Vesta's body in her car?

That séance is the last thing this town needs right now ...

Leslie blinked a few times and forced herself into action. She turned the corner and headed toward Java Joint, barely aware that her feet were moving.

By the time she reached the café's door, she knew what she had to do.

FIFTY-NINE

Tension and bodies thickened the air in Java Joint. Bailey scurried to fill orders, chiding herself for not calling in her weekend help a day early. People had crowded in after the press conference, chilled and frightened, seeking a hot drink and driven by the need to talk. Coats lay dumped over chairs, customers lined up at the counter, impatient with the slow service. Bailey tried to smile, but she just wanted to run home with her husband, lock the door, and pray. Worn and haggard from adjusting to new epilepsy medication, John had dragged himself to the press conference.

After which, he'd announced he would sleep tonight with a gun under his pillow.

Bailey's fingers trembled as she poured milk for Tanner Crayl's biggie latte.

"Take it easy, there, Bailey." Wilbur spoke up from his regular stool. "They want a coffee bad enough, they'll wait their doggone turn."

"That's right." Jake, sitting beside him, smacked a palm on the counter.

As she set the drink before Tanner, Bailey spotted Leslie in the doorway. Leslie took one look at the crowd, and her features caved. She started to back out, then glanced toward Bailey. Their eyes locked. Bailey read the mixture of weariness and anger on her face—and something else. A new jaw-setting determination,

253

although she didn't look too happy about mingling with so many people.

Bailey tried to smile, and knew it came out lopsided.

Leslie pushed the door all the way open and stepped inside.

"Leslie!" Angie Brendt waved. "How are you doing?"

Wilbur, Lucas, Ralph Bednershack, Tanner Crayl, Ray Whittlen, Carla, Jake, Bev, and more than a dozen other heads turned in Leslie's direction. S-Man even looked up from his computer.

"Hi." Unsmiling, Leslie held up a palm, as if to keep them away. "I'm here to help Bailey." She marched around the counter, eyes straight ahead, the stiffness in her spine saying she would tolerate no curious questions. She set her purse on a stool in the corner by the window, on top of Bailey's copy of the *Kanner Lake Times*. Then planted herself in front of Bailey, eyes fiery. "Okay, you obviously need help. What can I do?"

Bailey's heart quivered. She yearned to hug Leslie hard, then send her home, but resisted. Leslie had stitched her emotions into one bulging pocket, and an empathetic touch could be all it took to break the seams wide open. "Leslie, you don't have to do this. I know you've got enough on your mind. I'll manage."

"Now, Bailey, you just let her help." Wilbur shook a gnarled finger at her. "Running around like a chicken with its head cut off, you are."

Leslie ignored him. "No, you won't manage. I saw it on your face." She turned to the counter, whisked up the small pad of paper and pen. "Okay, everybody." She threw a no-nonsense look at the waiting customers. "I'm taking your orders and your money, then you can go sit down until your name's called. And be patient!"

"Now that's the spirit, you tell 'em, Leslie." Wilbur put a hand on his thigh, angling his head around to stare down the folks in line as if he owned the place.

Leslie started in. Minutes piled on top of one another as Bailey frothed drink after drink, pulled cookies from the display case, made a roast-beef sandwich. She and Leslie had no time to exchange a word. Gossip and speculation flowed from the tables and the two occupied counter stools. Wilbur and Jake exchanged enough opinions between them to equal three or four full tables. Where the missing victim might be found (anywhere from a basement to a closet to someplace in the woods), who the killer could be (someone mixed up in the hotel fight), and when he would be caught (likely not for weeks, God help the town). Although both men agreed the killer might also be shot dead at his next attempt since no one would be sleeping without a gun.

Echoes of John's vow...

Leslie's expression remained hard and focused as the coffee line finally dwindled. They'd almost made it.

"Hey, Leslie." A male voice spoke up, edged with anxiety.

Bailey looked around to see a grim-faced Sam Greene at the counter. "I hope this isn't what I think it is. I found it outside." He held out a piece of paper, folded twice, with Leslie's name printed on the top.

SIXTY

Leslie stilled, hand on the cash register. Her eyes whipped to the paper, fear spinning through her, then *poofing* away at the thought of Tommy Whittlen. Man, next time she saw that kid . . .

She heaved a sigh. "Let me guess; it was on the ground by the door."

Sam nodded, his arm still extended with the note. His dark eyes filled with questions. "Looks dirty. People must have walked over it."

Leslie glanced at Jake and Wilbur. They watched with twin rounded *O* mouths. Wilbur flattened his left arm on the counter, listing toward Leslie like a sailboat in the wind.

She looked back to Sam. "No doubt." She couldn't keep the irritation from her tone. "It's probably been floating around town since yesterday." With two fingers, Leslie plucked the paper from his hands with more than a little disdain and shoved it on a shelf underneath the counter. "Thanks, Sam."

Wilbur and Jake protested as one. Sam craned his neck, as if his line of sight could pull a downward U-turn and read the paper's contents. "Aren't you going to look at it?"

The two old men and Bailey, plus the three still standing in line—Spokane fireman Scott Murphy and Nels and Sally Huntsch—focused on her like hawks, awaiting an answer. Even though they must have heard at the press conference that yesterday's note was a prank, she could see the tension on their faces.

As if anything connected to her had to be tainted, another portent of tragedy.

Drat this. What was she doing here? She felt like some freak in a circus, gawking stares watching her every move.

Leslie waved an impatient hand. "It's just another prank, Sam. Bailey's got customers, and I need to help."

Bailey gave her a small smile and turned back to the espresso machine. Wilbur opened his mouth, but Leslie shot him a withering zip-it-mister look. Sam raised a shoulder, exchanged a glance with Scott Murphy, and backed off.

"Leslie, now—"

"Wilbur, *hush*." Leslie snapped. "Just don't say anything; I don't want to hear it." She ran a hand through her hair, trying to regain her focus. "Okay." She looked to Scott, who towered over her with his six-foot-four muscled frame—and stopped short at the expression on his face. His thin lips were pressed, large hands splayed on the counter, a cut over one knuckle. He returned her gaze with accusing eyes that pierced Leslie to the bone. She blinked, fighting her gut reaction to look away. Scott's raised chin, that down-the-nose stare zinged the memory of Myra Hodgkid through her brain. *Vesta was found in your car. Seems to me you should be looking to yourself for answers . . .*

Leslie went cold. She swallowed, her spirit breaking in two. Half of her seemed to float upward from her body, looking down in utter disbelief of what she had become to the town. *Does everybody blame me for what is happening?* Some more overt than others, to be sure. The other half remained rooted to the floor, every sense heightening. In a rush she felt her fingertips on the cash register, heard the gurgle of the espresso machine, saw Wilbur's and Jake's stares, smelled milk and coffee—each perception rubbed raw by the hardness on Scott Murphy's face.

His gaze dropped down, as if to indicate the ignored note under the counter, then kicked back up. For another long moment, they faced off.

Something cracked within Leslie, like a fragile tree limb weighted with ice. She raised her chin. "Do you want to order or not?"

He slitted his eyes further, taking his time to answer. "I'll have a biggie latte. Make it a double." He reached for his wallet, withdrew a five-dollar bill, animosity oozing with every movement. "Keep the change for Bailey. So she can hire some decent help."

Jake turned on his stool and heaved forward, practically in Wilbur's lap, to get a better look at the man and his gall. Wilbur shoved at his shoulder.

A seething retort leapt to Leslie's tongue. She held it back. Teeth clenched, she took the money from Scott, making sure their fingers didn't touch.

He glared at Leslie until Bailey placed the drink in his hands. On his way out the door, Scott stabbed Leslie with a final glance.

Wilbur stiffly cranked his torso around, watching the man take his departure. Then eased forward, shaking his head. "Man's elevator don't quite go to the top."

Jake's eyes couldn't bug any further. "That's for sure." He tapped the counter with two fingers, then leaned toward Wilbur conspiratorially. "Think he's the one?"

Yeah, well, throw Myra in there with him. Numbed, Leslie tuned the men out and asked Nels and Sally Huntch what she could get for them. Sally ordered, after ranting about Scott Murphy's "unbelievable behavior." As Leslie took their payment and opened the register one last time, the piece of paper beneath the counter seemed to rustle alive. Calling her name, taunting her to read, as if it knew her volunteer work was almost done, and no excuse remained for ignoring it.

Task over, Leslie pushed away from the counter, arms crossed, waiting for Bailey to finish the Huntches' mochas. Drinks in their hands, the couple turned toward the door, Sally with a parting smile at Leslie. Leslie smiled back tightly, feeling no warmth.

The note pulsed.

Bailey dropped into a chair she kept by the wall, wiping a hand across her brow. "Whew, we did it. Thanks."

"You bet."

"Good goin' there, Leslie, helping the ol' gal out." Wilbur winked at Bailey. "Now you gonna read that note or not?"

"Wilbur—" Leslie cut off with a sigh. "I swear, is there *ever* a time you can just mind your own business?"

He drew his head back in surprise. "I was only—"

"Oh, just forget it." She waved both hands at him.

She snatched the note from the shelf, grabbed her purse off the stool, and stuffed the paper inside, intent on making for the door. "Bye, Bailey. Keep these two in line, will you?"

Over by the wall, S-Man pushed back from his table, half rising, and beckoned to her.

"Thanks again," Bailey said. "So much. Go home and get some rest now."

And keep those doors locked. The unspoken words hung in the air.

Leslie nodded. "I'll just go say hi to Ted first." Skirting the counter, she sidetracked a few steps to grab Bailey's copy of the *Kanner Lake Times* off the stool. Rolling it up, she thwacked Wilbur on the head as she walked by.

Wilbur jumped. "Hey!"

Leslie chuckled. That felt good.

Ted pulled out the chair next to him, his expression typical S-Man—unsmiling, serious. She shook her head and slid into the seat across from him. "No, thanks, I'll sit here. With my back to everybody so maybe they'll get the idea and leave me alone."

He nodded.

She dropped her purse on the floor, tossed the newspaper on the table. It uncurled not quite fully. Ted's eyes grazed its cover page, bounced away, then pulled back in a staring double take. His face slacked. Two seconds ticked by. Three.

"Hey, S-Man." Leslie waved a hand in front of him. "You fall back into Sauria?"

He blinked hard, looked up blankly. "Sorry. I just …"

"Yeah, I know. You were just out of it, as usual." Leslie gestured toward the computer. "How can anybody write with all this noise in here?"

He pulled in a breath, let it out. "It's hard, even with *my* concentration. Thinking I might as well go home and work."

"I'll bet. You just have a couple weeks to go though, right?"

"Think so." His eyes drifted toward the newspaper, then away. "I'm tweaking the Saurian language right now. I have a loosely based mathematical formula of the Saurian alphabet for putting words together. Plus, they have to sound right." He rubbed a hand over his face. "I got letters and words and characters fuzzing up my brain."

"Yeah, well, that's better than dead bodies."

Ted looked at her more closely. "You hanging in there?"

"Barely."

He gestured with his chin in the general vicinity of her purse. "Don't want to sound like Wilbur, but you really should read that note."

"I know."

The air vibrated. Though she expected another Tommy prank, Leslie didn't want to look at the message. Not at all. Even now, knowing yesterday's note was written by a dumb twelve-year-old, she felt shivery remembering its words. How they'd stabbed through her. The guilt.

"Here." She hoisted over to snap the paper from her purse. "You do the honors."

Ted hesitated. Leslie shook the note before him. He accepted it with reluctance. Uncreased the two folds.

Leslie's heart skipped a beat.

He read without expression, then inhaled a long, slow breath. Coming from Ted, that was a *lot*. Goose bumps rose on Leslie's arms. Her mind whisked her to the previous night, to blackness and terror, and the undeniable sense of evil present.

She licked her lips. "That bad?" Her feigned light tone fell like lead.

Wordlessly, Ted turned it around, laid it before her on top of the newspaper. Her gaze yanked down of its own accord.

Vesta
kill tonight—or die
beat head
Don't you see what your words have done? Stop writing your
newspaper—now.

A tidal wave of sickness rose in Leslie's stomach. She snatched up the disgusting note, smacked it face down, and crumpled it. Pressed back in her chair, arms tight against her chest. Ted was staring at the newspaper again. Her legs shook, and her throat cinched so tight she could barely find her voice. If people weren't blaming her for real, they were taunting her. Even kids. She'd *had* it. "Forget *one* murderer in town. I'm going to kill myself a twelve-year-old."

Ted lifted his eyes from the paper, startled revelation in his features. They stared at each other for a frozen beat. "You mean you think it's another prank?"

Leslie huffed. "Of *course*!" How dare he even question it? "Don't you?" Her hand chopped the air. "And so nasty. Why does this kid hate me so much? But then, why should he be any different? I swear, half the town hates me right now." Tears bit her eyes. Great, now she was going to cry. She sucked in air with a small snort. "I don't care. I am *not* going to just roll over and feel sorry for myself anymore. I'm going to do something about this. Tonight."

His thick eyebrows bunched. "Tonight? What would that be?"

Her eyes widened. She hadn't meant to say that. "Nothing. I was just . . . venting, that's all."

"I don't think so."

"No, really."

"No, not." He leaned forward. "Leslie, you planning on doing something you shouldn't? 'Cause you're scaring me."

Scaring *him*?

Leslie felt a crack in her wall. She swallowed hard. Suddenly she so wanted to tell someone, to pour out everything she'd bottled up inside. Ted's eyes held hers, caring and concerned.

"Leslie." His tone pleaded. "You can trust me."

A hole broke through the wall. A brick shoved forward and toppled, then another. After that—no fixing it. Before Leslie knew it, the story was spilling in low whispers. A teenager's phone call, the séance, her discussions with Pastor Hank, and what she'd felt in her own bedroom last night. Even so the reporter in her held back Ali's name and the cabin's location. And she said nothing of the evidence Chief Edwards had told her about. But she did tell S-Man what she planned to do. "Something's going on in this town, Ted, something more than even the murders. It's dark and it's evil, and it's going to destroy Kanner Lake. I know it. I can *feel* it." She pressed a fist against the wadded note. "I'm not going to sit back and wait for somebody else to be killed. And I'm not going to play victim anymore. Bodies and notes wherever I go." The world blurred. "It's getting old real fast."

Ted did not take his eyes from hers, his expression taut. When her words ran out he stared at his computer, then slowly pushed it aside. "Have you told Chief Edwards what you're planning?"

"What am I supposed to say? 'Chief, you should know about a bunch of teenagers calling on ghosts.' He's got enough to worry about."

"Maybe he'd send an officer out there with you."

"No way!" Leslie exhaled in frustration. "First, the police are needed on the street. I sure don't want to pull one off patrol. Second, it's not like these kids are breaking the law. They're messing with the spiritual side of all this, not the legal side." She raked a lock of hair from her eyes. "Besides, I'll be a whole lot less intimidating to them than a police officer. I don't want to scare them. I just want to convince them to stop."

Ted surveyed her, his thoughts unreadable. "Leslie." His tone lowered, intense. "Listen to me. You can't be going anywhere by yourself after dark."

She crossed her arms up high and cupped both shoulders, chin resting on her wrist. Feeling like a defiant little girl before a parent.

"You hear me?"

She couldn't admit he was right. That she'd already considered this fact and hadn't quite decided what to do about it. "I have to go, Ted."

"Let Pastor Hank go."

"He's not supposed to know."

"Neither are you. Unless you're willing to give up this girl as your source."

"I'm not going to do that. I'm going to tell the kids ... something."

"What?"

Leslie closed her eyes. "I haven't figured it out yet."

"Leslie, this is not your problem to solve."

"Of *course* it is!" The words burst from her, and she glanced over her shoulder, afraid of the attention she'd drawn. Two tables of people were staring at her. She leaned across the table toward

Ted until her body practically touched the hateful note. "I did not ask for this!" she whispered vehemently. "I did not ask to find two people dead, and I did not ask to get ugly prank notes, and I did not ask for this girl to call me, and I *did not ask* for some evil *thing* to visit my room last night. But it's all happened, and, Ted, I will tell you one thing." Tears dropped onto her cheeks, but she paid them no heed. "I'm not going through another helpless night of panic. If what those kids are doing has anything—even the least little bit—to do with all this, I'm the only one who can stop it. And I will. I don't know how, but I *will*."

She glared at him, her breathing hitched.

A ghost of a smile played over S-Man's lips. He shook his head. "Leslie Brymes, you are something else."

He reached out and laid a hand on top of hers. It felt warm, strong. Leslie stared at it. Ted had never touched her like that. Her gaze rose, and his brown eyes held hers, two unfathomable pools. She sat spellbound, unable to move.

"Now I will tell *you* something." His voice was firm. "And no arguments accepted." He pressed her hand. "For your own safety, I am going with you tonight. I will make sure nothing goes wrong."

SIXTY-ONE

Six o'clock. The setting sun funneled between two hills, pulling down coral and gold. Behind them, cloud-ridden and ominous, the swathing shadows of night.

Vince walked down Sandy Westling's sidewalk toward his vehicle. The ISP techs and detectives were not quite finished processing the crime scene, but he couldn't stay. Darkness demanded another full-force patrol. This time two sheriff's deputies would help cruise the town.

Vince's footsteps muffled against the pavement, the sound of his own breathing loud in his ears. Up and down, the street lay deserted, folks fortressing themselves in their homes. For a surreal moment he felt alone, Kanner Lake's sole protector against lurking evil. His thoughts flashed to his son, Tim, in similar circumstances in war-torn Iraq, patrolling against invisible enemies.

Familiar pain pierced Vince's chest.

He reached his car. The coming night throbbed with portent. Vince's heart seemed to beat in rhythm. He slid into his vehicle and slammed the door, scrubbed his face hard with both palms. How long had he been up? Sleep was beyond him now; his overtired body craving yet unable to accept it, even if given the chance. He moved and spoke on sheer adrenaline, fatigue a thin, crackling glaze on the skin of his thoughts.

Where is victim number two?

He started the engine and headed for the station, where he would meet his four officers and the two sheriff's deputies to map out their patrol areas for the night.

The night. Never before had Vince dreaded it so much.

When he entered the station, he found C. B. alone.

"Hey, Chief." C. B. appeared at least half-refreshed from six hours' sleep, although Vince still noted faint circles under his eyes. "Leslie Brymes just brought something by. Thought you'd better take a look at it. She assumed it was another prank, but I don't know." He handed Vince an evidence bag labeled *Leslie Brymes, note #2, March 23.*

"Another one?" Tommy Whittlen only confessed to one. But then, Vince only confronted him with as much. Vince accepted the bag, opened it, and peered inside. C. B. fetched a pair of latex gloves, which Vince pulled on before extracting the note. He laid it on a nearby desk, bent over to read it. *Vesta . . .*

At the last sentence, chills cycled up his back. He straightened, jaw flexing.

"That look to you like another hoax by that kid?" C. B. asked.

"No." Vince's eyes riveted to the note. "Different tone. Different paper too. Plain white typing paper, like we found on the victim. It's block printing like Tommy's note, but that's common for someone trying to camouflage handwriting."

"Nothing in this that only the perp would know, though."

Vince nodded. "Could be a copycat. Or it could be the real thing." He held the note up to the light, searching for a watermark. Saw none. "Yeah. Could be the real thing."

He slipped the paper back into its bag. "Where did it come from?"

C. B. told him the details Leslie had related. None of which, unfortunately, narrowed the field much. That press conference had drawn a crowd of folks, many dispersing up Main to their cars when it concluded. Any one of them could have dropped the note.

Was the killer that close? Vince envisioned himself at the microphones, looking out over the knots of listeners and reporters. Had he seen this cold-blooded murderer?

A shudder knocked between his shoulder blades.

He closed the bag. "And Leslie had no idea who this could have come from?"

"She thinks it's a prank. Almost trashed the thing, she said, then thought better of it. No doubt the reporter in her. But the personal side? The young, scared twenty-one-year-old?" C. B. shook his head. "Scared witless, I think. And just exhausted. Doesn't seem to me she's thinking real straight about now."

Vince flexed his shoulders, then stretched his neck side to side. The sound of cars in the parking lot drifted to his ears. He focused out the window to see Frank and Jim pulling into parking spaces.

"Okay. I'll get this to the techs, then give Leslie a call to follow up. See if she's got any new thoughts of who might have sent it."

He stripped off the gloves, the *suck-snap* against fingers fraying his nerves.

By the time Vince, his officers, and the two deputies gathered for their strategizing session, his veins zinged with dread anticipation. They broke the town into seven sections, Vince assigning Leslie's parents' neighborhood to himself. After eleven o'clock, he would not stray far from their property. If that note was real, the killer indeed lurked close and might try, in Tommy's words, to leave another "present" for Leslie Brymes. Vince could only pray he would not catch his perp through such a Pyrrhic victory, for by that time another innocent victim would be dead.

The night thrummed as he and the other men made for their vehicles in the parking lot. Car doors slammed, engines started. One by one they pulled into the street and headed for their areas. Seven, thought Vince, against one—a killer who walked this world as invisibly as if he'd come from the next.

SIXTY-TWO

At six thirty, Bailey mopped the floor in Java Joint, all too aware of the growing darkness outside. With a café full of customers right up to closing, she hadn't been able to get a head start on cleaning. She'd locked the front door behind the last man out. Still, she didn't like being here alone. The silence rustled with menace.

Lord, get me home safe.

Bailey's cleaning followed a routine. Chairs were turned upside down, resting on tabletops. All surfaces and machines wiped. Cleaning the floor was her final job. She'd started behind the counter, then worked her way along its front and over to the rear wall. From there she walked down the short hall to the bathroom, restarted mopping, and backed her way out. Lifting the mop once more, she crossed to the far side and front of the café, cleaning that half toward the back wall. At the end she would have one strip down the middle, leading to the front door. At the door sat her purse, to be picked up as she exited. Bailey didn't like tracking footprints on a clean surface.

As she neared S-Man's usual table near the back, she spied a *Kanner Lake Times* on the floor. She smiled at the memory of Leslie rolling up the paper and whacking Wilbur on the head. Bailey rested her mop against the wall and leaned over to pick up the paper. Her eyes fell on the cover story about the hotel, vaguely registering a few boxed letters and words, then flicked to her watch as she straightened, paper in hand. Six forty-five. She looked over her shoulder. Night was falling fast.

She shivered at the thought of walking to her car after dark, even though it was close.

Bailey made a face at the newspaper. What to do with it? She couldn't cross the now-wet floor to the counter and throw it away. Impatiently, she rolled it up and stuck the end of it in her jeans pocket.

Ten minutes later, Bailey reached the front of the café, her task done. She leaned the mop against the wall, grabbed her purse, and hurried out, locking the door. Her car sat a short distance up the street. She scurried to it and slipped inside, pulling the newspaper from her pocket and tossing it on the seat.

She'd driven less than a mile when the boxed letters she'd seen on the front page flashed warning lights in her brain.

Did they say . . . ?

She couldn't push the thought from her mind.

Minutes later Bailey pulled into her garage. She cut the engine and hit the remote button to close the door. Then clicked on the overhead light, plucked up the newspaper, and stared at the bordered letters.

The words they spelled chilled her to the core.

SIXTY-THREE

She'd crumpled the note. *Crumpled* it.

He stalked the floor of his kitchen, anger and disgust oozing from every pore.

So much for reaching out to her. Giving her a chance.

He reached a wall, smacked a palm against it.

Maybe she wrote her articles knowing full well how the newspaper was used. She ought to be wallowing in guilt over causing Vesta Johnson's death. Instead she made excuses.

He pivoted, paced the other direction. Wishing the clock hands would move faster. Leslie Brymes deserved to be silenced, and his hands now itched to carry out the task—

A shadow moved in his peripheral vision.

Tamara.

He slid to a halt, heart tumbling over itself. Slowly, he turned his head. Just beyond the doorway to the living room, wisps of darkness swirled.

No!

He backed up, pressing against the wall, willing himself to push right through it, escape into the night.

The shadows undulated ... thickened. Gelled into solid form.

A body took shape.

In a heartbeat he regressed to six years old, hiding and shaking under the bed, Tamara lifting the coverlet. *I found you ...*

He drew his shoulders in, wishing for somewhere to run. Whimpers fell from his mouth.

A face materialized, blackened and burned.

Mother.

His knees turned to water.

She stood before him, donned in tatters of the robe she had worn on the morning she died at his hands. She pierced him with a stare, vengeful eyes smoldering. Her seared lips twisted in a hideous smile. "Did you think I would forget the curse?"

Vision crumbled away. He slid down the wall, to the floor, his mother's rasped demands digging hellish fingers into his ears.

When he awoke, he knew what he must do to survive.

SIXTY-FOUR

Seven o'clock. Chet, Kim, and Kristal would be coming any minute.

Ali had taken almost an hour deciding what to wear, finally pulling on jeans, a blue Abercrombie top, and white hoodie. Her emotions blew all over the place—from excitement about Chet to fear of the séance. She kept busy, putting on makeup and combing her hair. Trying to ignore the fear, even as her stomach fluttered. Now she stood in front of the bathroom mirror, staring critically. Trying to tell herself everything would be okay.

Wishing she could believe it.

She heard an engine out front. Ali peeked out the window and saw Chet's car pulling up to the curb. She sucked in a breath. *Here we go, no turning back now.* With one last look in the mirror, she walked to the bathroom doorway, flicked off the light—

A noise behind her—like a footstep.

Ali's head jerked. Her hand stilled on the light switch, eyes cutting left.

Turn around!

She couldn't move.

The air at her back expanded like a balloon full of hot breath.

No more sound, but she *felt* a presence. Could almost imagine it glaring at her.

From far away she registered car doors slamming—one, two, three. Voices on her front walk. Ali stood frozen in the doorway, her mind about to burst. *No need for a séance; the thing's already here . . .*

The air behind her pumped, swelled . . .

Ali whirled around.

Empty room. Counter, sinks, toilet—

The shower curtain hid the back half of the tub.

Ali's eyes glued to the spot. It was hiding there, she knew it. Waiting for her to rake back the curtain. Waiting to jump out . . .

The doorbell rang.

Her father's footsteps crossed the downstairs hall toward the front door. "Ali!"

Her breath came in little pants. She backed away from the bathroom. Reached deep inside herself to find her voice. "C-coming."

With a last glance at the tub, she wrenched away and scurried down the carpeted hall and stairs, legs shaking. Her feet hit the wooden floor as Chet stepped inside.

Ali's heart beat in her throat.

The next minutes all jumbled together. Somehow she introduced her friends. Then promised her parents they'd go straight to Kristal's house and gave Chet's cell phone number to her dad. Ali's parents wanted her home by eleven. Kristal said that was fine, fine, turning on her charm, smiling at Ali's parents as if the four of them planned to play Monopoly all evening. The next thing Ali knew she was outside on the sidewalk, buttoning up her jacket against the chilled night air.

As she trudged toward Chet's car like a prisoner to jail, she looked back at her parents standing in the golden, inviting light of their doorway. Ali wanted to run back into their arms. Forget the curse, forget her promise, and even forget these new friends. Just stay safe.

Ali, your own house isn't safe.

"Bye, Ali," Mom called. "Have fun."

Ali managed a feeble wave. "Bye."

Chet got into the driver's seat, Kristal up front with him. Trying not to show her disappointment, Ali slid in the back with Kim—and they drove off into the night.

SIXTY-FIVE

Don't you see what your words have done?

Leslie grabbed her pink jacket off her bed, jaw clenched. She didn't care what Chief Edwards thought—that note was another hoax. If it didn't come from that brat Tommy Whittlen, it came from some other lowlife. Someone blaming her for the murders, like stupid Scott Murphy, with his narrowed, mean eyes. Or one of Myra Hodgkid's minions. Who knew? The note *wasn't* true, that's what mattered. How unfair for anyone to suggest that something she'd written had led to these deaths. How all-out, unbelievably *unfair.* And now even Chief Edwards believed it.

Tears bit Leslie's eyes as she shoved her arms into the jacket. Crying just made her madder—which made her want to cry all the more. Her emotions had been on such a roller coaster for the last two days, by now she hardly knew up from down. Not to mention the lingering terror she'd felt just from stepping back inside this room. No way could she sleep here alone tonight. She and Paige planned to share the double guest bed—leaving a lamp on.

Don't you see what your words have done?

"No, I *don't* see," she said aloud, yanking her hair over the jacket collar. "I don't and I never will."

She threw a look at her reflection in the full-length mirror on the back of the bedroom door. Her eyes were red, cheeks flushed.

Her hair needed combing, and she'd forgotten lipstick. *So? People are dead out there; who cares what you look like?*

But she had to care.

Leslie drew herself up straight, took a deep breath. She couldn't let those teenagers see her looking so unnerved. She was supposed to be in control—the reporter who'd followed her own investigative leads to the hunting cabin. Who'd arrived there as someone concerned for the kids' safety, to warn them away from their own foolishness.

And if they didn't listen, she'd pull out a few threats and hope they believed her. Like telling the police.

She checked her watch. Ten after seven, almost time for Ted to arrive. Thank heaven he'd volunteered to take her.

Leslie walked over to the dresser, fixed her hair and makeup. As lipstick tube clicked down against wood, a word spoke in her head—*Pray*.

She stilled. Yeah, no kidding.

Leslie sank down on the bed, tucked both hands between her knees and lowered her head. The prayers flowed—pleas for the right words to say, for God's protection, for no one else to be killed, for this demon or ghost or whatever-the-world-it-was to go *away*.

When she pushed to her feet, she felt no better. In fact, she felt worse. Suddenly she realized how small she was, how inexperienced and ignorant of what she faced.

On impulse she picked up her cell phone, checked for Helen Communs's incoming number earlier that day, and hit *send*. Mrs. Communs answered on the first ring.

"Hi, it's Leslie Brymes. I'm just wondering—would you pray for me tonight?"

"Absolutely, dear. I've been praying for you all day."

"Good. Thank you. But I mean … especially this evening. Like in the next few hours."

Please don't ask me why.

"Yes. I will pray Jesus' power and protection over you. And, Leslie? Whatever you're up to, you do the same, hear now? Pray in Jesus' name. Aloud, as much as you can."

Fear flushed through Leslie. Mrs. Communs didn't even seem surprised at her call. "I will."

The doorbell rang.

"Thank you, Mrs. Communs. I need to go now."

"Good-bye, Leslie. Call me whenever you need me."

Leslie shut the phone and slid it in her jacket pocket. Exited her bedroom and headed for the door. Her parents and Paige weren't happy she insisted on going out, even though Ted would be with her. "We won't be gone long," she'd said. "We're just going to get something to eat and talk over this case. Ted's smart. He has some ideas."

Well, maybe a quarter of that was true.

She opened the door.

"Hi, Leslie." Ted stood on the porch, looking down at her with an enigmatic smile. "Ready to go?"

SIXTY-SIX

Ali bounced down Reckless Lane in Chet's car, the headlights cutting through darkness thick enough to touch. On either side, towering evergreens thrust into a clouded sky, turning the graveled, bumpy road into a tunnel through blackness. Ali clutched her hands in her lap, the *pop-grind* of rubber on pebbles raking her nerves. Nobody had said a word for the last few miles. The closer they got to the cabin, the more Ali's mouth glued shut.

Why had she ever said she'd come?

"There." Kristal pointed, her voice low.

Ali leaned around Kristal's head to see a narrow entrance ahead on the right. Chet slowed and turned. Their headlights swept across tree trunks and bushes, a pile of dead branches. A winding driveway.

After three curves, the driveway ended at the right side of a small, rustic wood cabin.

"First ones here." Chet pulled up until his bumper was even with the front edge of the cabin and cut the engine.

The abrupt silence rattled Ali's ears. Just seeing the cabin made her skin crawl. She couldn't imagine it would look much better even in daylight. Now it looked totally ... brutal. Like it lived and breathed, watching them through its windows, just waiting for them to come inside.

Ali, stop it.

She couldn't.

Was Chet going to turn off his headlights? That would make it so completely dark.

No one moved.

Kim shivered. "I don't like this already."

Chet focused out his window. "Yeah. This place feels …"

"Alive." The word slipped from Ali's mouth. There. She'd said it.

He nodded. "Yeah."

Kristal half turned in her seat, the back of her slick jacket whistling against the fabric. "Would you guys knock it off? This is scary enough." She blew out a breath. "Come on, let's get things set up. Nate and Eddie will be here soon. Chet, keep the headlights on."

Chet scratched his chin, like he was considering backing out. Ali's stomach quivered. He was supposed to be strong for her.

"Okay." He pulled the keys from the ignition. "Let's go." He opened his door, and the overhead lamp clicked on, a buzz warning him to turn off his lights.

They got out, moving as a tight group to the house, up the single step, onto the small porch. The air felt like weights on Ali's shoulders. She shrank back as Kristal pulled a key from her jacket pocket, inserted it into the lock, and pushed open the door.

The smell hit first. Musty. Smothering. The threshold yawned open like a cave. Ali couldn't see past the doorway. *It's in there, I know it.* She thought of the presence in her bathroom, and a chill ran up her spine. Maybe it was behind her—

She gasped and whirled around.

"What?" Kim pivoted too, then Kristal and Chet.

"Did you hear something?" Kristal threw panicked glances left and right.

Ali's eyes stabbed the forest. The car headlights, facing the other direction, did little to light the trees. Were those shadows moving around the trunks? There? Or there?

"Ali, what is it?" Chet's voice edged. "I don't see anything."

She swallowed. "Nothing. It's nothing."

Kim huffed. "Would you stop *scaring* us like that?"

"I'm sorry. I just …"

"It's okay." Chet tried to smile. "We're all a little jumpy."

Kim nudged Kristal's arm. "Let's go in and turn on the lights."

Kristal stepped into the doorway and felt around the corner. A light flicked on inside, then an overhead bare bulb on the porch. Whiteness spilled down on their heads, casting shadows under their eyes and noses. Ali blinked.

Reluctantly, she followed Kristal and Kim over the threshold, Chet behind her. Their breath fogged the air. Ali looked around the cabin. She stood in a small entry area, living room on the right and kitchen with eating area on the left. The living room was furnished with an old leather couch and two armchairs. Large burl coffee table and a couple of lamps. A geometric-designed red and black rug on the wood floor. Black wood stove in the rear corner. The eating area on her left held a round table with chairs and flowed back into the kitchen.

Ali stared at the table. Is that where they did the séance?

She gazed straight ahead down a hall, toward the back of the cabin. Two doorways on the right, one on the left.

Kim shivered. "It's colder in here than outside."

"We have to get the wood stove going." Kristal headed toward a stack of wood next to it. "Come on, Chet, help me." She turned to Kim. "Go get the rest of the lights."

Anxiety crossed Kim's face. She peered down the half-darkened hall, then looked to Ali. "Come with me."

Oh, great.

They walked together, Kim snapping on a switch to overhead bulbs. She peeked around the bedroom door on the right, then reached in to turn on its light. "Go on and do the bathroom." She waved a hand toward the door a little way down on the left.

The bathroom. Ali stared toward it. She could only see a couple feet past the threshold. She couldn't bring herself to move.

"Now what's the matter?"

"I just … In my house …" Ali licked her lips. She didn't want to tell Kim what she'd felt. Didn't want to tell any of them. It would just scare them more.

But guess what—she needed this séance to work more than the rest of them. After all, the thing had come to *her* house. And it could not come back. Did she want to sleep in her room tonight, knowing it was around?

What if it was there right now? What if it scared her parents? Her *mom*?

Dread welled up her throat. *God, please not that.* She'd do anything; she'd go through the séance for hours if she had to. Just get the thing away from Kanner Lake.

"Never mind." Kim tossed her hair. "I'll do it." She strode past Ali and smacked on the light. "There. And while I'm at it— *alone*—I'll do the back door too." She walked to the rear of the hall and turned its right corner. Ali heard three footsteps before seeing more illumination spill on the floor. Kim reappeared. "All right, done. I'll do the kitchen." She swept past Ali, her glare withering.

With a final glance toward the bathroom, Ali followed.

The front door opened, and Nate jumped inside, grinning. "Hail, hail, the gang's all here!" His cheeks were flushed. Eddie came in behind him.

"Hey, dude." Eddie raised his chin toward Chet. "I turned your car lights off."

"Oh, thanks, I forgot." Chet dusted off his fingers and shut the stove door.

"Okay." Kristal put her hands on her hips, black hair shining against white jacket. She lifted her chin in determination, even as fear flicked across her face. "Let's start the séance."

SIXTY-SEVEN

Leslie pressed against the back of Ted's passenger seat, arms folded, peering through the windshield for sight of their turn-off. Reckless Lane — how fitting. What was she doing out here? Even with S-Man she felt more vulnerable with every mile. He wasn't helping much anyway, with his taciturn silence. "Is something bothering you?" she'd asked. But he just shook his head.

The cloud-covered night obliterated the moon, the stars. Its blackness closed around the car like a monstrous mouth, swallowing the headlight beams. Disjointed scenes of the man in her bedroom jerked through her head. His shape. His hands ready to strangle. The hiss of her name. Twice Leslie started to tell Ted to turn back, but the thought of teenagers summoning pure evil closed her mouth.

Those kids have no idea the fire they're playing with. They think it's all just fun and games.

"There it is." Ted pointed.

A graveled road. Small white sign — Reckless Lane. How ironic.

"Yeah." Leslie looked at Ted's profile, taking in his full lips, the hair brushing his jacket collar, narrowed eyes. He caught her looking at him and flashed a half smile.

"You okay?"

She pulled in a breath and nodded.

Ted turned onto the lane, driving slower as they sought the cabin's driveway. Leslie leaned forward, hands on the dashboard. "She said it's the first on the right."

In less than a mile, they spotted it. They turned in and followed the curves until their beams washed across two cars parked one behind the other, about thirty yards away. To the left of the cars, a cabin, fully lit. Ted cut his lights down to parking beams as they'd agreed he would. Leslie wanted to surprise the teenagers. She didn't need them spilling out some back door into the forest.

"Thank goodness they've got the lights on. I was afraid they'd be doing this in the dark." Leslie found herself whispering, as if her voice alone might betray their arrival.

Ted stopped some distance from the second car and cut the engine. He turned to Leslie, laid a hand on her shoulder. "You sure you don't want me to come with you?"

Yes, she wanted him to. Even lit, the cabin looked creepy, surrounded by blackness. She didn't even want to walk from the car to the porch alone. "I'm sure." She pushed strength into her voice. "It's enough for me to show up unannounced. I don't want to scare them. Just convince them to go home—and stay there."

"Okay. I'll roll down my window. If you need me, just holler."

Leslie nodded. She withdrew her cell phone from the pocket of her jacket and turned it off. Slipped it back inside. This was no time for a call.

With a smile she didn't feel, she opened her door and slid out into the cold and hovering night.

SIXTY-EIGHT

Ali could feel the first hint of warmth in the cabin. Kristal took off her jacket and tossed it on the couch. The others did the same.

They gathered around the eating-area table, wood scraping wood as they pulled out chairs. "No candles this time." Kristal sat down and scooted her chair forward. She faced the front window, her back to the kitchen. "I'd just as soon do this with the lights on."

"No kidding." Kim settled on her left.

Yes, please! Ali couldn't be more relieved.

"Aw, it won't be any fun without flickering candles in the dark." Nate fluttered his fingers in a mocking *woo-woo*.

"Will you can it, Nate?" Kristal glared at him.

He dropped into the chair next to Kim. Ali sat on his left, facing into the kitchen, her back to the window. Chet was next to her, then Eddie.

Ali's gaze fell on a set of drawers next to the stove. "Kristal, is that message you saw still in there?" She gestured toward the kitchen.

"Yeah. I taped it right back where I found it."

Oh. The news squirmed down Ali's throat. To think that the written curse was here, so close to her. Did it really contain power? Was it the reason she'd felt so driven to pick up the note yesterday?

284

"Maybe we should put it here on the table," Eddie said. "Like to show we're not scared of it."

No, no...

"You're right." Kristal pushed back from the table. They all watched as she opened the middle drawer and knelt, reaching her hand deep inside. "I don't want to rip it." Her fingers made scraping sounds against the wood. "There." She pulled out a folded piece of paper and pushed to her feet. At the table, she unfolded it and laid it in the middle.

Ali's eyes riveted to the coral moon in the bottom corner. Something about that drawing. She'd almost swear the thing glowed...

Kim stared at it too, then raised anxious eyes to Ali.

"Okay." Kristal hit her palms against the table. "Let's call the spirit. When it comes, we can't show we're scared. We have to command it back to wherever it came from. Everybody ready?"

Everybody nodded but Ali. Nate stuck his chin out. "Yee haw."

Kristal held out her fingers to Kim and Eddie. Everyone joined hands. Chet gave Ali's a little squeeze, and a shudder ran through her. She looked toward the hallway but couldn't even see the first bedroom door. Anybody—any*thing*—could hide back there.

Kristal closed her eyes, not moving. "Dark Powers, can you hear us? Come back. Bring the spirit. We want you here. Come back now, send the spirit, come back now, send the spirit..."

Ali's fingers twitched. Nate gripped her hand tighter.

Everybody else joined in, their voices mingling and dark. They called the Powers over and over again until the words flowed together. "Show yourself ... come to us ... we call the spirit ... we want you here ..." The words started low, growing louder and louder.

The air pulsed.

A strange tension filled the room; Ali could almost hear it beat like distant drums. Suddenly she thought of the window at her back and the night beyond it. She imagined a dark fog moving through the trees, forming into shapes. Her muscles tightened until they trembled. She scrunched her eyes closed, silently pleading for the voices to stop, but everybody kept chanting louder and louder. "Where are you, spirit? ... Please come! ... You have to come! ... "

Ali felt it. Just like she had in her bathroom. Something dark and heavy — all around her. Pressing down, squeezing her chest. Her heart banged so hard she could barely breathe.

"Come to us, come to us, come to us ..."

The words vibrated and spun, around her head, her shoulders. Ali opened her mouth to yell for them to *stop*! but she couldn't make a sound. Then she heard her own voice joining in. Her lips moved and the words scraped up her throat, and she couldn't *stop* them. "Come to us, Dark Powers ... send us the spirit ... come, come, come, come ..." Her words came slowly at first, then faster, more intense. Her eyes squeezed shut as if they were glued. She wouldn't open them even if she could, terrified of what she'd see. Her voice got louder, she clutched Nate's and Chet's hands tighter, her mind numbing until she felt wrapped in a cocoon. Tremors started in her feet, then chewed their way up her knees, her thighs. On to her chest, then out to her arms and hands. Nate's and Eddie's hands shook too, like they were in the middle of an earthquake. The air filled with electricity, charges skimming across the back of her neck. The chanting got louder, louder, Ali's feet rammed against the floor, arms stiff on the table, pressure building in the air until her skin was going to *split*, and she would tear in two, right down the middle —

Something pounded hard on the door.

Ali yanked both hands free and screamed.

SIXTY-NINE

Vince cruised the dark streets of his patrol, up one block, down the next. His focus moved from the road to front yards, seeking furtive movement in shadows, at the corners of houses. Exhaustion wracked his limbs, even though it was barely past eight. After this night, he'd have to sleep. Forty-eight hours awake would render any man useless.

The air crawled with malice. Time and again Vince flicked a glance in his rearview mirror, half expecting to see an inhuman face.

Details and snippets chugged through his brain. The footprint, the hairs. Ghosts and notes and circled numbers. Vesta's sagging mouth and bloody head.

You think he's come back too, don't you? Wilma Redlin's parting shot about Henry Johnson.

No, I don't.

Did he?

How do you catch a killer from beyond this world?

Who among Vince's colleagues would even listen to such nonsense?

Vince drew a hand across his face. Didn't matter. His suspicions would remain tied to terra firma — they *had* to. These oddities of evidence, these feelings — they'd somehow be explained.

He reached a stop sign. Turned left.

Thank heaven Nancy was at Heather's again tonight. And that she didn't know—

His cell phone rang.

Vince had unclipped it from his belt, laid it on the seat. He lifted it before it could ring twice, checked the ID.

John Truitt.

He flipped open the phone. "Hello, John?"

"No, it's Bailey."

An edge to her voice. Not like Bailey. "Everything all right?"

"No. Maybe. I don't know. I found something in Java Joint tonight. Might be nothing, but it's been bothering me for over an hour. I mean it *can't* be anything, but ... John said I should call."

Vince pulled over to the curb, put his foot on the brake. "Tell me."

"It's a boxing of letters and words in the *Kanner Lake Times* newspaper. I think I need to show you." Briefly, she explained.

Whoa.

She was right; he needed to see for himself. The Truitts lived on the other side of town, which meant taking him off his patrol. But this was important.

"I'll be there in three minutes."

Throwing down the phone, he veered back onto the road and gunned toward the Truitts' house.

SEVENTY

A girl's scream lanced through Leslie's head. Without second thought, she thrust open the cabin door and barreled inside.

Dual senses hit her at once. A rolling, turgid evil in the air, and gasps on her left.

She swiveled to see six teenagers around a table, all heads twisted her direction, eyes wide and mouths agape.

For a moment nobody moved.

Leslie shut the door against the cold night air. She could hardly breathe. She flexed her shoulders, giving her lungs room. The atmosphere felt ... inhabited. Just like last night in her room. That thing was close. She could almost feel his fingers at her neck.

They had to get out of here.

"Well, I'll be danged, it's Leslie Brymes." A heavy-set guy spoke, his cheeks flushed.

"What are you *doing* here?" A black-haired girl jerked up her chin, eyes blazing.

"You've got to stop this séance and leave. Now!" The words scratched from Leslie's throat. "You have no idea what you're getting yourselves into."

Stunned silence.

The girl shoved her chair back from the table. "How'd you know about this?"

"I'm a reporter; it's my business to know."

The girl's eyes narrowed. "Someone must have told you." She shot an accusatory look toward a brown-haired girl with both hands at her mouth.

Ali.

Leslie strode to stand over Miss Black Hair, her legs unsteady. Thick air swirled against her chest. *Get out, get out, get out!* warned a voice in her head. "I don't know any of you, so don't go there." She spoke rapidly, a tremble in her words. "I *do* know more about these murders than you. And I had a not-so-friendly visitor in my room last night—thanks to your séances. You've got to stop. You're bringing evil to this town."

"We're trying to send the ghost back." This from the third girl, a blonde.

"It won't work. All you're doing is opening yourself up to some really bad stuff. And you're feeding the curse that was put on Kanner Lake." Leslie wanted to say more, wanted to tell them to ask God for protection, but her mouth snapped shut. Who was she to tell them anything? She hardly knew what she was talking about herself.

"Don't you *dare* blame us for what's happening!" Miss Black Hair shrilled.

"I'm not blaming you." Every breath oozed sludge down Leslie's windpipe. Couldn't they feel it? "Do you think I wanted to come out here at night? I'm here to help y—"

Movement in the kitchen caught her eye. Leslie snapped her head toward it. The teenagers jerked around.

On the floor, seeping through the worn wood. Blackened wisps. Circling, flowing. Thickening. Building higher. Malevolence seeped from it, wrapping around Leslie's limbs. The hair on her arms lifted straight up.

Air leaked from the heavy boy's mouth. His red cheeks drained white. "It's coming."

SEVENTY-ONE

He waited in the dark, pulse pounding.

Kill them and you will be free. His mother's poisonous words ran through his veins.

Anything for freedom now. *Anything.* He couldn't face the ghost of his mother a second time. Feared her more than death itself. He just wanted to be normal again. Get on with life. For that prize, he didn't care who he had to hurt, however young. Didn't care about all the blood he'd have to spill. Hadn't fate decreed it? Think of the information he'd heard, practically spoon-fed.

And if that wasn't enough — look at where that information had brought him.

The curse had come full circle. Swept through the town, back to the place once owned by his parents. By him. A place he knew corner to corner.

He reached under his driver's seat and withdrew a long sheathed hunting knife. An inheritance from his father, once kept in the very cabin that now pulled him in like sucking tentacles.

Kill them and you will be free.

He slid out of the car and clicked the door shut.

SEVENTY-TWO

Ali's hands crushed her mouth. She leaned to the right, staring wildly past Kristal to the tar-colored, moving mass. The air vibrated an evil that burned her limbs. *Get out of here!*

Her muscles locked up.

Seconds spun out. Ali heard everything in a jumble—Nate's whisper, Kim's gasp, breath sucked in Chet's throat. The substance whirled, then gathered up, up, into a column. Funneled into a figure. A chest, arms ... legs. A neck and head.

With a *whoosh* it solidified into a man.

Brown shirt and pants, stained red tennis shoes. The same wrinkled face with thick white hair that Chet had cut from the newspaper. The man leered, his features full of hate and meanness, his eyes a shiny black-green. He glared at Kristal, and his lips twisted into a hideous grin.

He's come to kill us.

Ali's limbs unfroze. She shoved her chair back, jumped to her feet—

The cabin flicked to blackness.

SEVENTY-THREE

Within five minutes of Bailey's phone call, Vince was leaning over the Truitts' kitchen table, a haggard John at his right, Bailey on his left. He'd reclipped his cell phone to his belt. The *Kanner Lake Times* lay unfolded before them.

Bailey pointed to the main article. "See what's boxed. If you put it together ..."

Vince's eyes raked in the heading and first few lines.

In̲v̲e̲s̲t̲ment or A̲ttack?

According to a source among those supporting the proposed Grayson hotel project, the group, in an effort to "kill all arguments against the hotel once and for all," tonight will determine a "winning plan of attack — or die trying." Their aim is to "beat the 'Give Kanner Lake a Break' faction and head off their wild arguments against his great investment."

The boxed words pulsed off the page. Vince stared, mentally scrambling for explanation. "Who did this, Bailey?"

She fisted her hands, pressed them together. "I think Ted Dawson. I noticed him looking at the paper after he and Leslie talked. It was unlike him. Usually he's so lost in writing his book."

Ted.

Vince absorbed the news. "The note that Sam Greene brought into Java Joint—did Leslie show it to you?"

"No. She seemed so upset about it, I didn't want to ask."

Vince fought to keep his poker face. Without reading that note, Bailey couldn't know the full significance of those boxed words.

"Did she show it to Ted?"

"I don't know. A short time after she left, he packed up his computer and was out of Java Joint pretty fast."

Vince straightened, focused without seeing on the wall. If Ted hadn't seen that note, no way could he know those words. And even if he had ...

"There's more." John reached for the newspaper and turned the cover back. "When I saw this, I knew we had to call you." He pointed to the continuation of the lead article on page three.

> ... in the block east of the town's sandy beach
> and west of Ling Street. But Hodgkid argues
> that the site would choke traffic ...

Fireworks of understanding burst in Vince's brain. Vesta—a circled one. Sandy—a three. *Page numbers.*

His eyes jumped to page two. No boxes.

Page numbers. There *was* no missing second victim.

But other articles filled that page. Who knew how many different names could be formed from combined words? One of the articles even contained a long list of petitioners supporting the hotel.

Would one of these people die tonight? More than one?

Vince straightened, adrenaline kicking through his veins. He had to call Leslie. Find out if Ted had seen the words on that note.

"Thanks." He folded the newspaper, snatched it up. "I'll need to take this with me."

John stepped back. "You think those boxed words—"

"Can't be sure yet. But you were right to call."

With a rising sense of urgency, Vince hurried out the Truitts' front door toward his car, unclipping his cell phone on the way to dial the Brymes' house.

Linda Brymes answered. Leslie was out, she informed him, even though they hadn't wanted her to go. She'd promised to return soon.

"Don't tell me she's alone."

"No, no, we wouldn't let her do that. She's with Ted Dawson."

Vince sank against his car. Fear chewed his spine as he focused down the street, thoughts racing.

Somehow he managed to end the call without petrifying Linda, even as data points added in his head. Ted Dawson, a single man with no alibis. Ted, at Java Joint when the second note was found outside. Ted, quiet and enigmatic, removed in his own world.

With trembling fingers, he punched up Leslie's cell phone number, hit *send*. The call rang once, then kicked to voice mail.

"No!"

He disconnected and tried again, not realizing he was praying until he heard his own voice. "Dear Lord, don't let anything happen to Leslie ..."

SEVENTY-FOUR

The cabin erupted in screams.

In the blackness, Leslie's heart froze.

Chaos followed—chairs shoved back and clattering, bodies stumbling. Someone rammed into Leslie and knocked her to the floor. "Get outside!" Something—a knee?—hit her in the head. She scrabbled away toward the kitchen.

God help me, Jesus help me . . .

"Chet, where are you?" a girl shrieked.

"Here, take my hand!"

Footsteps pounding toward the door.

"Lessslie."

An inhuman whisper behind her, piercing her ears despite all the noise. She whipped around. The thing's upper body was eerily lit in the darkness. Its hands reached out, thumbs touching, fingers flexed toward her throat.

Leslie shoved to her feet.

The sound of the front door opening, someone running into the doorjamb. "Umph!" A clatter on the porch.

Then another noise between her and the entryway, so horrible it froze Leslie's blood. The sound of fighting. Grunts and smacks, a cry of pain.

Leslie's brain warped into overdrive. She spun right, then left, not knowing where to go, what to do. Where was Ted? He should have heard the screams. Who was fighting? Where was the ghost or demon or whatever that *thing* was?

"God, help!"

"Aahh!" a boy's voice yelled.

"Chet, Chet, where are you?" Ali's cry.

"Nate! Eddie!" The sound of a punch. *"Help!"*

Panic ballooned in Leslie. Her lungs swelled nearly shut. She had to *do* something.

More scuffling. A heavy thud on the floor.

"Chet!" Ali screamed.

"Leslie." Cold fingers grazed the back of her neck.

She gasped, catapulted forward. Her left hand smacked into something hard. A chest? "Jesus, make it go!" (Had she screamed that aloud?) Someone grabbed her hand and yanked. She wrenched away, arms thrashing, one leg kicking. Fingers gripped her again. Not ghost fingers. Solid, hard. Then an arm. It spun her, pulled her close. She drove an elbow backward with all her might.

"Hunngh."

A man's groan. A clatter at her feet.

The thunk of a handle, the rattle of a long blade. *Knife.*

The killer was *here.* She was going to die.

Leslie's muscles exploded. She fought with a fury beyond herself, thrashing, pummeling the darkness, battling to survive. All sounds, all senses closed in, the world collapsed to the black space of her lashing limbs and her attacker's deadly hands. She sensed him warding her blows, stooping down. Seeking his weapon.

She stepped on something thin and hard. The knife? She kicked it, heard it slide across wood.

The man cursed. She felt him rise. Hands found her shoulders, sought her neck. She jerked backward. Her heel landed on a body. Leslie stumbled and crashed down on it. Air pushed from her windpipe.

Sudden car beams shot diffused light through the cabin.

Leslie twisted up to look at her attacker's face.

SEVENTY-FIVE

Voice mail again.

Oh, Lord, please.

Vince punched off the call to Leslie's phone, tried a third time. Same thing.

Her phone had to be turned off.

He took a deep breath, worked to steady his voice, and redialed her parents' house. It rang once, twice. *Come on, come on.*

"Brymes residence, this is Paige."

"Paige, Chief Edwards here. I'm trying to reach Leslie, and she's not answering her cell. Any reason you know it would be turned off?"

"No way, she never turns it off. Not even when it's charging at night."

Vince closed his eyes. "Why did she go out with Ted?"

"I don't know; it surprised me." Worry stole into Paige's voice. "Why? What's wrong?"

"Do you know where they went?"

"No. Chief, you're scaring me."

I'm scaring me too. "Does *anybody* know where they went?"

Paige's words cinched tight. "I don't think so. But you'd better tell me what's going on, or so help me, I'm going to track you down and find out."

"No, stay in the house." The words burst out, too harsh. He softened his tone. "I'm just worried for Leslie's safety. Keep trying her cell for me, okay? The minute you get through, tell her to call me." Vince snapped the phone shut, not waiting for a reply. He yanked open his car door, shoved himself inside, and reached for the radio to run down Dawson's vehicle. He had no time to waste.

Every man on patrol needed to be searching for that car.

SEVENTY-SIX

Ali froze in the cabin doorway, facing in, stunned at the sudden dim wash of light. *Eddie's car beams?* In one frantic second she saw everything—the back of a man, his arms up, fingers spread. Before him, Chet, crumpled on the floor. Leslie half on top of Chet, staring up, wild-eyed. A long, hideous knife, four feet away from them, toward the living room.

Behind Ali outside, Eddie shouted. "Nate, where's Chet?" Kim was sobbing. Kristal screamed, "My cell phone's in my jacket!"

The man lunged for the knife. Ali screamed. Chet lifted his head, dazed.

"No!" Leslie pushed up on her hands and knees, straining to catch one of the man's legs. She grabbed him below the knee. He tripped two steps and fell.

Footsteps pounded up to the porch. Nate and Eddie shoved past Ali, heads jerking from Chet and Leslie to the man.

The attacker snatched the knife from the floor and scrambled to his feet. Nate and Eddie rushed him, hitting him in the chest. The knife flew out of his hand. He staggered back and fell again. The guys jumped on top of him, punches flying.

Leslie went for the knife.

Nate jumped up and kicked the man in the head—hard. His shoe hit skull with a *thwack*.

Air seeped in a slow leak from the attacker's mouth. Both arms sagged to the floor.

He lay still.

Nate backed up to the wall, cheeks flaming red. Eddie fell on his rear and palms, breathing hard.

"Chet!" Ali sank to her knees beside him, tears blurring her eyes. She reached for his hand.

He blinked at her, clutched her fingers. "Yeah."

A whimper caught her attention. Ali swiveled to see Leslie, clutching the knife with both hands as if she'd never let go. On her feet, swaying, she stared wild-eyed at the man on the floor.

SEVENTY-SEVEN

Leslie's brain sludged into hardening concrete. Vaguely, she registered her fingers cramping around the knife, strands of hair caught in her mouth, the trembling in her legs. She couldn't tear her eyes away from the man before her. Just a few hours ago she'd stood feet away from him, looking into his eyes.

Why?

"Leslie!"

She blinked blurry eyes and turned to see another man stumble through the doorway. Blood clotted on the side of his head. His eyes raked over the teenagers, the figure out cold on the floor. He stopped, stunned, then pivoted toward her.

Jesus, don't let him kill me. Leslie raised the knife in a shaking fist and aimed it toward his heart.

He froze.

The knife shook. She fixed crazed eyes on him.

He held up both hands, palms out. "Leslie, it's me. S-Man."

She stared. Her throat convulsed in a swallow.

"Leslie."

She blinked. Her mind wouldn't work. "S-Man?" The name slipped from her mouth.

He nodded. Gave her a tiny smile. "Yeah." He took a limping step toward her.

Terror kicked through her gut. She jerked the knife. "Don't come near me!"

He stopped. "Whoa. It's okay now."

Okay? *Nothing* was okay.

"Hey." S-Man's voice dropped to a whisper. "Please. It's *me*."

The weapon shook. Where was her brain? Leslie couldn't *think*. Quivers moved up her arm, across her body, down her legs. She was going to collapse any minute. "I can't trust you. I can't trust anyone."

S-Man's eyes glistened. "I'd never let anybody hurt you."

Her mouth opened, but no more words came. Tears fell on her cheeks. Her focus drifted toward the attacker on the floor, then back to S-Man. "It's Sam Greene."

S-Man nodded. "Yeah."

"Vesta's neighbor. Her friend."

"I know."

"Why?"

Sorrow filled his eyes. "I don't know, Leslie. I just don't know." His voice thickened. He took a deep breath, held out both arms. "Please. Put down the knife. I want to help you. And we need to call Chief Edwards."

Chief Edwards. He would come. He would help. Leslie felt her face collapse. *The chief is going to be so sad.* Sam Greene was his friend.

A sound rose in her throat. Slowly, her hand came down. One by one her fingers relaxed. The knife slipped to the floor.

Leslie's knees buckled.

S-Man jumped to her side — and caught her.

PART FOUR

Confession

SEVENTY-EIGHT

He hunched on the thin cot of his jail cell, staring at the cold floor, hands clasped between his knees. The place smelled dusty and close. The side of his head still throbbed from where he'd been kicked, his arms and shoulders sore from the punches. He hadn't eaten in over twenty-four hours.

At night it was very dark.

He'd told Vince Edwards and the ISP detectives everything, their tape machine running. Confessed to killing Vesta Johnson and Sandy Westling, recounted his childhood. Vince placed a *Kanner Lake Times* before him, boxes around the cover page's words that were already branded into his brain. He shrank away. "Why did you need to draw the boxes?" He searched the chief's face. "Don't you see the coral crescent moons behind the words?"

Vince said no.

He didn't believe that, of course. The coral moons were there. On page one, the top of page three. And so many on page two — behind individual syllables, not to mention every hotel supporter listed in that article. Twenty-three names in all. He never could have taken care of all those people. What did his parents think he was, a cold-blooded killer? Just those kids at the cabin had been too much.

He stared at the floor, imagining his parents' charred faces. "I tried ... Leave me alone."

His pleas would do no good. Last night he'd heard them here.

"Hey, Greene!" The mat-haired guy in the cell across from him stood with one hand wrapped around a bar, the other scratching his large belly. Grinning like a fool. His sagging mouth revealed two gold teeth. "Don't worry, man, you'll breeze through your trial, everybody says so. You got insanity defense written all *over* you."

Sam turned his head away. *Insanity defense.* Even the lawyer who'd seen him earlier that morning had used those words. Well, hear this, world—Sam Greene wasn't crazy. He was plagued. Didn't he always know, deep inside, that one day his parents would demand their due? That he would be the one to carry out their curse?

Not until last night had it hit him—the morning he'd seen their message to kill Vesta Johnson marked ten years to the day since he'd condemned them to a fiery death.

A decade. He'd had that many good years in Kanner Lake. Enjoyed the town, lived off his inheritance. Slept soundly at night.

But in the end, the ghosts.

He would never be free of the ghosts.

SEVENTY-NINE

Late Sunday afternoon, Vince ushered Pastor Hank into his office and closed the door. "Please, have a seat." He indicated a chair opposite his desk.

"Thanks." Hank settled into it and clasped his hands, elbows resting on the chair's arms. Although he tried to smile, stress pulled at his face, the crow's-feet around his eyes etched deeper. Vince could only imagine how worn he felt after conducting Vesta's funeral just hours ago and facing Sandy's tomorrow.

Vince didn't feel much better. "I appreciate you coming in." He sank into his chair behind the desk.

"Glad to."

"I asked you here because, frankly, I've still got more questions than I have answers. The law enforcement issues of this case are all mixed together with the spiritual ones. And, on the latter, I've got to admit I'm way out of my league."

Pastor raised his eyebrows. "I may not have all the answers either."

"Fair enough." Vince surveyed his hands. Where to begin?

At least there was one part he *could* explain—the footprint. Just after Vesta and Wilma packed up Henry Johnson's clothes, Sam Greene hauled some trash to the dump. In all that garbage, what did he happen to see but Henry's old red sneakers. Sam had often argued with Henry, and he knew those shoes all too well. He told Vince and the ISP detectives that finding those shoes was providence spun by his dead parents. He knew he was to put them in his closet until the time came for their use, whatever that might be. A year later, he found a purpose—wear the shoes while killing Henry's wife.

For some reason on that day last week—maybe due sub-consciously to the ten-year anniversary of his parents' murder, and perhaps spurred further by his opposition to the proposed hotel—Sam Greene picked up his copy of the *Kanner Lake Times* and saw the coral-moon message from his parents embedded on the front page. In his warped thinking, he believed he was car-rying out his parents' curse through Henry Johnson's ghost. He even left the shoes on Vesta's back patio as a sign that Henry had returned from the grave.

So far, so good.

Except that Henry Johnson had shown up for real.

Vince raised his gaze to Hank. "When we talked yesterday, I told you about the evidence we haven't released to the public—and never will, by the way. The three white hairs at the crime scenes. We were interrupted before I could tell you the DNA test-ing will take a few weeks. But with what I know now, I don't doubt they'll match. What I want to know is how did they get there?"

Hank pondered the question. "Sam didn't leave them?"

"He claims to know nothing about them. And I don't know why he'd lie about that, because he's told us everything else." Vince shook his head. "I've tried to convince myself that Sam picked up the hairs on his jacket from somewhere in Vesta's house, and two brushed onto her body. Maybe the next night, as he wore the same jacket, the third hair fell on Sandy Westling's pillow. But that's pretty hard to believe, given how clean Vesta's house was. And that Henry died fourteen months before. The techs didn't spot any other hairs like that in her home."

Pastor Hank gave him a penetrating look. "And the alternate explanation?"

"Even harder to believe. But it doesn't stand alone. We got six teenagers, plus Leslie, who insist they saw Henry Johnson's ghost in that cabin. Leslie felt a presence more than once before that. I felt it myself. You said you've sensed a darkness over this town. Then I hear Sam Greene's stories of his childhood, and the spirits and the curse. I can partly believe the curse was a self-fulfilling prophecy, given Sam's mental instability. But that still doesn't explain the hairs. Or the ghost."

Hank nodded slowly. He ran a hand across his mouth, as if taking a moment to put his thoughts in order. "I had a similar talk with Leslie about the ghost part. I don't believe that's what she and those kids saw, or what you felt. I believe it was a demonic spirit taking the form of Henry Johnson. That it was attracted by the séances, and the curse, and all the dark forces that Sam Greene's parents chose to surround themselves with."

Vince rubbed his fingers across a dent in his desk. "Why Henry's form?"

"Because demons are liars. They exist to create havoc. If Sam Greene wanted to pose as Henry Johnson's ghost to carry out some curse on the town, Henry Johnson is what the town would get."

Vince could accept that. "But what about the hairs? If they're really from Henry ..."

Pastor Hank lifted a hand. "That's the hard one, isn't it. All I can say is, demons are supernatural beings. They can take any form they choose, and they're not stuck in our dimension. How do they fly into pigs and send the animals throwing themselves off a cliff into the sea, as the Bible says they did? For that matter, how do angels do what *they* do?" He leaned forward. "Vince, these things are beyond our understanding. Our human minds are finite. I'm not going to tell you I can explain everything in rational terms. But one thing I know—because God's Word says it over and over—Jesus is stronger than any demon. The Bible says they flee at His name. Do you know that thing in the cabin disappeared when Leslie screamed the name *Jesus* aloud?"

Sudden weariness swept through Vince, and his throat tightened. He placed a thumb and finger at his temples. "I just want to know it won't come back."

"It won't. Many people in this town are praying against it." Pastor Hank's tone was firm. "Leslie's in counseling with me now, by her choice. And I'm meeting regularly with the kids involved, as you asked me to. I've also vowed to start teaching more from the pulpit about these issues; I've been lax on that."

Vince pressed back in his chair, a burn in his eyes. Man, he was on the edge. A hundred times a day he saw Sam Greene's tortured face. Part of him still couldn't believe what had happened. "Kanner Lake's *my* town, Hank. *My* responsibility. I fight against crime, perpetrators I can see and touch. This whole thing..." He shook his head. "This thing really got me."

"Chief." Hank slipped out of his chair, leaned across the desk on his knuckles. "You did your part. God did His." He waited until Vince met his gaze. "Now hear what I'm telling you. It's over."

EIGHTY

After dinner the first evening back in their own house, Leslie and Paige slid into the Explorer to drive across town for a visit with Ali. They'd promised to go. The girl was busted but good—grounded for a solid month. Leslie could understand her parents' stunned fear. Cops at the house, statements taken, all the hounding media. Excluding herself, of course. But really, after Friday night's trauma, did the kid need more punishment?

Leslie fought her fatigue. Maybe by the summer she'd catch up on sleep. Maybe by 2010 her lingering fear would subside. You just don't stare a demon in the face and fight a crazed killer all in the same night, then bounce back like nothing happened. On top of that, she'd had one TV interview after another. Which left her with that nagging, biting ambivalence. Did being on TV feed her old ambition? Oh, yeah. Was she leery of that ambition? Double yeah.

Somehow she and God had to figure this thing out.

Paige turned right at the end of their street. "You and Ali have really become friends, huh." Leslie had gone over to Ali's yesterday and met her parents.

"She's lonely. Besides, shared dire circumstances can do that to people." Leslie pushed her fingers into Paige's shoulder.

"No kidding. *How* many times has S-Man called you since Friday?"

"I wasn't talking about S-Man."

"I was."

Leslie drew her jacket tighter and looked out the window. "So? He did take a nasty hit to the head on my account."

Sam Greene had parked off the side of Reckless Lane and made his way through the dark up the driveway. Clutching a thick piece of branch, he yanked Ted's door open and pulled him out of the driver's seat onto the ground before Ted could react. A single blow with the branch knocked Ted cold. Ironically, Ted could thank the rising chants of the teenagers for his life. Before Sam could draw his knife, the sound of those voices pulled the unhinged man toward the cabin in a frenzy. He popped the inexpensive lock on the back door, slipped inside, and tripped the fuse box.

Thank heaven Ted came to when he did.

Paige threw Leslie a knowing look. "He likes you."

"S-Man? You're crazy. Besides, he's, what, about ten years older than I am?"

"Who cares? He's also really nice. And kind of cute."

"Yeah, in a Stephen King, laconic, head-in-the-clouds sort of way."

"He's not always like that. Just when he's writing."

"He's *always* writing."

"He's almost done."

"Then he'll start another book. That's what writers do."

But Leslie couldn't really knock the writing. If Ted hadn't been thinking all day about letters and words in his Saurian language, Vesta's name in the newspaper headline may not have jumped out at him. Followed then by other words from the note he'd just read. Then he even made the connection to the numbers one and three. Ted Dawson was smart, all right. And he did care about her feelings. He hadn't wanted to tell her then, knowing how guilty she already felt. He'd simply convinced her to take the note to the police, thinking he would talk to them himself— after watching over her that evening.

Leslie heaved a sigh. "Besides"—she wagged her head—"Frank's the guy for me."

No response.

"Right?"

Paige fussed with the heater vent by her door. "Right."

They arrived at Ali's house. Leslie introduced Paige to Ali and her parents. Mr. and Mrs. Frederick looked wary. In a way, Leslie couldn't blame them. Move to a quiet town, and the next thing you know, two girls who've been plastered on TV thanks to their murderous adventures are befriending your daughter. Life was not exactly predictable.

On the other hand, Leslie had done her part to save Ali. And she vouched for Paige.

Ali led them upstairs to her bedroom and closed the door. The three of them plunked down on her bed. Ali's eyes fell on her backpack, lying on the floor. She drew her legs under her. "I sure am glad that note's out of there. It almost seemed ... like it had a heartbeat or something."

The police had taken it as evidence. The curse note in the cabin too.

"Has Kristal decided to forgive you for lying to them?" Leslie didn't even try to hide the disdain edging her voice. Kristal was far too big for her britches.

"About not throwing away the note, yeah. After everything that happened, that was kind of minor. But they'll never know I called you. I'm just letting them think we started talking after Friday night. They've got too much on their minds to think that one through."

Yeah, like a bit of unwanted notoriety.

Ali plucked at a thread on her bedspread. Then looked from Leslie to Paige with a sigh. "You both are so pretty."

Leslie *tsk*ed. "Look who's talking."

"I'm not pretty."

"Yes, you are."

"Okay, then I'm ... uncool. I don't do makeup very well. Or hair."

"Shoot, we can fix you up, girl. Fix you up for Chet." Leslie grinned. "Right, Paige?"

"You bet."

Ali laughed. "Great."

They fell silent. Weariness pulled at Leslie, and her smile crumbled away. She really needed to get to bed early tonight. Sleep for a week.

At least she was still breathing.

She scooted backward to lean against the headboard and closed her eyes. A tired prayer filtered through her mind.

"You okay, Leslie?" Ali's voice.

"Yeah."

"What are you thinking?"

Leslie rolled her head from side to side against the wood. "Just thanking God for who He is, Ali. Just thanking Him for who He is."

EIGHTY-ONE

www.kannerlake.blogspot.com

SCENES AND BEANS

Life in Kanner Lake, Idaho—

brought to you by Java Joint coffee shop on Main

Monday, March 26

Thank You For Your Notes

It's Bailey with you this morning. Wilbur was supposed to be up, but as you know, we've had a very difficult weekend, and I felt I'd better say a few things. Before all of this began last week, Wilbur was working on his post. (And giving me trouble about it—can you imagine that?) I will put it up in the next few days.

So many of you left concerned comments to my post on Friday. Then over Saturday and Sunday—I suppose as you heard further information on TV—I see that you left more. All of us here in Kanner Lake thank you for your kindness. We are slowly emerging from our shock. But to tell the truth, the weekend seemed very long as we struggled to understand. We still could use your prayers.

I'm not going to comment on what happened. You've seen it all in the news anyway, and if you've been with this blog for any length of time, you know this is not the place to foment more talk. Kanner Lake has never been about tragedy. As long as I've lived here, it's been a wonderful town, with beautiful surroundings. Until last summer, we'd seen very little to shake us up. Now it feels like we've been to hell and back. But God is good. And with His help our town will restore itself.

So many of you asked about Leslie. I know she looked shaken and worn in her Saturday interviews. Those clips have run again and again—I saw them on many different channels. But she wants me to tell you she is recuperating emotionally and will be fine. You know Leslie; she's a fighter.

In the past you've seen a few posts here about the proposed hotel in Kanner Lake. Some of you wondered in your comments what these murders might do to that project—will they scare away the investor who wants to build here? It's too soon to tell. Talk is rampant, and I wouldn't blame the investor if he decides to pull his project off city hall's table. But whatever happens, you know I remain Kanner Lake's cheerleader. You can visit here in the future and maybe stay in a new hotel, or you can enjoy the B&Bs around town and on the water, as before. Either way, we want you to come see us. You'll love the beauty of the area. Water sports in the summer, snow sports in the winter. Not to mention the friendliness of the town. (Please, please remember that what happened here recently is so far from what this town is usually like.) It has been such a joy to meet those of you across the country who've come into the café to say hi.

Thank you again, all of you, for your encouragement and love. And mostly for your prayers.

Until next time, from Java Joint,

—Bailey

Posted by Bailey Truitt @ 7:00 a.m.

ACKNOWLEDGMENTS

My hearty thanks to all the wonderful North Idahoans who have embraced this series and supported me in placing my fictional town in your beautiful part of the country.

Special thanks go again to Tony Lamanna, Spirit Lake, Idaho, chief of police, for reading this manuscript (as he did with *Violet Dawn*) and offering help with the law enforcement aspects of the story.

And my appreciation again to Terry and Marilyn Cooper, owners of the real Simple Pleasures (at 221 Sherman Avenue in Coeur d'Alene, Idaho) for once again allowing me to feature their store. The merchandise mentioned in this story is sold at Simple Pleasures. Visit their Web site at www.simplepleasures-cda.com.

Finally, a second go-round of thanks to aspiring novelist Stuart Stockton for allowing me to use his science fiction novel, *Starfire*, for S-Man. May *Starfire* find its publishing home.

Be sure to read book three in the Kanner Lake series, *Crimson Eve*.

ONE

"Is a heinous murder any reason to devalue such a glorious piece of real estate?"

The words rolled off the man's tongue in a luscious English accent, with a hint of tease. He was pure James Bond. Cocky and dashingly handsome (a good British description, what?).

Carla Radling flicked a glance at his left hand. No ring. But then he'd already intimated he was single. A real estate developer, he'd said over the phone yesterday. And apparently rich, although no proper English gentleman would stoop to such a tactless description of himself. He was "seeking a beautiful and private piece of property near water as a second home," and the half-page ad in *Dream Houses* had caught his eye. If he liked the place, he was prepared to pay cash.

To think she'd complained about the high cost of the ad.

Behind them, the heavy wrought-iron gates of the estate belonging to the late Edna San, world renown actress, closed with a muted clang. Carla steered her Toyota Camry down the impressive driveway curving through forest. Her client, David Thornby—although James Bond was so much more apropos—dignified her front right seat like no other passenger before him. His legs, clad in impeccable beige silk trousers, were apart in that indisputable I'm-a-confident-male position, his left arm draped over the console, fingers casually drumming the leather.

The fabric of his navy sport jacket boasted a weave that surely had set him back a couple thousand.

Carla emitted a small laugh at David's "heinous murder" remark. "Devalue? Not in my book. And so far, for this property, it hasn't. But often that's what happens to the homes of celebrities caught in a scandal—or murder. Seems to give would-be buyers the willies to picture the crime occurring in their living room."

"Technically, it didn't occur here, correct? Edna San was taken out of the home, with no one being sure exactly where she was killed."

That accent truly was to die for. "Right. The news was where they found her, not where she was killed." But enough of this morbid topic. "The property has only been for sale a little over a year. That's not a long time given its price for this area. I told Edna's heirs I fully expect that someone out of the area will buy it."

Carla rounded a curve in the wide driveway, and the actress's magnificent two-story home of wood and stone swept into view. A front porch with thick round pillars ran its entire length, the arched and mullioned windows giving it a castlelike quality. Perfect for a well-bred English gent.

David drew in a breath. "It's stunning. And look at that view."

Kanner Lake sparkled some one hundred yards beyond the backyard of the house, its waters tinged crimson in the last rays of sunset. Carla caught a glimpse of it through the side yard as she pulled up to the front of the house.

"Yeah, isn't it great? Like the ad said, a large private dock and three-hundred feet of sandy beach. Plus, with the forest all around you, it's completely private."

Carla slid another look at David, registering the body language. Torso leaning forward, anticipation etching his face. The man liked what he saw.

Something twinged in her stomach—a warning niggle that such obvious excitement didn't fit the demeanor of a suave British gentleman. Weren't they supposed to be understated sorts?

Carla pushed the thought away. What did she know about English behavior?

She rolled to a stop close to the wide porch steps and cut the engine. "Wait till you see the inside."

He smiled at her as his hand found the door latch, and his steel blue eyes twinkled. *Twinkled*. Carla hadn't known a pair of eyes could do that—not outside the romance novels she used to read as a teenager.

How old was this guy? Maybe forty?

Please, oh, please, buy this house, you beautiful male specimen. Then marry me quick.

"Thanks for letting me leave my car outside the gate." His eyes still held hers. "This was far more of a treat, being free to ogle while you drove in."

"No sweat. We aim to please."

They mounted the three curved flagstone steps side-by-side, David a good eight inches taller than her five-six frame. An aura of power and control emanated from his every move, his back straight as he walked, chin high and eyes alert. He ran his knuckles down the huge carved door as Carla, trying her best to appear unaffected by his charm, slid her key into the lockbox. She removed the lock, pushed back the door, and waved him into the entryway. "After you."

He stepped over the threshold onto gleaming tile floor, Carla following. David's head tipped back to admire the grand curving staircase to their left.

"Truly stunning."

Carla hung back, giving him time to admire the sights from where he stood: a formal living room on the right, furnished in white leather couches and Persian rugs, rich wood wainscoting on the walls.

"Of course if you don't like Edna San's taste in furniture, you could always—"

"I do like it, very much." David's voice held an almost hushed quality, as if he dared not disturb the perfection of the house. "Makes it easier to buy a second home when it's turnkey like this."

"Well, that's good." Carla dropped her keys into her purse. "Since Edna's son and daughter didn't seem to care a whit about taking anything. Other than the china and some photos of Edna with Bette Davis and other movie cohorts."

"I thought Edna San hated Bette Davis." David stepped into the living room and leaned down to inspect the fifteen-thousand-dollar rug.

Carla shrugged. "Didn't all the legendary female movie stars hate each other? It's a cat thing."

"Cat?" He spoke the words with distraction, his back to her and eyes still focused on the rug.

"Yeah, you know how women . . . " Carla eased up beside him, and he focused on her without straightening, eyebrows raised. Those eyes were something else. Carla mushed her lips together. "Never mind."

He flashed her another smile, sending a tingle down Carla's spine.

"So." She pointed toward the entryway, her gesture a little overdone. "How about if I show you the kitchen and dining room."

"Yes, certainly."

In the large kitchen David nodded and murmured approval as Carla pointed out its long list of amenities. He stood back while she opened cabinets, the refrigerator. A voice inside her whispered this was odd. Prospective buyers typically inspected every nook and cranny.

Must be a man thing. The guy probably didn't even cook.

Down a short, wide hall off the kitchen they stepped into the formal dining room. A highly polished cherry wood table lay beneath a sparkling crystal chandelier, the matching hutch elegant despite its emptiness after Edna San's children had claimed its dishes and goblets. On the hardwood floor spread another luxurious Persian rug. Carla walked around to the other side of the table, gesturing toward the large back windows. "Great view of the lake."

David put his hands low on his hips and nodded. "Splendid." His gaze fell on Carla across the table, one side of his mouth in a slight curve. "And so are you."

Carla blinked. The statement was spoken with such gentlemanly aplomb. For a moment she wondered if he merely referred to her skills as a realtor. But the approving expression on his face said otherwise.

He sighed. "It's such a shame."

Carla was half tongue-tied. It had been years since any man had so mesmerized her. "What's a shame?"

He spread his hands. "You. This place. That I can have neither beauty."

Whoa, where had *that* come from? She tilted her head. "You can't?"

"No. Unfortunately things aren't quite as I represented."

It took her a second to realize the accent had vanished. The guy now sounded as American as her coffee-drinking pals down at Java Joint.

Carla stared at him. *What* was going on? Her mind fastened on the behaviors she'd chosen to ignore—his request to leave his car outside the gate, his excitement, the refusal to touch anything. Her spine tingled anew. This time it wasn't so exciting.

"You're not British." She refused to allow a tremble in her voice, even though the ten-minute drive to town suddenly seemed a trip to the moon. What was she thinking, coming out here alone near dusk? After all the trauma Kanner Lake had seen in the past year.

But good grief, he'd sounded so *normal*. Not to mention anxious to buy.

His lips spread in a slow smile. "No."

Fear flushed through Carla—and that ticked her off. She raised her chin. "Well, how about that. So how much of what you told me *is* true. Are you a real estate developer?"

He shrugged. "It seemed like such a respectable line of work at the time."

"At what time?"

"When I called you."

She stuck her tongue between her lip and top teeth, surveying him with an I've-had-enough look. "Okay, let's cut the games. Just what are you, then?"

His graceful right hand slid into his coat pocket. "To use the vernacular, vulgar though it is"—his voice carried a light, engaging tone—"I'm a hit man."

He withdrew a handgun and aimed it at her heart.

Brink of Death

Brandilyn Collins

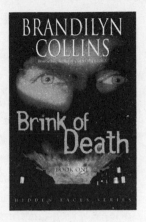

The noises, faint, fleeting, whispered into her consciousness like wraiths in the night.

Twelve-year-old Erin Willit opened her eyes to darkness lit only by the dim green night-light near her closet door and the faint glow of a street lamp through her front window. She felt her forehead wrinkle, the fingers of one hand curl as she tried to discern what had awakened her.

Something was not right . . .

Annie Kingston moves to Grove Landing for safety and quiet — and comes face to face with evil.

When neighbor Lisa Willet is killed by an intruder in her home, sheriff's detectives are left with little evidence. Lisa's daughter, Erin, saw the killer, but she's too traumatized to give a description. The detectives grow desperate.

Because of her background in art, Annie is asked to question Erin and draw a composite. But Annie knows little about forensic art or the sensitive interview process. A nonbeliever, she finds herself begging God for help. What if her lack of experience leads Erin astray? The detectives could end up searching for a face that doesn't exist.

Leaving the real killer free to stalk the neighborhood . . .

Softcover: 0-310-25103-6

Pick up a copy today at your favorite bookstore!

Stain of Guilt

Brandilyn Collins

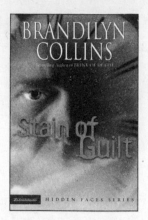

As I drew, the house felt eerie in its silence. . . . A strange sense stole over me, as though Bland and I were two actors on stage, our movements spotlighted, black emptiness between us. But that darkness grew smaller as the space between us shrank. I did not know if this sense was due to my immersion in Bland's face and mind and world, or to my fear of his threatening presence.

Or both . . .

The nerves between my shoulder blades began to tingle.

Help me, God. Please.

For twenty years, a killer has eluded capture for a brutal double murder. Now, forensic artist Annie Kingston has agreed to draw the updated face of Bill Bland for the popular television show *American Fugitive.*

To do so, Annie must immerse herself in Bland's traits and personality. A single habitual expression could alter the way his face has aged. But as she descends into his criminal mind and world, someone is determined to stop her. At any cost. Annie's one hope is to complete the drawing and pray it leads authorities to Bland — before Bland can get to her.

Softcover: 0-310-25104-4

Pick up a copy today at your favorite bookstore!

Dead of Night

Brandilyn Collins

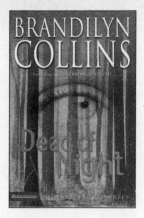

All words fell away. I pushed myself off the path, noticing for the first time the signs of earlier passage—the matted earth, broken twigs. And I knew. My mouth turned cottony.

I licked my lips, took three halting steps. My maddening, visual brain churned out pictures of colorless faces on a cold slab—Debbie Lille, victim number one; Wanda Deminger, number three . . . He'd been here. Dragged this one right where I now stumbled. I'd entered a crime scene, and I could not bear to see what lay at the end. . . .

This is a story about evil.

This is a story about God's power.

A string of murders terrorizes citizens in the Redding, California, area. The serial killer is cunning, stealthy. Masked by day, unmasked by night. Forensic artist Annie Kingston discovers the sixth body practically in her own backyard. Is the location a taunt aimed at her?

One by one, Annie must draw the unknown victims for identification. Dread mounts. Who will be taken next? Under a crushing oppression, Annie and other Christians are driven to pray for God's intervention as they've never prayed before.

With page-turning intensity, *Dead of Night* dares to pry open the mind of evil. Twisted actions can wreak havoc on earth, but the source of wickedness lies beyond this world. Annie learns where the real battle takes place—and that a Christian's authority through prayer is the ultimate, unyielding weapon.

Softcover: 0-310-25105-2

Pick up a copy today at your favorite bookstore!

Web of Lies

Brandilyn Collins,

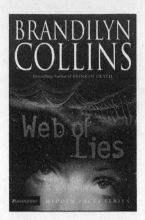

*She was washing dishes when her world
began to blur.*
  *Chelsea Adams hitched in a breath,
her skin pebbling. She knew the dreaded
sign all too well. God was pushing a vision
into her consciousness.*
  *Black dots crowded her sight. She
dropped a plate, heard it crack against the porcelain sink. Her
fingers fumbled for the faucet. The hiss of water ceased.*
  God, I don't want this. Please!

After witnessing a shooting at a convenience store, forensic artist Annie Kingston must draw a composite of the suspect. But
before she can begin, she hears that Chelsea Adams wants to
meet with her—now. Chelsea Adams—the woman who made
national headlines with her visions of murder. And this vision is
by far the most chilling.

  Chelsea and Annie soon find themselves snared in a terrifying battle against time, greed, and a deadly opponent. If they
tell the police, will their story be believed? With the web of lies
thickening, and lives ultimately at stake, who will know enough to
stop the evil?

Softcover: 0-310-25106-0

Pick up a copy today at your favorite bookstore!

Eyes of Elisha

Brandilyn Collins

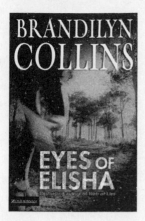

The murder was ugly.
The killer was sure no one saw him.
Someone did.

In a horrifying vision, Chelsea Adams has relived the victim's last moments. But who will believe her? Certainly not the police, who must rely on hard evidence. Nor her husband, who barely tolerates Chelsea's newfound Christian faith. Besides, he's about to hire the man who Chelsea is certain is the killer to be a vice president in his company.

Torn between what she knows and the burden of proof, Chelsea must follow God's leading and trust him for protection. Meanwhile, the murderer is at liberty. And he's not about to take Chelsea's involvement lying down.

Softcover: 0-310-23968-0

Pick up a copy today at your favorite bookstore!

Dread Champion

Brandilyn Collins

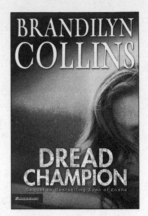

Chelsea Adams has visions. But they have no place in a courtroom.

As a juror for a murder trial, Chelsea must rely only on the evidence. And this circumstantial evidence is strong — Darren Welk killed his wife.

Or did he?

The trial is a nightmare for Chelsea. The other jurors belittle her Christian faith. As testimony unfolds, truth and secrets blur. Chelsea's visiting niece stumbles into peril surrounding the case, and Chelsea cannot protect her. God sends visions — frightening, vivid. But what do they mean? Even as Chelsea finds out, what can she do? She is helpless, and danger is closing in . . .

Masterfully crafted, *Dread Champion* is a novel in which appearances can deceive and the unknown can transform the meaning of known facts. One man's guilt or innocence is just a single link in a chain of hidden evil . . . and God uses the unlikeliest of people to accomplish His purposes.

Softcover: 0-310-23827-7

Cast a Road Before Me

Brandilyn Collins

A course-changing event in one's life can happen in minutes. Or it can form slowly, a primitive webbing splaying into fingers of discontent, a minuscule trail hardening into the sinewed spine of resentment. So it was with the mill workers as the heat-soaked days of summer marched on.

City girl Jessie, orphaned at sixteen, struggles to adjust to life with her barely known aunt and uncle in the tiny town of Bradleyville, Kentucky. Eight years later (1968), she plans on leaving — to follow in her revered mother's footsteps of serving the homeless. But the peaceful town she's come to love is about to be tragically shattered. Threats of a labor strike rumble through the streets, and Jessie's new love and her uncle are swept into the maelstrom. Caught between the pacifist teachings of her mother and these two men, Jessie desperately tries to deny that Bradleyville is rolling toward violence and destruction.

Softcover: 0-310-25327-6

Pick up a copy today at your favorite bookstore!

Color the Sidewalk for Me

Brandilyn Collins

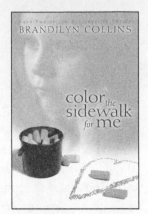

As a chalk-fingered child, I had worn my craving for Mama's love on my sleeve. But as I grew, that craving became cloaked in excuses and denial until slowly it sank beneath my skin to lie unheeded but vital, like the sinews of my framework. By the time I was a teenager, I thought the gap between Mama and me could not be wider.

And then Danny came along. . . .

A splendidly colored sidewalk. Six-year-old Celia presented the gift to her mother with pride — and received only anger in return. Why couldn't Mama love her? Years later, when once-in-a-lifetime love found Celia, her mother opposed it. The crushing losses that followed drove Celia, guilt-ridden and grieving, from her Bradleyville home.

Now thirty-five, she must return to nurse her father after a stroke. But the deepest need for healing lies in the rift between mother and daughter. God can perform such a miracle. But first Celia and Mama must let go of the past — before it destroys them both.

Softcover: 0-310-24242-8

Pick up a copy today at your favorite bookstore!

ZONDERVAN®
.com

Capture the Wind for Me

Brandilyn Collins

One thing I have learned. The bonfires of change start with the merest spark. Sometimes we see that flicker. Sometimes we blink in surprise at the flame only after it has marched hot legs upward to fully ignite. Either way, flicker or flame, we'd better do some serious praying. When God's on the move in our lives, He tends to burn up things we'd just as soon keep.

After her mama's death, sixteen-year-old Jackie Delham is left to run the household for her daddy and two younger siblings. When Katherine King breezes into town and tries to steal her daddy's heart, Jackie knows she must put a stop to it. Katherine can't be trusted. Besides, one romance in the family is enough, and Jackie is about to fall headlong into her own.

As love whirls through both generations, the Delhams are buffeted by hope, elation, and loss. Jackie is devastated to learn of old secrets in her parents' relationship. Will those past mistakes cost Jackie her own love? And how will her family ever survive if Katherine jilts her daddy and leaves them in mourning once more?

Softcover: 0-310-24243-6

Pick up a copy today at your favorite bookstore!

Three ways to keep up on your favorite
Zondervan books and authors

Sign up for our *Fiction E-Newsletter*. Every month you'll receive sample excerpts from our books, sneak peeks at upcoming books, and chances to win free books autographed by the author.

You can also sign up for our *Breakfast Club*. Every morning in your email, you'll receive a five-minute snippet from a fiction or nonfiction book. A new book will be featured each week, and by the end of the week you will have sampled two to three chapters of the book.

Zondervan *Author Tracker* is the best way to be notified whenever your favorite Zondervan authors write new books, go on tour, or want to tell you about what's happening in their lives.

Visit *www.zondervan.com* and sign up today!

ZONDERVAN®

ZONDERVAN.com/
AUTHORTRACKER
follow your favorite authors